# THE
# EXILE OF
# GIGI
# LANE

Also by **Adrienne Maria Vrettos**

*Sight*

*Skin*

# THE
# EXILE OF
# GIGI
# LANE

**Adrienne Maria Vrettos**

MARGARET K. MCELDERRY BOOKS
New York    London    Toronto    Sydney

MARGARET K. McELDERRY BOOKS
An imprint of Simon & Schuster Children's Publishing Division
1230 Avenue of the Americas, New York, New York 10020
MARGARET K. McELDERRY BOOKS is a trademark of Simon & Schuster, Inc.
For information about special discounts for bulk purchases,
please contact Simon & Schuster Special Sales at 1-866-506-1949
or business@simonandschuster.com.
The Simon & Schuster Speakers Bureau can bring authors to your live event.
For more information or to book an event, contact the Simon & Schuster Speakers
Bureau at 1-866-248-3049 or visit our website at www.simonspeakers.com.
Book design by Sonia Chaghatzbanian
The text for this book is set in Adobe Garamond Pro.
Manufactured in the United States of America
10 9 8 7 6 5 4 3 2 1
Library of Congress Cataloging-in-Publication Data
Vrettos, Adrienne Maria.
The exile of Gigi Lane / Adrienne Maria Vrettos.—1st ed.
p. cm.
Summary: Returning for her senior year at an exclusive private school and poised to
become the new "Master of the Universe," a teenaged girl falls from social glory and
must scrabble her way back to the top using strategic effort and the help of her best
friend.
ISBN 978-1-4169-2433-3 (hc)
ISBN 978-1-4391-6068-8 (eBook)
[1. Popularity—Fiction. 2. Cliques (Sociology)—Fiction. 3. High schools—Fiction.
4. Schools—Fiction. 5. Humorous stories.] I. Title.
PZ7.V9855Ex 2010
[Fic]—dc22
2009015401

FIRST
EDITION

*For Wren,*
*who chewed on the very*
*first draft of Gigi*

# ACKNOWLEDGMENTS

## My deepest thanks to:

Jeff, *illy*.

My mom and dad and big brother for their love and support, and for sharing with me their love of books; my aunties and cousins for making Girls' Weekends so wonderful; my whole family, North and South, for their love, support, and laughter; my amazing friends Chloe, Clint, Danielle, David, GT, Kate, Maria, Shawna, Suz, and Tara; Miriam Cohen, Ellen Tarlow, and Dorita for being there from the very beginning; the whole TADN crew; all of my friends at 557 Broadway, especially David Levithan and Lisa Sandell for keeping their office doors open; and Rachel Coun, for her support.

Gigi wouldn't be the Swan she is today if it weren't for the support, patience, brilliance, and encouragement of my agent Tracey Adams and my editors Emma Dryden, Lisa Cheng, and Karen Wojtyla. Special thanks to Emily Fabre, Carol Chou, and everyone at McElderry Books. You have made my dreams come true, and I can't ever thank you enough.

*"Nothing is more deceitful,"* said Darcy, *"than the appearance of humility."*

—Jane Austen, *Pride and Prejudice*

# CHAPTER ONE

## Who Says Dung Can't Be Fun?
## First-years' final duty announced!

### (You'll want to hold your noses for this one.)

*I'm Gigi Lane and you wish you were me.*

Oh my *God*, that has to be the most powerful affirmation in the history of the world. Dictators don't have affirmations that good.

I tap my fingers on the steering wheel to its undeniable rhythm. *I'm Gigi Lane and you wish were me.* I could rule the world with an affirmation like this. But I think I'll start with Swan's Lake Country Day School for Young Women.

My head nods, my fingers tap, my butt muscles pulse to the music of my affirmation as I cruise the predawn streets of Swan's Lake. I stay on Pleasant Street, aptly named because, according to *The Guide to New England Private Schools*, it "winds its way up and down the wooded hills of Swan's Lake, interrupted only by picturesque hilltop farms."

It's at the top of one of these hills that I pull over to the side of the road for a much needed moment of what my mom, in her bestselling self-help book *Meet Your Tweet: The Girlie Bird's Guide to Finding Her True Heart's Song*, calls an affirmation confirmation.

Turning off the car, I slip off my seat belt and get myself into the official Girlie Bird affirm and confirm meditation pose: legs crossed, arms bent to form the "wings that will carry you home."

I close my eyes, steady my breathing, and listen to my heart. *I'm Gigi Lane and you wish you were me.*

I wake up when my head hits the steering wheel, and frantically look at the clock, relieved to see I was asleep for only two minutes. I yawn and rub the crust out of my eyes. Thank God for natural beauty. Otherwise I'd look a wreck after three nights in a row of just a few hours' sleep.

I yawn again, rest my head against the steering wheel, and gaze out the window over the valley to the wooded hill on the other side. Rising up from the early morning mist, standing proud and tall and sure, is the reason I've spent the last seven months in a hamster wheel.

It is a mansion made of brick and marble and limestone, a gorgeous patchwork of architectural styles, its two turrets standing guard on either side of the steepled roof.

From here, in the dim light of dawn, I can barely make out

the stone steps leading up to the double doors. And above the front doors: a circle of stained glass, twelve feet in diameter, inlaid with the pattern of the Swan's Lake crest. I wait, holding my breath. Beyond the school I can see the sun inching its way above the horizon, and in just moments it is shooting through the stained-glass crest, glinting and sparkling, sending all the colors of those carefully cut pieces of glass spinning out across the valley, and straight into my heart.

I know that there are those who are bitter about their own academic experiences (gym class rejects, etc.), who think that my love for Swan's Lake marks me as a pitiable yet attractive creature who has gotten so caught up in the circus that is high school that I truly don't care about anything else.

I ask you this: What else is there?

And please don't bore me with "There is life *after* high school," that medicating sentiment clung to by girls who cry in the bathroom at school dances. Of course there's life after high school! There is college and all that's beyond. But I'm not in college, am I? No! I'm nearing the end of my third year of high school, and may I be stricken with cystic back acne and a lazy eye if I waste one minute of my high school career pining for the future like some pathetic nerd. If there's one thing I hate about nerds, it's their inability to live in the moment.

The future is *now*! Why is it only the pretty people who realize this?

I glance at the clock again. If I don't pick up my best friend, Deanna, and get us to school by five a.m., there'll be hell to pay.

They hate it when we're late. Fiona says it makes her question her selection decisions, and she *hates* questioning her decisions.

Swan's Lake is like any other high school. We have the usual cliques: the Greenies, the Gizmos, the Deeks, the Bookish Girls, the Glossies, the Cursed Unaffiliated, and so on. And, like any other school, there is a top secret group of senior girls that work with an international network of alumnae to keep the Swan's Lake power structure intact.

Also like at any other high school, the Glossies and the Cheerleaders are top tier: You can't get any more popular. Until senior year, that is.

From your very first day of kindergarten at Swan's Lake, you hear the rumors. A whisper on the jungle gym, a low murmur on the story time rug.

As the years go by, the rumors gain traction. Details. There is a secret club, they say, and everyone knows its name, but only its members are allowed to say it out loud. You relish the danger of whispering it to one another in the last bathroom stall, the one marked OUT OF ORDER. "The Hot Spot," you whisper with gummy-bear breath, pulling the end of your braided ponytail out of your mouth.

By the time you're in eighth grade, your braids abandoned for carefully brushed curtains of hair, your skin nicked and scabbed from newly gained permission to shave your legs, a precious few inches of actual cleavage pushing against your crisp, white triangle bra, by this time you know that every year the Hot Spot has a leader. She is called Head Hottie, and on the day you are taken across the street to tour the Upper School, you see her. She is standing on the landing at the top of the grand staircase that stretches up from the main entrance to the first-floor classrooms. There is a girl on either side of her. Together, the three make up the Hot Spot. They are watching you, all of you, as you file through the front doors, trying not to gasp at the car-size chandelier hanging overhead. The Head Hottie watches as you're led into the front office. She studies each of you and then whispers something to the girl standing on her right. The girl nods and makes a note in the back of an oversize, leather-bound book.

It's called the Hottie Handbook, and there is only one copy, bound in black leather, handed down from Head Hottie to Head Hottie every year since Swan's Lake was founded.

If you're lucky enough to be one of those eighth graders whose name was written down in the back of that book, and if you're further lucky enough not to have your name crossed out later due to an unfortunately horizontal growth spurt or a sudden increase in ugliness, you will be like me. One of the chosen.

A Hottie Hopeful. Who cares that being chosen means spending your junior year proving your worth and your loyalty by performing maddening duties like using Wite-Out on any piece of paper in the recycling bin that has less than three lines of text on it? It's Fiona's right to make us do these things. She's Head Hottie, and Cassandra and Poppy are her second and third in command. We're their Hopefuls. We'll do whatever it is they want us to.

Exhaustion and paper cuts are temporary. The Hot Spot is

forever. Once you're in, you're in for life. Like the mob, but with better fashion and less murder. As soon as you make the jump from Hopeful to Incumbent, you become part of the *Network*. It sounds so . . . classified. And it *is* classified. Fiona won't even tell me how exactly it is the whole *Network* thing works, except to say, "Shut your piehole, Lane! You'll know about the Network when I decide you need to know about the Network."

Want a Swan transferred to a vocational high school with a major in industrial plumbing because you don't like the way she laughs? Done. Freeze the family assets of a Swan who fouls you during gym, causing her tuition check to bounce? No problem. Have a Swan deported, even though she was born in Kansas? Enjoy your "native" Ireland, Katie Pretovka!

Head Hottie is always the most popular girl in school, closely followed by her second and third: in my case my best friend, Deanna, and our hanging participle, Aloha. There is no way someone with substandard social standing could handle, much less deserve, the sort of power we stand to inherit.

I am sure that I am not the only one who is sick and tired of the vulgar media backlash against popularity. Filthy propaganda texts like *Mommy, Why Don't They Like Me? How the Quest for Popularity Is Killing Our Daughters*; snuff films profiling the "evil" popular girl who ends up publicly humiliated at the hands of a vindictive nerd; photographs, collages, folk music, sculpture, dance . . . there is an *endless* list of tools "artists" use to slander, defame, and otherwise vilify popular girls.

And you know what I say to them? *You're welcome.*

Without popular girls like me, artists would have nothing to rail against, nothing to lament in whiny songs, no angst or anger or *feeling*.

At least art is benign. What's harder to handle is the myths.

### Myth #1. Popular girls are the reason you're unhappy.

No. *You* are the reason you're unhappy. In my mom's best-selling self-help book *Chicken No More: The Girlie Bird's Guide to Facing the Truth* she says that what holds most people back from success is—get ready—themselves. She says if you can't face the truth about your shortcomings, you will never overcome them. I will give you an example: Daphne "Dog Face" Hall. She's a classic Art Star, one of those girls that wear Converse sneakers and are always crying in the art room. I have done my best to verbally hold the mirror of truth up to Daphne, and she still refuses to truly see herself for the horror show she is.

"*Your eyebrows are taking over your face, Daphne.*"

"*I can see your panty line, Daphne.*"

"*You have weird man-hands, Daphne.*"

"*That bra makes your back fat stick out.*"

"*Here's some zit cream.*"

"*And deodorant.*"

"*And mouthwash.*"

I've given that girl a whole drugstore's worth of product, and she still insists on coming to school looking like a "Before" picture of an ugly-girl magazine makeover.

**Myth #2: Popular girls are secretly anorexic cutters cracking under the pressure of having to be perfect.**

To this I say, "Ha!" Pressure just makes popular girls get better grades and grow bigger boobs. Anyone who can't handle the pressure doesn't deserve to be popular and will be weeded out by those who do deserve it soon enough.

**Myth #3: Popular girls will peak in high school.**

They will show up to your ten-year high school reunion and have back fat, a bartending job at Chili's, and a smoker's cough. Aw, the sweet lies whispered at bedtime by parents of sobbing loser children.

**Myth #4: Popular girls are just like everyone else. They get pimples, have fat days, and feel misunderstood.**

We don't get pimples. And we don't have fat days. Or gas. Also, we look pretty when we cry, we never get athlete's foot or gingivitis, and we always ace pop quizzes.

**Myth #5: Popular girls are heartless wenches that delight in the degradation and humiliation of other people.**

We are not monsters. We don't kick kittens or trip blind people. If we're mean to you, it's because you deserve it. It's because you've shown a lack of respect, forgotten your place, forgotten *us*. Keeping you down is part of our duty, just like keeping us up is part of yours. The underclass are not expected to have the aesthetic gifts and natural fashion sense that popular people have, so they don't have to strain themselves popping zits or trolling the Internet for sales on fashionable clothing. For all their whining, they are *happy* with the way things are. They have their place, and so do we.

By the time I flash the peace sign to Max, the overnight guard at the entrance of the gated community where Deanna lives, the sun is rising, lighting up what looks to be a perfect early spring day.

I pull into the driveway of Deanna's humongous house and thank God for small favors the ass-ugly Jones Family Minivan is in the garage. Ugly is contagious, even for cars.

The minivan was a gift from one of Deanna's sponsors during her superstar gymnast days. The Jones Family Minivan, as it was officially called, or the JFM to us, got a little rickety after being driven all over the country to get Deanna to her competitions. But Deanna's mom couldn't afford another car when she had to go back to work selling paper products, so the JFM is still limping along.

I give the horn a quick tap. The light in Deanna's room is on, and so is the one in the kitchen. I honk again, louder this time.

"DEANNA 'DEAR HEART' JONES, IF YOU DON'T GET YOUR ASS OUT HERE, I'M GOING TO KICK YOU IN YOUR ONE GOOD KNEE! Good morning, Mrs. Jones!" I call sweetly as Deanna's mom opens the front door and waves to me. I blow her a kiss and then flip down the sun visor so I can check out my bangs in the mirror. I look back to the house, ready to raise holy hell if Deanna doesn't get outside, when I see her giving her mom a kiss good-bye.

Deanna "Dear Heart" Jones.

My best friend, and the girl formerly known as America's New Olympic Hope.

She walks gingerly down the steps and limps across the front lawn toward my car, her feet making trails in the morning dew. She's wearing an adorable but dangerously short cream-colored baby doll dress with gray knee-highs, a pageboy cap perfectly askew over her signature short pixie-cut hair. She looks like a sexed-up version of Tiny Tim. Without the crutch.

"What's wrong, gimp?" I say out the window. "Run out of horse tranquilizers?"

"I showed the neighborhood kiddies how to back-handspring, and my knee went all wonky on me," she chirps, getting into the car. "It'll be good once I'm busy enough to ignore the pain."

I open the glove compartment and pull out a Shake It Cold chemical ice pack, which features a picture of eleven-year-old Deanna in her leotard giving the thumbs-up sign. I shake it up and hand it to her.

"Are you all right to go to school?" I ask, eyeing the swell of her right knee. Seeing the scar still makes my stomach go sour.

She slaps the ice pack on her knee. "Ohmygosh, this is nothing! Once, during a competition, I sprained my ankle so bad it swelled up bigger than my head!" She gives a half-second shudder at the memory and starts dancing in her seat. *"Whaddup, Gigi, let's go to school, got to get educated, don't be a fool!* I brought Pop-Tarts, is Aloha meeting us at school?"

"Yes, you spaz, she's meeting us. God forbid she actually does what Fiona tells her to. She *knows* Fiona wanted us to come to school together for the rest of rush."

"Blah, blah, black sheep," Deanna groans, handing me a strawberry frosted Pop-Tart and taking one for herself. "Be nice, you know you love her."

I hold the breakfast pastry in my hand, feeling its weight. "Do you know how many calories are in this?"

"Zoink!" Deanna plucks the Pop-Tart out of my hand and takes a huge bite out of it. She hands it back. "There, now it's half the calories."

"Thanks?"

"Did I ever tell you how I wasn't allowed to eat enough food to grow boobies?"

I take a bite of the Pop-Tart. It is ridiculously good. "Really?"

"True story." Deanna stuffs the rest of her Pop-Tart in her mouth. "Now I'm trying to eat my way to double-Ds. How am I doing?" she asks, sticking out her still very flat chest.

"Wow," I deadpan, "those are huge."

"You lie and I love you for you it," she squeals, leaning over to kiss me on the cheek, before twirling her bangs into a perfect point hanging between her eyebrows. "Oh! Did you read the *Trumpet* yesterday?"

"I could never find it!" I smack the steering wheel, remembering my frustration. "And I wanted to look after school, but . . ."

I trail off, sighing, and finish my Pop-Tart.

"But you had a special top-secret meeting with Fiona?"

I try for a noncommittal shrug.

"Wait," Deanna says, "you didn't even call me last night. How late were you out with the pretty little fascist?"

"Late," I grumble.

"Why?"

"You know I can't tell you—"

"Can it with the goody-two-shoes bit, sister, and spill. What'd she make you do this time?"

I sigh. "She had me stealing toilet paper from all the rest-stop bathroom stalls between here and New Hampshire."

"She's a freaky deeky!" Deanna howls with laughter. "Did she tell you why?"

I shift in my seat, trying to stretch out the knot between my shoulder blades. "To try and get me arrested? I don't know. She barely said two words to me the whole time."

Deanna reaches over and digs her fingers into my back. "So you just drove around all night, not talking?"

"Oh, she talked. *Ow!* Not so hard!" I try unsuccessfully to move from Deanna's reach without letting go of the steering wheel. "She just didn't talk to *me*. She sat in the backseat and whispered on the phone. *Ow!* I said not so . . . uuugggggghhhh."

The knot releases, I turn into Jell-O.

"That's the spot, right?" Deanna giggles, the fingers of one hand knuckling deep between my shoulder blades. "Could you hear what she was whispering about?"

She pats me on the back, the massage over. I give a happy shudder. "Paint color, I think."

"Score!" Deanna punches the sky. "I bet they're painting the DOS for us!"

"I hope not. She kept talking about the color red, and I'd like to picture the DOS awash in a creamy beige."

"For *real!*" Deanna agrees. "Very relaxing. Speaking of, I heard there's a giant fountain in the DOS with a statue of Ms. Cady as Poseidon in the middle."

"Just how big do you think the DOS is?" I laugh.

Deanna grins. "If it's big enough for a pool, how could it not be big enough for a fountain?"

"You have a point."

"Did Fiona buy you snacks at least?"

I snort. "She made me buy them. I think I got a chemical burn from eating too many Atomic Fire Balls. Where was the *Trumpet,* anyway?"

*The Trumpet of the Swan* is our school newspaper, run by a clique called the Voice of the People, otherwise known as the Vox Foxes. They dress in pencil skirts, silk blouses, and pumps, with sheer stockings. They tend to move only as a group, and cruising down the hall wearing coordinating matte red lipstick, they look like a formidable army of secretaries from a 1960s typing pool.

"In Ms. Cady's coat closet. The one next to those wooden

telephone booths at the end of the second-floor science wing. It was down in the left toe of her trout-fishing waders."

Every morning the Vox Foxes hide the one and only copy of that day's *Trumpet* somewhere on campus. They stopped printing out the full circulation after the Greenies climbed up the south turret, housing the Vox Foxes offices, and chained themselves to the roof until the Foxes agreed to save the earth by cutting their circulation down to one. Since the *Trumpet* started out as a paper venture, tradition dictates that it stay that way. Publishing online just isn't an option.

Usually, the first-years find the *Trumpet*, running around before homeroom yanking open closet doors and crawling under the sagging armchairs in the library, giddy and brimming with innocent joie de vivre. Once they find it, word spreads, and usually at some point during the day everyone takes a few minutes to read it, standing with their head inside the shade of a floor lamp or holding themselves up as long as possible on Ms. Cady's chin-up bar, the *Trumpet* taped to the ceiling above.

"So what'd the *Trumpet* say?" I ask.

Deanna bounces up and down with laughter. "It announced the final duty for the first-years! Holy guacamole, those poor pooper-scoopers are going to *stink!*"

"Wait, what are you talking about? What's the duty?"

First-year duties are the other tradition at Swan's Lake. It may seem a bit coarse to have first-years do things like find and clean *only* the windows shaped like triangles, or have a contest as to who can find and dust the longest line of uninterrupted chair rails, but it really teaches first-years the ins and outs and ups and downs of Swan's Lake.

"So," I ask again, "what's the duty?"

"It's doodie duty!" Deanna shrieks. First-years always work from basically the same list of duties all year, supervised by the sophomores. But the last duty for first-years is one the sophomores get to think up, and it's traditionally something absolutely ridiculous and seemingly impossible. "They have to fertilize all the flower beds with cow poop! *And* it's BYOP—they have to bring in the stinky stuff themselves!"

She howls with laughter, slapping her good knee. "Oh, and the *Trumpet* also said that the ballot box for Founder's Ball queen is up outside Carlisle's office."

"Why do they even bother with a ballot box? Everyone's going to vote Fiona as queen, and Cassandra and Poppy as her court."

"Tradition, I guess." Deanna shrugs and then turns her shrug into a shimmying dance. *"And that's gonna be us next year! The queen's court, baby!"*

My cell phone rings, and when I see it's my dad, I hand the phone to Deanna.

"Hi, Dr. Bruce!" she chirps, and then, "Oh! And hi, Dr. Lane!" She moves the phone away from her face to whisper, "It's both of them." She listens and says, "I know, it *is* an early wake-up! Student Council, you know. Oh yes, she's right here, but she's driving, so she can't talk." Deanna laughs. "I *know* you approve, Dr. Lane!" She lifts the cold pack off her knee and pokes at the scar with her free hand. "It's fine, hurts a little in the morning."

A minute later she's off the phone, reporting to me what they said. "Okay, so your dad is stuck at the hospital working a double. He'll be home around three and will most likely pass out, but you should wake him up when you're ready for him to cook dinner."

I look at Deanna.

"To which your mom said, 'Oh, honey, you don't have to pretend you two aren't going to order out again. Just try to at least nibble a piece of lettuce along with the pizza.' And then your mom said she misses you guys so, so, so much. She's in Vancouver, it's beautiful, and she thinks you should all go there next winter break for some snowboarding. And she thinks you should bring me. Well, she didn't say that exactly, but it was, you know, inferred. Even if all I do is sit in the lodge, show off my scar, and have cute board dudes buy me cocoa." She thinks for a second. "Let's see, I think that's all they said. Oh"—she bats her eyelashes at me—"they both love you, and are proud of you, and want you to affirm and confirm before you start the day, because you're their little Gigi Bird, and they want you to fly."

I laugh. Deanna is the only person allowed to indulge in some light teasing about the fact that both my parents have bought into my mom's self-help theories big-time. My mom says when you tell someone your power statement, it takes away its power. But Deanna says she doesn't need her gymnastics power anymore, so at this very moment she giggles, presses her index fingers to her temples, and murmurs her old affirmation, "Super gymnastic powers . . . go!"

"You know you need a new power statement," I remind her. "My mom can help you come up with one if you want."

Deanna shrugs. "High school is cake compared to gymnastics. No special powers needed."

"If you say so."

*I'm Gigi Lane and you wish you were me.*

We crank up the stereo and are on our way.

# CHAPTER TWO

**Free\* Haircuts!\*\***
\*If you have shoulder-length or longer hair
\*\*We get to keep the hair.

**(Do-Goods, we're looking at you—bald kids need your help!)**

"Good morning, Ms. Cady!" we both scream as we pass the stone statue of our school's founder sitting proudly atop a rearing horse that guards the bottom of the school driveway. Two first-years, one dangling precipitously from the horse's towering left hoof, and the other sitting atop Ms. Cady's shoulders, look up at us as we pass, their polishing cloths paused.

We're a few minutes early, so we park and blast the heat.

I'm exhausted but antsy, shifting in my seat so I can see the parking lot entrance. "They should be here by now."

Deanna yawns and stretches, taking the ice pack off her knee, poking her scar, and tossing the ice pack back in the glove compartment before leaning back and closing her eyes. "We could take naps until they get here."

"I hope Aloha doesn't show up," I grumble. "Maybe that way Fiona would boot her out of the Hopefuls."

"Be nice," Deanna says, her eyes still closed. "You know Aloha is the best choice for our third. She's been our friend forever."

I try to bite my tongue, but words come out. "Not forever. You and I have been friends *forever*. Aloha's a transfer student. There is no forever, past or future, in our friendship."

"Gigi Lane." Deanna opens one eye and glares at me. "You're being a total butt-wipe."

I pout. "So?"

"So, we've talked about this. Is Aloha your friend?" Deanna, both eyes open now, pokes me when I don't answer. "Gigi!"

"Yes, she's my friend."

"Why?"

"Come on, Deanna." I groan, now regretting the fact that I walked right into a Deanna "Dear Heart" Jones love lesson.

"Gigi, why is Aloha your friend?"

I rush my oft-recited answer out in a sigh: "Because she's funny and smart and *kind of* pretty, and when we were ten, she helped us carry that dog that got hit by a car all the way to the animal hospital and then cried when it died."

Deanna nods. "Very good. I bet your heart grew two sizes just by saying that."

I snicker. "And because who else are we going to pick for our third? Daphne 'Dog Face' Hall?"

She tries not to, but Deanna giggles. "Or Heidi," she says, breaking into a devilish smile.

"Ick. No." I shudder. Heidi is in our year and is on the path to becoming Head Cheerleader, a position that any Swan with barely above-average looks and moderate intelligence would be thrilled with. But earlier this year, when Deanna, Aloha, and I were tapped as Hottie Hopefuls, and Heidi wasn't, she threw a fit. Flying pom-poms; furious scissors kicks; obscene, nonsensical cheers through her tears. It was hilarious. It was all just further proof she wasn't ready for the popularity pressure cooker that is the Hot Spot. "That would have been a total disaster," I say, a little giddy at the thought.

"*Total* disaster. Ooh, there's Aloha." Deanna points out the window.

I look down the hill and see Aloha's black Jeep screech into the parking lot. It roars up the hill and screeches again as she parks next to us, lurching to a stop, her hair flying in front of her face, her forehead almost hitting the steering wheel. Totally unfazed, she rolls down her window, and I roll down mine.

"Whaddup, tramps?" Aloha doesn't look at us, but at her own reflection in the visor mirror as she pops open a tube of lip gloss and smooths it on. "Are we early or are they late?"

I grimace as I watch her pucker her lips and make a kissy face at her own reflection. "Aloha, where the hell have you been?"

Deanna pokes me and mouths the words, *Remember the dead dog!*

I sigh and start again. "You know Fiona wanted us all here on time."

"Slept in," Aloha purrs, flipping the visor back up. "What?" she says with a smirk. "Afraid Fiona will lay into you for not 'controlling your fellow Hopefuls'?"

"Just get in the car," I growl.

"Hi, Aloha!" Deanna calls. "Get in, I brought you a Pop-Tart!"

"You're the tart, you tart!" Aloha calls back with a wink. She gets out of the Jeep and then makes a point of standing right by my window, smoothing down her hair and straightening her outfit.

Dear God, her outfit!

"Take it easy, Gigi," Deanna murmurs, leaning over me to roll up my window. "Just don't look at her."

I nod. And keep nodding. I'm still nodding as I say through gritted teeth, "But, Deanna, she totally stole my style."

"Dude," she cautions, "we cannot keep having this discussion. You guys have a similar look. That's all. Neither one of you is a style snatcher."

I glance out the window to where Aloha is picking an invisible piece of lint off of her vintage 1970s high-waisted jeans. "Oh, come on!" I whisper-yell. "She knows I have that exact same pair of jeans! What if I had worn them today? What then?"

"Then you would have popped your trunk and grabbed the spare outfit you keep exactly for that kind of emergency."

I shake my head. "But I shouldn't have to!" I hiss, trying to keep my voice down. "She knows as well as you do that 1970s nondisco, nonpolyester, nonhippie, non-bell-bottom fashion is my thing! I was the first one to grow out and feather my hair, and I was the one that started wearing those high-waisted jeans she's trying to cram her fat ass into, and I've been wearing dangly gold pendant necklaces for *years*. Plus, I have blond hair, which *clearly* works better for that sort of hairstyle. Her brown hair looks like feathered doggie doo-doo."

"Are you done?" Deanna groans.

I shrug. "Maybe."

"She'll be sweating in jeans today," Deanna finally offers. "It's chilly now, but it's going to be a high of sixty-two."

I glance out at Aloha, who is retucking her chocolate brown silk shirt into her jeans, a snug argyle sweater-vest with a deep V-neck over it.

"I suppose my dress *is* more suitable to the weather." I grin with a deep breath, smoothing down the fabric of my vintage micromini. "She'll stink up that silk before lunch."

"Exactly!" Deanna agrees.

"She's going to smell like roadkill! Thanks, Deanna." I pat her on her good knee. "I feel loads better."

Aloha gets into the car, flipping her feathered hair as she does. "I cannot wait for this rushing bullshit to be over with."

I whip around to glare at her. "If you hate it so much, you can drop out right now."

Aloha shrugs and takes the Pop-Tart Deanna is holding out. "Nah. You'd miss me too much. Besides, if I dropped out, then I'd have to go be a Glossy or a Cheerleader, and there's no way I'm going to demote myself."

I can't even look at her. "You shouldn't be so flippant," I snap. "You should show some appreciation."

"For what? The honor of picking up Fiona's dry cleaning?"

*I'm Gigi Lane and Aloha wishes she were me.* "Forget it. You just better hope they don't find out how lacking you are in sisterhood. Ms. Cady would be—"

"Ms. Cady was a tramp." Aloha laughs. "Why would I care what she thought of me?"

"She wasn't a tramp!" I turn around again. "She had lovers! And she chose not to limit herself by getting married and giving up all her rights!"

"She was a spinster hag!" Aloha shouts gleefully, clearly loving the fact that I'm so riled up.

Deanna levels a glare at both of us and orders, "Be nice."

Aloha pats her on the head. "Sorry, Dear Heart. Didn't mean to sully your delicate sensibilities."

"That's okay." Deanna shrugs. "You guys just drive me bonkers with your stupid faces."

We're all still laughing when I see a familiar sleek sedan pull into the driveway. "There they are." I wipe my eyes and wonder how, once again, Deanna has made everything okay.

The Jaguar slows as it passes us, my stomach twitching at the tinted windows, knowing they are looking right at us. "Let's go."

We get out and follow along behind the car as it parks, like we're Secret Service agents following the president's car in a parade. We take our places—Deanna and I on the driver's side,

Aloha on the passenger, all of us standing three steps back, our hands clasped behind us. "Like butlers," Aloha snorted the first time they made us do it, to which Fiona responded by making us address her only in pig latin for the rest of the month. When the engine shuts off, we glance at one another and then reach out at the same time and open the doors.

Fiona Shay sits in the driver's seat. She is putting on lipstick. She doesn't even look at me. "We're not ready yet." Next to her is her second in command, Poppy, and in the backseat sits Cassandra.

We close the car doors in unison and barely have time to step back into position before there are three quick knocks on the driver-side window from inside the car. We all reach out quickly and open the doors again. This time they get out.

Fiona steps so close to me I can smell her perfume, the brand of which I never find, no matter how many bottles I sniff at the mall. The scent is like a mix of gardenias and oligarchy.

"You'll wash the car," Fiona orders quietly, looking directly into my eyes. "And clean out the trunk. And when you're done, you will wait outside the DOS for further instructions."

Aloha pretends to stifle her groan when Fiona mentions the Den of Secrecy, and when Poppy, Cassandra, and Fiona all level their stares in her direction, Aloha just smirks at her shoes.

Fiona looks at me. "Control your Hopefuls, Lane."

I nod, swallowing against the dryness in my throat. "Aloha," I say, turning toward her. "School song. Five times."

Aloha snorts.

Fiona glares at me, raising her eyebrows.

"In Latin," I add, "and backward."

Fiona nods her approval and walks away, followed by Poppy and Cassandra. We stand watching them, their perfect hair, their perfect posture, cutting a perfect silhouette of popularity for us to step into next year.

Aloha stops reciting as soon as the three are in the building, and wrinkles her nose. "This car smells like ass."

"It's got a bad case of the funk," Deanna agrees, kicking a piece of something smooshy off the front tire. "Did she make you drive through the dump on the way back from New Hampshire?"

I shake my head. "We used my car for New Hampshire. I dropped her back here to pick up her car."

"Why'd you go to New Hampshire?" Aloha asks.

"That's classified and you know it," I snap. "Go get the hose."

Aloha stares at me for a long moment.

"The hose, Aloha," I say firmly.

After she stomps off toward the shed, Deanna sighs.

"What?" I ask, already defensive.

"You could have told her," she reasons. "You told me."

I shrug. "She doesn't deserve to know. You saw the way she acted, she was a total embarrassment."

"She's just being herself."

"Exactly," I agree. "An embarrassment."

The car *does* stink, inside and out. We take turns holding our breath and leaning into the trunk, the portable hand vacuum bucking as it sucks up bits of glass, metal, and unidentifiable gunk. We spray the whole trunk down with carpet cleaner and scrub, and then stretch an extension cord from the basement so we can blow-dry it with the emergency hair dryer I keep in my trunk.

By the time we're done, it's almost 7:00 a.m., and we still have to find the Den of Secrecy, the Hot Spot's secret meeting room. There are tons of rumors about what's inside—a tanning booth; a movie theater; a trampoline; hammocks slung between imported palm trees; a 360-degree mirror box so you can check out what other people really see when they look at your ass; a pool; a kitchen loaded with goodies; a bathroom fully stocked with every cream, lotion, and serum you could ever wish for; and a walk-in closet filled by the *Network* every spring and fall with fashions so forward no one outside of Europe has even seen them yet.

The deal is Head Hottie gets the key to the DOS the first day of senior year. Unless the Hopefuls can find it before the end of the Founder's Ball. If we find it first, we get to spend the rest of the year hanging out in the DOS with this year's Hot Spot.

"You scabs ready for another exercise in futility?" Aloha asks once we're on the landing of the narrow back staircase.

"Perk up, pups," Deanna chirps. "I bet this time we find it."

Aloha rolls her eyes. "It's so cute the way you're delusional."

We decide to look on Founder's Path, the long hallway that marks the old path from the main house to the shed where Swans built Ms. Cady's stunt plane. Now it leads from the senior locker wing to the main entrance of school in the original mansion. Dusting the two dozen Ms. Cady portraits that line Founder's Path is one of the first duties first-years get, and I remember staring in awe at the various images as I ran my dust cloth over the lines and curves of the gilded frames.

"Let's check behind the paintings again," I decide once we're there, peeking behind an eight-foot-tall portrait of Ms. Cady standing next to a giraffe. "Knock on the wall, see if it sounds hollow. There might be a hidden door we missed last time."

Aloha snorts. "You really think Fiona hoists herself through a hole in the wall to get to the DOS?"

"Shut your piehole and knock, Aloha," I snap, moving on to peek behind a cubist rendition of Ms. Cady jumping out of a biplane. "Unless you have a better idea."

Aloha leans on the wall in front of me, blocking my way. "Oh, I have *lots* of ideas, Gigi. You have no idea what great ideas I have."

I hear someone walking up behind me and turn to see Daphne "Dog Face" Hall stop dead in her tracks, as if my gaze has frozen her to the spot.

"Gross!" I gasp, looking at her.

She blinks.

Deanna looks up from the portrait she's checking to shoot me a warning look, and starts hurrying toward us. "Hey, Daphne," she says with a smile, "what's up?"

"Um . . . ," Daphne mumbles. "I'm just going to the art room."

I can feel a familiar, prickling heat rush up over my scalp. I make a shooing motion with my hands. "So, go then."

Daphne doesn't move, she just stares at me, *blinking.*

The heat lets loose and washes over me, sinking into my skin, incinerating my insides until my ears whoosh with the sounds of liquid fury.

"Get your fat ass off Founder's Path, you stupid, ugly troll," I hiss. I step closer to her, going in for the kill. "You're using the wrong moisturizer, and you have stubby eyelashes."

"Dude!" Deanna says, smacking me on the arm. "Don't be a dick!"

Daphne backs away and then turns, breaking into a herky-jerky train wreck of a run toward the arts wing.

"She started it," I huff, my body cooling as Daphne runs out of sight.

"She's got a face like a popped zit." Aloha yawns.

"You're both evil tarts," Deanna says, "and you're going straight to hell."

Aloha nudges Deanna with her hip. "Then why are you friends with us?"

Without thinking, Deanna says, "Because if I wasn't around, they'd burn you at the stake for bitchcraft."

"Oh, crap," Aloha groans. Too late, I see Ms. Carlisle, our headmistress and resident fashion don't, walking toward us. There's a reason that in the "Letter from the Headmistress" section of our brochure there's just a picture of the nameplate on her office door.

28

She's wearing a lavender skirt suit that I am sure is made of polyester. She adjusts her giant vinyl purse, causing the suit jacket to fall open.

"Ew!" Aloha laughs into her hands, covering it with a fake sneeze, as we all try to look away from Ms. Carlisle's too snug skirt. Its waist is directly beneath her chest, and the skirt squeezes its way down her pouchy stomach, over her bulging thighs, to end in a hideous, flouncing petal-cut hem at her knees.

"Good morning, ladies," she crows, smiling so wide her smudged plastic glasses slip down to the tip of her nose. I try not to flinch at the brown stains on her snaggled teeth. I can't believe *that's* the public face of Swan's Lake.

"Good morning, Headmistress," we answer in unison.

"And what are you ladies up to so early this morning?" Ms. Carlisle starts rifling through her ugly purse, digging in up to her elbow.

"Student Council meeting," Deanna says brightly.

"That's nice, dears. You know, Ms. Cady was a big fan of the saying 'The early bird gets the worm.'"

Aloha grumbles, "She probably ate them."

If Ms. Carlisle hears, she doesn't show it. We rush out a quick good-bye as she pulls out her office key, and make our way to the main entrance.

We pass by the main double doors to school, and through the mottled colors of the stained glass we can see the two rows of first-years with morning duties lining up on the front steps.

"Poopers. Foiled again." Deanna sighs. "We're *never* going to find the DOS."

"Nonsense," I snap. "We're not going to be the first Hottie Hopefuls in the history of Swan's Lake to not find the DOS before the Founder's Ball. Now, where are they?"

"Here." We look to where Fiona is walking down the wide, curving main staircase into the entrance hall, her hand running lightly along the dark, polished banister. Cassandra and Poppy follow. "We're here." Cassandra glowers at us as they reach the bottom. "Where were *you*?"

"We finished the car," Deanna offers.

Poppy clucks her tongue. "You were supposed to find us in the DOS."

"Yeah, well, we tried." Aloha smirks. "But we were interrupted."

"You'll have to try harder," Fiona says. "If you don't find it, how in the world do you expect to use it next year?"

"Wait, *what*?" I jump forward. Fiona narrows her eyes at me. I take a step back. "You said we'd get the location on the first day of school next year. That's what you read to us from the Hottie Handbook."

"Yes, that's true," Fiona admits after a moment. "But no Incumbent has ever had to wait to be *given* the location. Usually the Head Hottie Hopeful would have found it by now."

Aloha snorts and I shoot her a quick glare.

"You're too late now anyway," Poppy informs us. "The first-years are here. You'll be supervising them in cleaning the

Oriental rugs from the underclassmen locker hall. We've given the second-years the morning off from supervising. Find us in the DOS before first period."

Aloha snorts again, and Deanna makes a squeaking sound.

Fiona focuses her gaze on me. "I suggest you advise your fellow Incumbents that snorting like a pig or making sweet little baby sounds will not get them out of their responsibilities. If they would rather not be in their current position, they are welcome to clear the cliques and find another home for senior year."

This shuts even Aloha up. Clearing the cliques is this completely humiliating process that transfers go through where they spend a week or so with each clique until they settle somewhere near the bottom. Transfers never get top tier. *Well, most of them don't,* I think, trying not to snarl at Aloha's platform wedge sandals. Fiona and the others walk up the staircase, not looking back at us.

"Do you think the DOS is upstairs, then?" Deanna wonders.

"Could be," I say. "But we've searched up there a dozen times."

Outside the front doors the first-years have started singing our school song, which, following tradition, they will sing louder and louder and more and more obnoxiously until we let them in.

"'We are the sisters of the swan!'" they sing. One of them kicks the door.

Aloha laughs. "Cheeky little brats, aren't they? Should we let them in or make them chew through the doors?"

"'We weave a tapestry of sisterhooooooood!'" the first-years scream from outside, slapping their palms on the mottled glass inlay.

I nod at Deanna, and she pulls open the doors. Immediately the singing stops, replaced by gasps and squeals of "Dear Heart!" and the mob of girls pushes through the doors, breaking formation in a thundering scuff of ballet flats to surround Deanna.

"Are you leading duties today?" they ask, their legs still too long for their bodies, their chipmunk cheeks just beginning to thin, their bangs finally growing out from the blunt short cuts that mothers of unfortunate junior-high girls insist on. "Can you teach me to do a back kickover?"

They are giggly, and earnest, and young. Until they see first me and then Aloha watching them. They swallow their giggles, try to settle their breath. They change the way they stand, the way they tilt their heads. A hush falls over them. They stare at us, flushed and gulping.

It's like I'm watching the incarnation of my affirmation. I'm Gigi Lane, and every single one of these Swans wishes they were me.

"The rugs in the underclassman locker corridor need to be beaten," I inform them, thrilled at the low, no-nonsense sound of my voice. "There are three rugs. Four of you to a rug. You can bring them out to the garden by the kitchen; there are ropes already strung up for you to hang them. Grab brooms from the kitchen supply cupboard to beat the dust out. Stay away from the Deeks' courtyard; we don't want to have to pay a ransom to get you back. You will return the rugs to position by first bell. Understood?"

They all nod. I stand there, not moving, not speaking for a long moment. Beside me I see Aloha smile at me. I wink at her. "Dismissed."

They scatter like marbles.

A couple of weeks later I'm running down the hall, hoping to get back to Human Biology so I can finish the final before the end of class. Fiona texted me halfway through to tell me to report to the DOS *immediately*, ignoring the fact we still haven't found it yet. We're not allowed to leave class during finals, and Ms. Blackwell refused until I showed her my test and whispered in her ear all the answers to the questions I'd yet to finish. When she finally nodded her approval, I dashed out of class and frantically started running up and down the halls, hoping that by some merciful stroke of luck I'd stumble upon the DOS, but instead I stumble over Beatrice.

"Shit!" I yell, almost knocking her over, my shoes pulling up the long Oriental rug as I skid to a stop. She grabs my arm, keeping me from falling.

"Hello, Gigi," she says when I've righted myself.

"Hey, Beatrice. What's going on?"

"Nothing of note." She helps me straighten the rug. "We're on a bit of a stakeout." She looks behind her, and I see the rest of the Vox Foxes leaning in a line against the lockers, one high-heeled foot apiece propped behind them, looking like a chorus line.

"Ladies." I nod.

Fiona says there's a long history of camaraderie between the Voice of the People and the Hot Spot, so I've made it a point to talk to Beatrice and the other Vox Foxes whenever I get the chance. There's a bit of doublespeak involved, since rushing the Hot Spot is supposed to be a secret endeavor.

"How's the end of the year going?" Beatrice asks.

"Well." I laugh as I catch my breath. "Actually, I'm running around like an idiot. How about you?"

"Oh, much better than you." She chuckles. "We get to *stand* around like idiots. Are you looking for Fiona?"

"Maybe . . . ," I falter, not wanting to break the first rule of the Hot Spot, which is, of course, don't talk about the Hot Spot.

"I think she's talking to my sister." Beatrice's older sister, Beverly, is a senior, the current editor of the *Trumpet*, and the head of the Vox Foxes.

"Where?"

"You think she'd tell us?" Beatrice sighs.

I sigh. "All right. Well, if you see them—"

"Heads up," Beatrice interrupts, turning on her heel to join the other Vox Foxes against the lockers.

Fiona's voice comes cracking down the hall. "Where have you been?"

I groan, and Beatrice gives me a pitying look as her sister

and Fiona come walking quickly toward us. "I had to stop waiting for you and go to the meeting without you."

"Foxes, let's go." Beverly doesn't stop walking, and the Vox Foxes fall in line behind her.

Fiona looks at me with such derision there's nothing I can do but affirm and confirm. *I'm Gigi Lane and you wish you were me.*

Fiona looks at her watch. "Don't you have a biology final to finish? You know our GPA requirements."

"You were going to take me to a meeting?" I can't help but be excited by this turn of events. Meetings mean power. "Are the Foxes in trouble?" I mime a one-two punch. "Did you have to put them in their place?"

"Gigi," Fiona snaps, "there is more to the Hot Spot than 'putting people in their place,' as you put it. We have a school to run."

I nod eagerly. "I understand."

She tips her head and studies me. "Do you really?"

"Of course!" I try for a confident tone, but to be honest, I'm a little taken aback by the intensity of her gaze.

She dismisses me with a wave of her hand, and I take off at a run back to biology.

I'm tearing around the corner into the arts wing when I actually do knock someone over.

"Son of a bitch, that *hurt!*" Aloha yells, hopping around on one foot, her hands gripping her shin.

"What are you doing here?" I gasp for breath. "You know the GPA requirements for Hottie Hopefuls! You should be in class."

"Relax, Gigi," she sneers, "I'm just going to take a tinkle, if that's okay with you."

"Aloha," I groan, "relax, okay? Do we really have to show our teeth whenever Deanna's not around?"

"Aw," Aloha says, laughing, "but what would we have in common if we didn't hate each other?"

"I . . . I don't hate you," I stammer, shocked at her words. I've always thought Aloha and I had a sort of sibling rivalry that resulted when one sibling was better looking and more success-ful than the other. There's not real hatred involved, just well-warranted jealousy.

"You don't hate me?" She feigns shock. "Let's hug and get matching Best Friends Forever necklaces! Oh, wait"—her face warps into a glower—"you already have matching BFF necklaces with Little Miss Sunshine."

"Deanna and I both really like you—"

"Cram it, Georgina," Aloha snaps. "The only reason I even talk to you is because I want into the Hot Spot."

I clear my throat. "First of all, my full name is only for emer-gencies. Second of all, I'm glad to know your true feelings. I'll make a note of them."

Aloha laughs in my face. "You do that, Gigi. You make *all the notes* you want."

We part ways without another word, and I'm almost back to my class when I hear a lackluster "She's got spirit, yes she do! She's got spirit, how 'bout you? It's Gigi! It's Gigi!"

Heidi moves limply through the cheer, her ever-ready pom-poms barely swishing as she raises them over her head before resting her hands on her hips and smirking at me.

"I'm late, Heidi. I don't have time to talk."

"Well, don't let me keep you," she says. "I was just doing my duty, paying my respects to the future of Swan's Lake."

I shake my head. "You're going to have to get over it, Heidi. You know there could only be three of us."

"And you let a *dirty transfer* in as your third."

"It wasn't my choice."

Heidi laughs. "Oh, Gigi, I know Aloha was the least of two evils in your mind. A transfer, yes, but without my—what did you call it? Trademark desperation?"

I step closer to her. "You'll want to watch your tone, Heidi. Cheerleaders may be top tier, but they're not untouchable." I lower my voice. "Remember when we were first-years, and the *you-know-whos* got that Cheerleader convicted of tax evasion? She spent two years in jail, sharing soap and sleeping with a sharpened comb under her pillow, before her lawyers got her off. That's the *Network*, Heidi. No one is untouchable."

"Oh, I know that, Gigi." Heidi smiles, showing all of her teeth. "No one is untouchable."

"I . . . I've got to get to class." I curse myself for stammering.

"You . . . you do that," she says, her smile too big for her stupid face.

"I will," I say, turning on my heel, the weight of her envy threatening to slow me down as I quicken my steps.

I groan loudly when I see Daphne "Dog Face" Hall coming from the opposite direction. She sees me and flinches, dropping her hall pass. I walk quickly toward her, and by the time she's picked up her pass, I'm standing right in front of her. "What are you doing?" I ask.

She holds up the hall pass and gulps.

"What are you, nine?" I snap. "That timid-little-girl act stops working once you get boobs. Now, I ask you again, what are you doing here?"

"You . . . you don't own the halls," she stammers.

I laugh in her face. "Right. You just keep telling yourself that."

"Why . . . why do you hate me so much?" she whimpers, fat tears pooling in her eyes and sliding down her cheeks.

"Oh my God," I groan, disgusted. "Don't *cry*! What the hell is wrong with you? Why must you cry every time we have one of our little chats?"

"I . . . I don't know."

"Well, I do. You cry because you're weak. Have you read my mom's book?"

Daphne shrugs.

I shake my head and sigh. "I keep telling you, read *Meet Your Tweet*. It'll change your life."

"Okay," she says quietly, her gaze fixed on the floor.

I reach out and lift her chin. "You said that last time, remember? Why should I believe you?"

"I'll . . . I'll read it."

"Good. Buy a copy. Don't get it from the library. My mom

doesn't get royalties if you get it from the library. Understood?"

She nods.

"Good. Now, run along."

As she turns, Daphne shoots me a millisecond-long glare of pure hate.

I remind myself of what Fiona told me at our first private meeting. *Their hatred isn't real, Gigi. They hate us the way first-years hate duties. They act like they hate us, but they know this school would fall apart without us.*

Lunch period is the time when the kiss-butts show themselves. Since the Hot Spot spends lunch in the DOS, it's our time for the teeming masses to pay their respects to the future leaders of Swan's Lake.

"Hi, Gigi!" I look up to see Margot Danesi standing at my elbow.

I'm sitting with Aloha at our usual spot in the cavernous dining hall, waiting for Deanna to buy her lunch. I didn't mention my altercation with Aloha to Deanna, and since then Aloha and I have kept a stony silence between us.

I glance at Margot and go back to my salad. "Hello, Margot."

Margot is a Do-Good, one of those community-minded pretty girls with admirable dental hygiene who volunteer for things like reading porn to the blind. She's a third-year and she's set to take over the Do-Goods in the fall. She was first in line for the hair-donation fund-raiser, and since then has been growing out a pixie cut that exposes the nape of her neck in the most tawdry way.

She's dressed in the Do-Goods' usual uniform: buttoned-up collared shirt, below-the-knee skirt in a fabric too heavy for the season, and the sort of sweet ballet flats first-years wear. She's added a silk scarf around her neck.

"You know, Margot," Aloha observes, "I don't think God would be *that* upset if you unbuttoned the top button on your blouse. After all, he gave you that rack, and I'm sure he wouldn't object to you airing it out once in a while."

Margot turns bright red. "Oh, Aloha, you card!" She laughs uncomfortably. "I swear you're going to get me in trouble!"

I sigh. "Oh, Margot, you know you never swear. Jesus hates a potty mouth."

"That's true," Margot murmurs in agreement.

"Hey, Margot!" Deanna says, sliding her tray onto the table and sitting down. "How's the pious life treating you?"

"Great!" Margot answers. "How are you?"

"Did you need something, Margot?" I ask, smiling, before Deanna can answer. "Because we have, you know, *business* to attend to."

Margot's eyes widen. "Oh, of course. *Business*. I was just saying hello."

"I'll make a note of it."

I peek out one of the basement windows, its bottom sill just inches above the asphalt of the student parking lot. It's past eight at night, and in the purple light I can see three dozen first-years and seniors spreading manure in the flower beds on the far side of the lot. That's the other thing about the first-years' last duty—seniors always show up to help them finish. It's an added bonus for the sophomores, who are stuck in that awful middle-child position of not being the youngest or the oldest in school. This way they get to think up a task gross enough to punish both the babies and the seniors.

"Aw, look at the little kittens pushing the poop!" Deanna laughs, getting up on her knees to look out the window next to me. We're sitting on a stack of old gym mats, watching Aloha try to fix the furnace.

"Do you really think old Gertie had this in mind when she talked about the 'service of sisterhood'?" Aloha's voice echoes from deep inside the furnace. "I thought she meant giving soup to dirty people and mercy-killing stray dogs." She steps back, her face smudged with black ash. "I can't see a damned thing in there."

"Well, look again." I hand her down a flashlight and fight a yawn. "There has to be a reason it's not working."

"I don't understand why we need a furnace in summer." Aloha ducks back in for another look. "Carlisle's the only one that'll be here, and I bet she doesn't wash her hands after she goes to the bathroom anyway."

"Is the flue open?" Deanna asks, looking again at an ancient set of instructions we found jammed into a crack by the furnace.

"Is *your* flue open?" Aloha snorts, standing up again.

"Don't be dirty. The flue, it's like the opening chimney thing." Deanna leans forward to hand Aloha the instructions. Aloha glances at them and throws them over her shoulder.

I sigh and slide off the mats. "Step aside."

"Gladly." Aloha yawns, climbing up next to Deanna.

I stick my hand in, feel for the little lever described in the instructions, and pull. "It's stuck." I grunt, pulling harder this time.

"Oh crap," Deanna gasps.

I just stand there looking at the dirty metal lever in my hand.

"I think that's supposed to stay in the furnace." Aloha laughs.

I groan, squatting down on my heels, dropping the bar, and holding my head in my gritty hands.

"Gigi?" I hear Deanna slide down from the mats onto her good leg. "Are you all right?"

I nod and hold up one finger, still covering my face with my hands. "I just need a second." Affirm and confirm. That's all I have to do. Affirm and confirm. *I'm Gigi Lane and*—

"Why's she mumbling?" I hear Aloha jump off the mats. "She's not freaking out, is she? Because she can't freak out—the Founder's Ball is only four days away, and we still have to find the DOS if we want to get sworn in. Gigi!" I flinch as Aloha claps her hands right next to my ears. "Gigi! Snap out of it!"

I peek between my fingers to see Deanna crouching down next to me as best she can, with her bad leg sticking out in front of her. "We're really close, you know that, right? Just a few more days and we'll find the DOS and get sworn in, and then rushing will be over forever."

"But the thing broke!" I cry, raising my head and limply lifting the broken lever. "And I don't know how to fix it and I don't know why we have to in the first place! I don't know why we have to do any of the things they've made us do!"

Deanna pats my shoulder. "Aw, buck up, camper! It hasn't been that bad."

"Hasn't been that bad!" I jump up, tears pricking at my eyes, motioning wildly with the lever. "Cassandra forces Aloha to do her accounting homework, like some common playground bully!"

"I do hate the spreadsheets," Aloha grumbles.

"And Poppy forces *you* to have lunch with disgusting Whompers and Gizmos!" I say to Deanna.

She laughs. "They're not that bad, Gigi."

"Those people are cretins!" I screech. "And Poppy just makes you talk to them because she thinks it's funny!"

Aloha points at me and looks at Deanna. "Make her chill out!"

"I'm chill!" I yell at her. "I'm just . . . I'm just having a *moment*, okay? Is that allowed? Am I allowed to have one moment when I'm not absolutely perfect? Now, hand me the damn instructions!"

# CHAPTER THREE

**Die, You Swiney Vine!**
**Climbing vines take over South Gate**

**(Whompers, out with your swords!)**

The envelope is there, on the pillow next to me, when I open my sleep-crusted eyes. I stare at it for a long time, my head ringing with lack of sleep. It's Founder's Ball day, and I know what the envelope means. It means it's been worth it. And it means my trials are over. The envelope is a smooth, solid weight in my hand. I flip it over, my heart jumping as I run my fingers over the red wax seal. A flame. Of course. It cracks in half when I lift the flap, and before I take out the card inside, I carefully peel off the two sides of the seal and lay them on my bedside table.

7:30
Basement

"It's really happening," I whisper aloud, pressing the card to my chest, trying to ignore a strange prickling feeling of coming doom. *Lack of sleep*, I tell myself, pasting on a smile and hoping it takes root. "It's really going to happen."

My cell phone rings.

"Gigi?" Deanna squeals. "Did you—"

"Yes!" I echo her tone, giving a fist punch in the air for effect.

Deanna squeals again, and I can hear the bedsprings squeak as she bounces. "Aloha, too! She just called me! We're coming over!"

Deanna is still in her polka-dot pajamas when she pulls up to the gate at the foot of my driveway in the JFM. She comes running up the flagstone path, clapping and jumping into my arms. My dad comes outside, looking like he slept in his scrubs, a crease from his pillow across his unshaven face.

"Urgl . . ." He clears his throat and rubs his eyes. "Everything okay, girls?" He blinks at the morning sun, as though he's trying to remember what day it is.

"Everything's *great*, Dr. Bruce!" Deanna grins.

My dad looks at me questioningly. "What's the good news, Gigi?"

"We're just pretty sure we got into the Spirit Society for next year, that's all."

"Aw, that's great, honey," my dad coos, hugging me. I rub my cheek against the fabric of his scrubs, a feeling I have loved since I was a little kid. "I have no idea what that means, but

45

I assume it'll look good on your college applications, so good for you."

"Whaddup, you tarts!" We all turn to see Aloha sauntering her way up the path to the front porch, twirling her car keys on her finger.

"Hey, Dr. Lane." She winks at my dad. "How're tricks?"

My parents have never been big on Aloha's marked lack of respect for her elders. "Things are fine, Aloha. And how are you? How are your parents?"

"They're fine. Getting ready to book their Hawaiian vacation this summer. You know, their annual celebration of my conception."

My dad tries to cover his grimace by smiling. "And what will you be doing while they're in Hawaii?"

Aloha shrugs. "Hanging out."

He shoots me a look to let me know that is *not* what I'll be doing all summer. "Gigi will be working on her college applications this summer, and volunteering at the clinic at the hospital."

"Bummer." Aloha shrugs. "You guys eat yet?"

"I'm going to get a few more hours' sleep before my shift." My dad lays his hands on my shoulders. "Your mom and I expect *lots* of pictures of you in your Founder's Ball gown tonight. We know you're going to look beautiful." He gives me a kiss on the forehead and goes inside.

"So I guess they don't care that we haven't found the DOS yet." Aloha winks at me. "Lucky for you."

"Lucky for *all* of us," Deanna corrects firmly. "None of us could find it."

Aloha shrugs. "Whatever. What's the deal for hair and makeup?"

"We have to be there at seven thirty tonight." I lean against the banister and cross my arms, pressing my hands up under my armpits to keep from scratching out Aloha's eyes. "That means we can still keep our four o'clock hair and makeup appointments, but then we'll only have, like, an hour to come back here and put on our dresses."

"Do you think they'll have the dresses delivered here?" Deanna asks. One of the privileges of being Head Hottie is that you get to choose the dresses that the Hot Spot *and* the Hottie Incumbents wear for the Founder's Ball, so that when we make our entrance, we are a vision of uniformity.

"I'm sure of it," I answer. "Fiona asked me where we were getting ready, so she knows we'll be here."

"Cool." Aloha stands up and stretches. "It's settled, then. Let's go stuff our gullets at Friendly's."

It's one of the happiest days of my life. We scream our heads off on the way to Friendly's, windows rolled down, singing along with one of Deanna's old *Set It Off!* playlists she used to listen to before gymnastics competitions. When we get there, Deanna is mobbed by the Saturday breakfast crowd, and she poses for picture after picture, looking adorable in her pajamas ("It's kind of like a senior prank," she says, even though she's the only one wearing them), and the cooks in the kitchen decorate her pancakes with an American flag made out of strawberries, blueberries, and whipped cream. Aloha stifles her inner wench, and we manage not to fight for the entire breakfast.

Once we get to Jean-Claude's salon, however, it's a different story.

"How's your mom doing, love?" Jean-Claude asks as he lays his cool, dry hands on my cheekbones, straightening my head and studying my bangs before moving behind me to comb out my hair.

"She's good," I answer. "She just left on a summer seminar tour."

On either side of me sit Deanna and Aloha, deep in conversation with their own stylists. Blythe, who is so obviously a former Glossy (beautiful face, mannish hands), is working on Aloha. She nods as Aloha explains the intricacies of her split ends. Deanna's stylist is a woman named Leech who wears tangerine-colored T-shirts she cuts the collars out of in order to show her chest tattoos.

"Good for her." Jean-Claude pulls his fingers through my hair. "So, what are we doing to your gorgeous hair for the big dance?"

I repeat exactly what Fiona said in her voice mail this afternoon. "Romantic updos, please." My stomach jumps at the thought of what dress might match such a sophisticated hairstyle.

Leech makes a barfing sound. "That go for you, too, Dear Heart?"

"Yep, just leave the pixie point."

"I cannot wait until I can chop that thing off." Leech scowls at Deanna's bangs, which come to a sharp point between her eyebrows.

"Chillax, Leechie!" Deanna chirps. "In a few months we can burn my contract *and* my bangs."

"Thank *God*," Leech groans. "Those devil-juice people can't be paying you enough to keep this."

"Hey!" I huff, faking offense. "First of all, it's called Razzmatazz Energy Elixir, and second of all, I *gave* Deanna that haircut."

Leech wiggles her tongue ring at me. "You should be shot for it."

I gave Deanna her first pixie point by accident in third grade, right before a competition. She won, the gymnastics press lost their minds over her haircut, so she kept it. When she got super famous, all of her sponsors put it in her contract that she had to keep the pixie point. It's seriously, like, against the law for her to get a haircut.

"Blythe," Jean-Claude says, glancing at Aloha's stylist. "Are you all set for a romantic updo?"

"We're doing edgy rocker," Blythe answers. Aloha smiles at me in the mirror. Blythe, watching her own reflection, pulls at Aloha's locks with her hairy knuckles, making it hang straight.

"*Excuse* me?" I ask, trying to swivel my chair, but it's all jacked up and my feet aren't touching the ground. Jean-Claude comes to my rescue and turns my chair for me so I can glare at

Aloha. "Not doing romantic updo? You heard the message from Fiona!"

Aloha doesn't have Blythe swivel her chair. Instead she just turns her head to smile at me. "Gigi, do you *really* think Fiona cares? Seriously, what's she going to do? Disband the *you-know-whos* because I refuse to get a cliché of a hairstyle? It's not like I'm Lydia Jarmush or something."

I'm speechless, a prickly, angry heat shooting up my neck to my cheeks. "Don't joke about Lydia Jarmush," I finally hiss.

"Seriously, Aloha," Deanna scolds, "it's superbad mojo to say her name in mixed company."

Leech sighs. "Fine. I'll ask. Who the hell is Lydia Jarmush?"

Deanna and I exchange a look. "She used to go to Swan's Lake," I explain. "But she was kicked out."

"Cool." Leech nods her approval. "I like her already. What'd she do?"

I try to remember the story that Fiona and the others took turns reading us from the Hottie Handbook.

"She and her boyfriend threw some kind of secret school dance," Aloha says dramatically, "and everyone lost their minds."

"Why would she do that? Stay still, please," Jean-Claude murmurs, twisting and pinning tendrils of hair around the crown of my head.

Aloha shrugs and goes back to her magazine, bored of the conversation. "Maybe because our dances aren't coed and she wanted to dance with her rebel boyfriend."

"Wait, boys aren't allowed at the Founder's Ball?" Blythe looks positively scandalized. "You should invite some, just for fun."

"Don't be crass," I snap. Leech, Jean-Claude, and Blythe exchange an amused look in the mirror. "I wouldn't expect you to understand," I tell them, "but tradition is everything at Swan's Lake, and boys weren't at the first Founder's Ball, so there's no reason for them to start attending now."

"That Lydia person doesn't sound so bad," Leech says, shrugging. "You'd think she threw pee at the gym teacher or something."

We all look at her.

"For example," she says with a grin so devilish it shows her gold tooth.

Blythe ends the conversation by turning on the razor and letting it snip and snap at the ends of Aloha's hair, giving her a thoroughly ridiculous asymmetrical cut complete with blue streaks that make her look like a cartoon character.

I grip the steering wheel on the way back to my house, squeezing it as hard as I can, wishing it would just crack like pretzels in my palms. My teeth grind together, and I take loud, deep breaths through my flared nostrils.

*I'm Gigi Lane and you wish you were me. I'm Gigi Lane and you—*

"Oh, get over it, Gigi," Aloha says from the backseat, not even bothering to raise her voice, looking me dead in the eye in the rearview mirror. "You're breathing like a bull in heat. And you're acting like a child."

Deanna starts fiddling with the stereo.

"I am *not* acting like a child," I growl. "*You* are acting like a total jerk."

Aloha yawns. "I'm just tired of you bossing me around."

"And what exactly do you think next year is going to be, huh?" I ask, raising my voice. "I'm going to be Head Hottie, you idiot! If you want to be in the Hot Spot with me, you need to answer to *me*."

Aloha laughs. "It's just pathetic. This is, like, the biggest thing that has ever—or will ever—happen to you. Do you really think anyone cares that you're going to be Head Hottie? Popularity is so twentieth century, Gigi. Nobody cares anymore. Except for you."

I look quickly to Deanna.

Aloha laughs again. "And don't fool yourself. Deanna doesn't care about this crap. All she wants is to hang out with you and have"—she starts imitating Deanna's voice—"'a super dooper senior year, just like all the others girls.' As if all those 'other girls' have to spend their Saturdays at the mall, making a big show out of drinking Razzmatazz Energy Elixir just so they can make good on a contract that's the only reason their mom can pay the mortgage on their house."

There is a good chance I will tear this steering wheel off and use it to beat Aloha over the head. I look for a place to pull over.

Deanna switches off the radio and turns to face Aloha.

"Aloha, what has gotten into you?" Her eyes brim with tears. "Why would you say that?"

"Oh, can it, midget," Aloha scoffs. "I'm immune to your America's Sweetheart act. Gymnastics isn't even a sport, it's just a way for flat-chested girls to get some exercise."

I yank the wheel to the right, sending half of my car up onto an embankment. "Oh my God, are you on drugs?!" I screech, snapping off my seat belt, kicking open my door, and jumping out of the car to face Aloha, who has calmly gotten out herself. "You don't talk to her that way!" I yell, pointing at Deanna and trying not to move enough to make my hair fall down.

"What are you going to do?" Aloha says with a defiant smirk, the jagged edges of her hair swaying in the breeze. "Hit me?"

I tighten my fists.

"Please," Aloha teases, stepping closer. "Do it. Show some *real* sisterhood. Ms. Cady would be so proud."

"Why are you doing this?" I whisper, my fists still gripped tight. "You're going to ruin everything."

"Would you two wackadoodles get back in the car?" Deanna calls from inside. "You're *both* the queens of the universe, okay? Can we stop with the pissing contest?"

I can't even speak. I just growl and get back in the car.

"It's heavy!" Deanna grunts, lifting the end of the huge covered garment rack that is waiting for us on my front porch when we get back to my house. Aloha leans against the railing as I lift the other end.

"Ooof. Jesus. It *is* heavy." We manage to cram it through the front door, but only when Aloha decides to move her lazy ass and help push.

I hate that Aloha's in my house. I hate that she's going to the fridge to get herself a Diet Coke. And I hate that I have no choice but to let her stay.

The mood is icy, and too quiet.

"Let's see what we've got here." Deanna's voice is tight with the sort of reedy sound it gets when she's trying not to cry. She pulls the large fabric cover off the garment rack, exposing three huge white garment bags.

"What the hell is this?" I pull at one of the bags. They are *enormous*, each one the size of an armchair.

"Yessss!" Aloha purrs, yanking down the zipper on one of the bags, her soda dangerously close to what I now see is a vibrant blue silk. I open the bag farther.

"But what the hell is it?" I poke at the fabric. "Why is the bag so big?"

"Here." Aloha rips an envelope off the hanger. "It comes with instructions. This one's yours. See?" she says, pointing to my name on the envelope. "Gigi."

Deanna has unzipped another bag and found a similar dress in a gorgeous deep raspberry color. The envelope in that bag has her name on it. "Oh, wow," she gasps, unfolding the instructions. "They're, like, Victorian prom dresses." She holds up an identical instruction page to the one I'm holding. There's a diagram on it of a woman wearing knee-length underwear, a series of progressively larger hula-hoop-looking things encircling her from hip to ankle. "Oh." Deanna giggles. "Great. They have hoops."

"I think they're fricking amazing," Aloha coos, opening the last bag and pulling out a truly gorgeous emerald green dress. "Classy, you know? None of this micromini hooker wear that leaves your ass in the wind."

Deanna glances at me, seeing if I'm going to react to Aloha's very obvious insult to the dress I wore to the winter formal.

"We should get these on," I say, pulling my dress from the rack.

*Fiona Shay would never steer us wrong,* I tell myself. It takes two hands to drag the garment bag up to my room. Deanna comes up with me, and Aloha, without a word, goes into the guest suite downstairs. I have no idea how she'll manage to get her dress on, because it quickly becomes obvious that these dresses are a two-person job.

"I guess this is why they had lady's maids back then." Deanna gives a weak laugh as I work my way up the row of buttons on the back of her dress. "Hey, do you think Ms. Cady had lady's maids?"

"No way. You know Ms. Cady only wore trousers."

In a fit of flat-chested fashion-crisis genius, Deanna cuts off a swatch of the sheer white gauzy curtain from my window and simple-stitches it over the plunging neckline of her gown, covering for her lack of cleavage.

# CHAPTER FOUR

**Hey, Gizmos–Squash That Bug!**
**Swan's Lake computer system down**

**(We know you think you're smarter than the rest of us—prove it!)**

*Fiona Shay would never steer us wrong,* I assure myself again, looking at Deanna and me in the mirror, our skirts so huge we both have to lean in to fit in the reflection.

Our waists are cinched, and all the chest God gave me is shoved up so high it looks like it's trying to make contact with my chin. Deanna pokes at one of my boobs. "Boing! I could do a double back handspring off those things."

"We look okay, right?" I ask her reflection, a feeling of unease chilling the pit of my stomach.

Deanna looks at me. When I don't look back, she grabs my wrist and tugs until I do. "Gigi, we look amazing. *You* look amazing."

I nod, taking a deep breath. "It just feels different than I thought it would. Aloha's throwing a shit fit, we're wearing dresses made for people without internal organs, and—"

"None of it will matter," Deanna says firmly. "In two hours none of that will matter. We'll be in the Hot Spot. We'll have the key to the Den of Secrecy. We'll have the Hottie Handbook. And more than that, we'll have *the Network*."

I nod again, though her mention of the Den of Secrecy makes me feel a little sick.

"Get your head in the game, Lane!" Deanna barks, stepping in front of me and snapping me out of my thoughts. "I'm going to scissors-kick you in the face if you don't stop your bellyaching and enjoy the best night of your life."

"You're right!" I force my voice into a yell.

"You're right I'm right!" Deanna yells back. "Now, affirm and confirm!"

I nod and stare at myself in the mirror. *I'm Gigi Lane and you wish you were me.* I think it again and again until my heart changes its rhythm to match the words. This is going to be the best night of my life. It has to be.

Aside from her stupid hair, Aloha looks adequate.

The only problem is that we can't fit in my convertible or Aloha's Jeep. The dresses are too big, the roofs too low. And we could open the roof of my convertible, but then there'd be too much wind resistance from our enormous skirts. Deanna would end up getting caught in a strong breeze and blowing all the way to Boston.

We try every limo company we can find, but they are all either booked up or so far away they couldn't get here in time.

So we go to the Founder's Ball in the Jones Family Minivan.

"Oh my God, look at the Ugly Ducklings," Aloha snickers when we get to the center of town, and we all turn to see the Swans from the elementary school standing on the picnic tables outside the general store, craning their necks to get a look up the hill. You aren't allowed up on the hill for the ball until you're a first-year, and even then first-years and sophomores have to perform duties like opening the doors, and they aren't allowed to even sneak a peek inside the ballroom.

I have been looking forward to this night since before I had boobs. But now, craning my neck to see Swan's Lake, with its crumbling bricks and sagging gutters, it feels like this isn't grand enough a place to have this night play out. I push the thought out of my mind. *I love Swan's Lake,* I tell myself. She is the grande dame. My old lady. She is stately, and regal, and timeless. And next year she's going to be my responsibility. Socially speaking, of course. I look over as Deanna pats my hand.

"What a pile of crap," Aloha snorts, leaning forward from the backseat between Deanna and me to look at the school from the student parking lot. "Who puts a widow's walk on a Georgian mansion? No wonder enrollment is down."

I grit my teeth. *I'm Gigi Lane and you wish you were me.*

● ● ●

58

No one answers my first knock on the door at the bottom of the basement stairs.

"Dude, I can't believe the DOS is in the basement. How could we miss it?" Deanna whispers.

"I bet it's not. I bet they're going to make us fix the furnace again," Aloha snorts.

I knock again. Nothing. Aloha reaches past me and bangs on the door with the palm of her hand. This time there is a click as the handle turns, and the door opens just a crack. Deanna grabs both of our hands, and a moment later the door is pulled wide open. Inside, the furnace glows red through its iron smile, barely lighting up the pile of old gym mats and the outline of the rest of the random cast-off junk. We step in, waiting for our eyes to adjust to the darkness.

"Oh, for Pete's sake, is that a door?" Deanna whispers, nodding toward the mats. And sure enough, next to the pile of mats is an open door.

"How did we not see that before?" I whisper back.

"Because we're ding-dongs. And the mats were in front of it," Deanna groans, keeping her voice low.

She grips my hand and pulls me forward so I'm leading the way. It's dark through the door, but not totally pitch black. The furnace in the basement gives off enough light to see shadows, enough to see that we are in a small room made smaller by a jumble of broken school desks and athletic equipment stacked ceiling high, leaving just a small square in the middle of the room for standing.

"This can't be it," Deanna whispers. It is musty in here, and my eyes start to itch and my nose starts to run. I am two seconds away from sneezing my hair out of its careful design when a bookcase in the corner moves. None of us gasp; we just hold our breath and watch as it moves again, swinging open to reveal a dark doorway.

"Whoa," Aloha says, not whispering at all. "Sweet!"

I can feel Aloha flinch slightly the moment before she starts to move, and I step quickly forward, getting to the hidden door a split second before she does. I pull it the rest of the way open. It's heavy, and I end up having to use two hands, my high heels slipping and scraping on the dusty cement floor until the door is open wide. I wipe my sweating palms on my dress and look at Deanna and Aloha.

They are just silhouettes in the darkness, bulbous in their gowns, Deanna's hair a tower, Aloha's a shaggy mop. I should say something, I know I should. Something inspirational, something to mark the months and months of hard work we've been through to get to this moment.

I swallow dry air and clear my throat, but no words of inspiration come. This doesn't feel the way I thought it would. There is no magic in this moment. I feel a cold crush of dread descend on me, and I try to shake it off. *I'm Gigi Lane and—*

"Are we going in or what?" Aloha whispers loudly.

I know I should ignore her and finish my affirmation, but I don't. I just nod and lead the way into the room.

I walk quickly, thinking I'm going to have to take several

steps forward to make room for Deanna and Aloha, when I am stopped by the corner of a table.

"*Ooof.* Whoops, sorry," I mutter as Deanna runs into me and starts cracking up.

"I just bounced off Gigi's dress butt!" she whisper-laughs as Aloha runs into her.

"Shhh!" I hiss. My thigh throbs where it hit the corner of the table, and I can imagine the green blue bloom of a bruise growing there. I am dizzy in the darkness, and I lay the tips of my fingers on the table to steady myself, trying not to let the words *Wrong, wrong, wrong, this is all wrong* from running through my head.

I frantically scan the room, hoping to see the shadows of plush couches, crystal lamps, a fireplace, a television, a private kitchen . . . anything that would make this place closer to what we thought it would be instead of what I am realizing it is. A small room. A very small room. Small enough so it feels like the air I am breathing is coming right out of someone else's mouth. I am gripped with the fear that the lights will turn on and we'll be looking at a couch with three broken legs and a table made out of milk crates under a spray-painted sign that crookedly spells out DEN OF SECRESY.

I slip off one shoe and gingerly lower my toes to the floor. *Please be a cashmere rug imported from Italy, please, please, please,* I think as I touch the cold cement floor.

"Um . . . Gigi?" Deanna murmurs. "Did you just take off your shoe?"

I slip my shoe back on.

"Freak show," Aloha mumbles, and it's like I can feel her smirking at me.

*Maybe this is another anteroom,* I think, trying to comfort myself. They'll open up another door, and it will lead to a huge room, the *real* DOS. It will have an inverted-dome ceiling, just like the ballroom, and it will be built entirely of white marble, with huge windows flooding it with beautiful light. The bookcase door closes behind us, and the room becomes pitch dark.

We wait. Deanna and Aloha eventually move to either side of me, the rounded hips of their dresses brushing against mine. We hold hands. Deanna laces her fingers through mine, palm to palm, and gripping hard. Aloha basically flops her dead-fish hand into my palm, leaving me to hold it, her fingers curled and motionless and cold.

We aren't alone in the darkness. I can hear people breathing, but after a while it is hard to hear over the pounding of my own heart.

*The bodies of three girls were found in the basement furnace room of Swan's Lake Country Day School for Young Women. They apparently died of disappointment.*

There is a rustle, a sound like the extra blanket being stretched up to your chin the first cold night of fall, and then there is a sharp click. A flame rises out of a lighter, whoever is holding it still in darkness. The flame rises and then curves as it dips deep inside something opaque—the edge of a tall, thick white candle. When the candle is lit, a warm white glow spreads from the table I bumped into. The light doesn't reach far, but we can now see the silhouettes of three figures on the other side of the table. They are wearing monkish cloaks, in a thick gray fabric, with tulip arms and oversized hoods that reach over their faces, so that only their chins and bottom lips show in the flickering light.

We all know it's Fiona, Poppy, and Cassandra, but the way they stand so still, so silent, makes the hair on the back of my neck stand at attention. Their arms are hidden, crossed in front of them and tucked into their sleeves.

*Open the next door,* I think, scanning the too-close walls of the room. *Please, open the next door.*

"The Hopefuls will bow."

The voice scares me so badly I automatically start an *I'm Gigi Lane,* before I'm interrupted by the voice coming again. It is a screeching, distorted, terrifying voice that echoes off the walls and scrapes up our spines. Every undepilatoried hair on my body stands on end, vibrating from the echo of that horrible voice. *It's a recording,* I tell myself, *it's just a recording playing through a speaker behind us.* But then my stomach lurches as I feel someone's hot breath breathing in my ear, and that awful voice says again, "The Hopefuls will bow!"

Deanna squeezes my hand so hard I think I hear it crunch, while Aloha jumps, her hand slipping out of mine. I am actually thankful for the chance to bow, to close my eyes and try to keep my hair-heavy head from spinning. Who *was* that? If all three Hotties are standing in front of us, who is behind us?

I bury my face in the bulging skirt of my dress, breathing

in its scent, trying to calm myself. Still doubled over, I turn my head, and in the candlelight I can see Deanna looking right back at me, her eyes crossed and her tongue sticking out. I smile nervously and wink at her and turn my head to look at Aloha. I'm startled to see her staring right at me, like she was just waiting for me to look her way. She slowly raises her eyebrows, and my heart goes cold. Someone blows out the candle, and the room is dark again.

"The Hopefuls will stand." This time it is the Hot Spot that speak. All of them at once, their voices creating an uneven harmony. We stand up straight, and they fall silent for so long that I flinch when they speak again, interrupting what sounds like the beginning of a snore from Aloha.

"Who was our founder?" they ask.

"Ms. Cady." We answer automatically, just like we did in baby-school spirit class.

"And what is our motto?"

"For the good of our sisters is for the good of our school. For the good of our school is for the good of our sisters."

*Is this it?* I think. *Is this our initiation?* It feels so sudden, so unremarkable, so totally devoid of the sort of ceremony I was expecting. *Wait!* I want to scream. *Please, just slow down!*

This time only the person in the middle speaks, and as soon as she does, I can hear it's Fiona. "From this moment forward you will live by that motto until the day you die by that motto. The Hot Spot are the keepers of secrets. We are the chosen protectors of our school."

I try to pay attention, swallowing back disappointed tears.

"You must never tell"—this time it is Poppy speaking—"the things we will teach you."

"Repeat after us," the chorus chimes, again in unison.

*Please wait,* I beg silently, *please just slow down and make it last.*

> *"Never will we share your secrets.*
> *Never will we betray your trust.*
> *For you are our school, our home, our hope, our heart.*
> *We are in your service; we are in your debt.*
> *We are your sisters, we are your daughters,*
> *we are your Swans."*

We repeat, line after line, and by the end I give up fighting to keep my voice above a whisper, and instead just mouth the words, afraid that if I do speak, I'll cry.

"Gigi." I snap to attention when I hear my name. It's just Fiona talking now, and I watch the sharp tip of her chin as she speaks. "Do you swear to uphold the secrecy and sanctity of the Hot Spot?"

I struggle to push my voice above a whisper. "I do." In the back of my throat there is the bitterness of knowing that the "ceremony" I had so looked forward to is coming to a truly anti-climatic end.

Fiona goes down the line, asking each of us.

And then she says something that stops my heart.

"We were not alone in this room."

I'd forgotten, for a moment, the voice.

Again the Hot Spot speak in chorus. "And you will not be alone at Swan's Lake. You will be watched, and you will be assisted. And you will be judged.

"We have something for you," the chorus drones. Fiona pulls her hands out of her sleeves. In one hand she holds an ancient-looking brass key. The candlelight reflects off its polished surface, and then she tips her palm. I reach out my hand and catch it as it falls.

"The Den of Secrecy is yours. From this moment on you are part of the Hot Spot. Do not disappoint us."

I can't stop myself. "*This* is the Den of Secrecy?" I blurt out.

Fiona smiles and shakes her head. "Of course not. You'll see the DOS after the Ball."

"Oh. Of course." I gulp, slightly relieved. I try to keep my voice low, in the spirit of what should be a solemn occasion. But I can't help but ask, "And what about the Hottie Handbook?"

I hear Fiona move, and a second later the room is flooded with ugly fluorescent light.

I think I can actually feel my heart breaking.

"You'll get it after the ball," Fiona says with a shrug. She strips off her heavy gray robe, and Poppy and Cassandra do the same, revealing ball gowns just like ours.

"Can't we just give them the handbook now?" Cassandra groans.

"Oh, come on, let's give them one more night of freedom. You know the rules," Fiona says firmly, and I'm grateful at least to hear her familiar Head Hottie tone of voice. "The handbook changes hands at midnight."

"So are we done here?" Poppy yawns. "I want to go dance."

Fiona moves toward the door. "I think we're good. Let's go get my crown."

"Wait!" I cry out, stepping in front of her. "That's it? That can't be it. What about the ceremony? What about the initiation?"

Fiona cocks her head to the side. "That was the ceremony."

"And you were initiated," Poppy agrees. "You said 'I do,' right?"

"I just . . . I just thought . . . ," I stammer.

"You thought it would be . . . *more?*" Fiona asks, a wry smile playing on her lips. "The *more* comes later. *This*"—she motions to the small room, the robes lying in a heap in the corner—"this is just a stupid tradition. So is the Founder's Ball. The real fun, and the real work, comes next year." She moves closer to me, her eyes sparkling. "The DOS. The handbook. The Network. That's the stuff that will really get your heart pounding."

*Believe her,* I tell myself, wishing I could make butterflies flutter into my stomach, wishing I could shake the feeling that Fiona is just telling me these things so I won't ruin her night. Cassandra and Poppy stare uneasily at Fiona, like they, too, are unsure if Fiona's reassurance will take root. Poppy opens her mouth to speak, but Fiona silences her with a slight shake of her head.

"Next year, Gigi," Fiona says with a smile. "Next year is *your* year."

I can feel Deanna and Aloha watching me, waiting for my reaction. I don't want to ruin this for them, I don't want to cry and ask, *Why doesn't this feel better?* I want this night to be the night we've dreamed of. So I smile, and I let Fiona's words sew up my broken heart. But I can't help that there are gaps between the stitches.

I let everyone else go ahead of me as we climb single file up the back staircase to the senior hall. I need the momentary solitude of being last in line, of being unwatched long enough to gather myself, only to lose myself in the rhythm of climbing. *I'm Gigi Lane and you wish you were me. I'm Gigi Lane and you wish you were me. I'm Gigi Lane and I wish I were me.* I wish I were the me I imagined experiencing this night—filled with joy, glowing with power, feeling like a puzzle piece had just clicked into place inside of me.

Fiona kicks open the door at the top of the stairs, and I hear hollow echoes of music from the ballroom inching toward us. Everyone else runs the rest of the way up the stairs, bursting into the senior hall and laughing as they twirl their way toward Founder's Path. I try to make my body dance, but it will barely move. I have to hurry to catch up, and Deanna reaches out her hand midtwirl to pull me along with her.

Ahead of us are the huge wooden doors leading into the ballroom. The two first-years on door duty are hunched over the keyhole and giggling, shoving each other to get a better view. They jump when Fiona clears her throat, and then quickly smooth down their tuxedos and place their white-gloved hands on the brass door handles. Fiona nods, and they open the doors, their cheeks flushed and eyes wide as we stream past them into the ballroom. The stars shine through the concave glass ceiling, their sharp points blurring as if they were shining through water.

Fiona leads us through the crowded ballroom, the air already close with heat from the dancing Swans. My eyes scan the perimeter, and I see the Do-Goods on punch bowl duty. Margot, wearing a cap-sleeved sweater and A-line skirt, straightens the glass cups waiting to be filled, and then blushes and smiles when another Do-Good compliments her. Next to the punch table, in a little knot, are the professors, having an animated conversation and ignoring the students. We follow Fiona onto the dance floor, the grooving bodies making a path for us, whispering to one another in our wake, surrounding us once we stop in the middle of the dance floor. As soon as we stop, as if by design, the song ends and fades to silence, and all eyes turn to the small stage at the front of the room. It glows under an arbor of potted saplings strung with lights. At the front of the stage is a microphone stand, and Ms. Carlisle steps out from among the saplings to stand behind it.

I glance off to the side and see a table with the sound and lighting equipment on it, and Gadget, this year's Head Gizmo, whispering instructions to Farley 2.0, Head Gizmo Incumbent.

The music softens to silence, and a soft spotlight opens on Ms. Carlisle.

"My Swans," she says, waving her hands. Titters ripple

through the crowd as the light gives full effect to her dress, a dung brown sheath that goes down past her knees, cinched unattractively around her beanbag waist. Her hair hangs limp against her face, her smudged glasses sliding down her nose until she pushes them up again.

"My Swans," she repeats. "The moment you have been waiting for has arrived!" Most people glance over at Fiona, who stares ahead like she doesn't notice—or doesn't care. Ms. Carlisle continues, "Your votes have been counted. And you have chosen your queen." She holds up a cream-colored envelope, pops the seal on its closure, and pulls out a card. She reads it and then smiles her brown-toothed grin. I look back to Fiona as Ms. Carlisle shouts, "Fiona Shay, come and get your crown!"

The cheers startle me, and it takes me a moment to join everyone's applause. Cassandra and Poppy give half smiles and golf claps, but then start screaming themselves as soon as they're named to the queen's court. It's like I'm cheering for myself, for who I am going to be next year. I'm trying to cheer loud enough to make this moment what I thought it would be, like if I can "woo-hoo" loud enough, it will warm the chill that settled in my stomach the moment we walked into the basement.

But then I feel something on my arm. A slick, slimy something. I turn to look, and that hog-bellied troll Daphne Hall is standing right next to me. *Sweating* on me! The unexfoliated point of her fat elbow just poked me, leaving a slug-trail swath of slime on my arm.

I stare at the slick spot, horrified and sickened that my night has just gotten even worse. "What the hell!" I hiss at her. "Get away from me!"

I hiss louder than I want to, and Daphne isn't the only one that looks at me—everyone in our immediate area does. "She slimed me." I laugh uncomfortably, looking at Deanna, showing her my elbow. Deanna wrinkles her brow and gives me a slight shake of her head.

"Ew." One of those annoying Glossy girls who is always kissing up to the Hot Spot leans close to me as she continues to clap for Fiona and her court. "That's just *wrong*. I love your dress, by the way."

The Cheerleaders, never wanting to be outdone by the Glossies, rustle their pompoms as they push closer to me. "She's *disgusting*, Gigi Lane, and she just *touched* you!" I turn to see who it is that spoke, and see Heidi nodding solemnly at me.

Beyond Heidi, I see Beatrice Linney being shoved forward by her sister. "Go get that story!" her sister hisses, and Beatrice reluctantly pulls out her notepad and slips the pen out from behind her ear.

I want to say, *There's no story here!* because suddenly I wish I hadn't said anything to Daphne, suddenly I just want to undo it, to go back to everyone watching Fiona and Poppy and Cassandra on stage so that I can stand here in the safety of the darkness and affirm and confirm until I feel okay again.

But everyone's looking at me—even Daphne shows no sign of slinking away.

Aloha leans in and whispers in my ear, "Jesus Christ, Gigi,

everyone's watching! You need to take care of business *now*, or everyone's going to think they can walk all over the Hot Spot next year." I pull away to look at her, and she murmurs, "If you can't handle it, I'll take care of it for you."

"That won't be necessary." I turn to Daphne. Even though Carlisle is now laying the ceremonial sashes on Poppy and Cassandra, all eyes in the immediate vicinity are on me. *I'm Gigi Lane and you wish you were me.* I try to feel the fire that usually fills me with rage enough to tear her down, but I feel nothing.

"You know what, Daphne," I say, struggling to speak loudly.

"Gigi, don't," Deanna whispers, trying to slip her arm through mine. "You don't have to prove anything."

I pull away. "You know what, Daphne," I start again, pausing long enough for her to react. I just can't believe she's still standing here looking at me. *Run away!* I scream at her in my head. *Turn around and run away.* She doesn't, so I have no choice but to keep going. "You really should just off yourself and save us all from having to look at your face." I say it loudly, loud enough for everyone in the crowded room to hear, even the teachers, who make the same disapproving clucking noise as the Do-Goods, even the Cursed Unaffiliated and the Deeks, watching from the shadows, and even Fiona, Poppy, Cassandra, and Ms. Carlisle, standing on stage. Every single one of them hears me.

Daphne's head jerks back like I flicked her weak chin, and her eyes go wide and focus on mine, a familiar look of hurt making them shine with tears. There. It's done. I've put her in her place. I'm struck with the irrational hope that she'll do something this time, that she'll finally fight back, that she'll give me the chance to take my anger about this night out on her. But she just blinks at me, her face slack, and looks around like she doesn't know where she is. Finally she pushes away through the crowd.

It's the lost, utterly dejected look on her face that gives me the first hot, prickly feeling on my skin, the feeling that something has gone terribly, terribly wrong. I refuse to look at Deanna, even though I can feel the heat of her stare as much as everyone else's.

"I have something to say!"

There is a collective murmur of confusion as everyone turns to the stage to see who's talking.

My stomach falls to my ankles. It's Daphne, in her discount dress, standing in front of the microphone. Fiona and Ms. Carlisle and the rest of the Hot Spot, apparently shoved out of the way, stand behind her, looking annoyed and confused.

"I . . . I have something to say!" Daphne grips the microphone stand with both hands, like it's the only thing keeping her upright. I look at her and realize that I've spent the past ten years making sure that I never looked her full in the face. I would always focus my eyes on one tiny offense—her eyebrows, her snaggletooth, her fat ankles. But now . . . it's like seeing a turtle pulled out of its shell. Seeing her, totally exposing herself to the whole school, makes my stomach churn.

"Just shut up, Gigi Lane!" Daphne yells, even though I haven't said anything. The microphone feeds back in a squealing whistle, and people cover their ears, ducking as if they can dodge the sound. "You just shut up. You . . ." She laughs a little, shaking her head. "You just don't stop, do you, Gigi?" She sniffs, and I can see tears rolling down her face. "What is it you want from me? I don't talk to you, I don't look at you, I don't *care* about you. And yet every day there you are. Letting the whole world know just how repulsive you think I am. Why do you care, Gigi? Why do you care that I'm fat? Or that I'm poor?"

Well, she *is* a little chunky. But wait . . . she's poor? In all of my private meetings with her, Daphne never mentioned it. I look at Deanna, horrified. *I didn't know that!* I mouth to her, trying desperately to remember if it's against Hot Spot policy to make fun of poor people.

"Or that I'm an orphan."

"Oh, shit," I whisper, my breath sucked out of me. That one's definitely against the rules.

"Or that I have learning disabilities."

I look to Fiona, who looks like she is going to fly off the stage and murder me dead. I close my eyes. Oh no. Oh, please no.

"So, good for you!" Daphne sobs. "You made the poor, dyslexic orphan cry! You must really be proud of yourself, Gigi." She takes a shuddering breath. "But this is it," she says with a hiccup, "so you look. You look at me!" she screams into the mic, and even though I don't want to, my eyes pop open. "I read your mom's book, just like you told me to, and guess what? I discovered the truth about myself! You're not better than me, Gigi Lane! You're not better than any—"

The end of her sentence is cut off because she drops the mic on the floor. It pops and snaps and growls as it rolls on the stage, before Carlisle finally picks it up and puts it back on the stand.

You know how in the movies when someone makes a really moving speech, the people in the movies will do the slow clap? Like, one person will start clapping really slowly, and then more and more people will join in until there's this thunderous applause and cheering and whoever just made the speech is flushed and smiling and happy? I've always liked those scenes; they give me a happy little shiver down my spine. But I never thought about how bad it would be to have people do the slow clap not *for* you, but *at* you.

It is the most horrible experience of my life.

Until I get home.

# CHAPTER FIVE

**Who Can Guess Ms. Cady's Favorite Number?**
**Here's a hint: It's a number found on bills**
**in denominations over twenty.**
**Think you know the answer? Drop an example**
**of whatever bill you think it is in the front office!**

**(Guesses are non-returnable.)**

"There's no time!"

Fiona Shay, the girl who plucked me from (relative) junior-class obscurity to succeed her as next year's master of the universe, is shrieking at me from where she kneels inside my walk-in closet. She is waving one of my pink slippers. I can't tell if she wants to hit me in the face with it or if she wants me to pack it. She chucks the slipper at my head. It bounces off with a soft *foof* and lands in the suitcase lying open on the bed. I manage to catch the other slipper as she whips it in my general direction, her skirt wobbling with the effort.

"For the love of all things holy," Fiona screeches, heaving herself up by grabbing on to a summer dress that hangs neat and perfect inside a clear plastic garment bag, her Founder's Queen crown slipping down over one eye. She shoves it back up on her head and yanks the dress off the hanger, garment bag and all, and thrusts it toward me. "Does everything you have look like it came out of my dog's butt?"

This can't be happening. This *cannot* be happening. I need to say something. It's like I've swallowed my tongue and it's flopping around in the pit of my belly. I know what I need to do. I need to affirm and confirm. That's what my mom would do. *I'm Gigi Lane and you wish you were me. I'm Gigi Lane, and even if I was just totally humiliated by Daphne "Dog Face" Hall at the Founder's Ball, you STILL wish you were me.*

Right?

I can feel my face, already a mask of dried tears, start to go all crinkly again.

I look at my bedroom door, wishing Deanna would come bounding through with her trademark pluck and charm. But there's no Deanna. She's back at the ball, along with Aloha; ordered by Fiona to stay behind and "smile, for God's sake! Smile and act like none of this ever happened!"

"I have other things I could wear," I mumble thickly, squinching up my nose to keep from crying. "If I just knew where I was going."

"There's no time!" Fiona screams again, and then she starts yanking things willy-nilly off the hangers and shelves in my closet and tossing them onto the bed. "You have really screwed things up, Georgina Lane," she growls, now stuffing two flower-girl dresses, a wet suit from my trip to Belize, and my seventh-grade Halloween costume into the suitcase. "You better thank your lucky stars that we already swore you in to the Hot Spot, because the sort of *display* we all saw tonight is most definitely *not* Hot Spot behavior, nor is it the sort of behavior becoming to a young woman of Swan's Lake!"

"Wait!" I gasp, the lump in my throat threatening to break my neck. "That wasn't my fault. . . ."

"Bull balls! Whatever you did to that *Daphne* girl was enough for her to totally demolish you! In front of *everybody*! At the last Founder's Ball I'll ever attend! You went too far, Gigi!"

*Stay calm, Gigi.* I take a deep breath and try for a smile. "But you said—"

Fiona narrows her eyes at me and lowers her voice to a growl. "Don't you put this on me, Gigi Lane! I never told you to go ballistic on the poor girl."

She starts quoting by heart from the Hottie Handbook, "'Though the verbal intimidation and punishment of sister Swans may be necessary in order to maintain order and obedience, excessive cruelty weakens the reputation of the Hot Spot and Swan's Lake Country Day School for Young Women, therefore jeopardizing both the Hot Spot's power at Swan's Lake and the reputation of Swan's Lake as a whole.' We are not mean girls, Gigi! What you did"—she shakes her head—"what you did crossed the line. It's not just a few people that think you're the devil, Gigi. It's everyone. If I had any idea you'd been *torturing* that used-tampon of a girl . . ."

She leaps up on the bed, and for a second I think I'm going to die in a borrowed ball gown, but instead of stabbing me with her corsage pin, she closes the suitcase and plops her bony butt down, bouncing a couple of times to cram the clothes in. Her hoopskirt flies up, and from where I stand, it looks like she's being eaten headfirst by a giant whale. She slaps the skirt down, pinning it between her knees.

"Zip!" she yells. I zip the suitcase, trying to avoid getting a stiletto in the eye as she lifts her legs so I can zip around them. It gets stuck halfway around, and she shoves me away and works on it herself.

"This," she says, grunting with effort, "is not how I wanted to end my senior year at Dear Olde Swanny, and I am sure it is not how you wanted to start yours."

Fiona stands up, still on the bed, narrowly avoiding bumping her head on the chandelier above. With the palm of her hand, she carefully pats away the sheen of sweat that's gathered on her forehead. She smooths her dress and takes a deep, shuddering breath. She's screamed off most of her lipstick, and the sweat has sent the rest of her makeup south, so it's starting to gather in the creases of her neck. She lifts a hand to yank a long pin out of her hair, knocking into the chandelier with her elbow, and in the swaying light her hair comes tumbling down around her shoulders like a black waterfall. Sweaty and without makeup, Fiona Shay is still the most beautiful girl I've ever seen.

"You'll be Head Hottie next year, Gigi." Fiona's voice is syrupy sweet, the light swinging her face into harsh brightness and inky shadows. "This is for the best."

"But I don't understand. Why do I have to leave tonight?"

Fiona laughs, a short, barking huff. "'Why do I have to leave tonight?'" Her imitation is so accurate, and so sharp, that I can only swallow in response. "You have to leave tonight because I don't want to have to look at your face all summer in the DOS."

"No, no, no, no, no . . . Fiona, please," I beg, "I'll do whatever you want." My mind is racing. "I'll cut my hair. I'll shave it right off. . . ." She looks at me, no emotion in her face. "I'll stop waxing my upper lip and grow a handlebar mustache, I won't use deodorant for a month, and I'll wear dollar-store perfume, please, Fiona, punish me however you want, you just can't make me leave!"

She looks at me for a long time, her head cocked to the side, and I'm suddenly embarrassed at how desperately I want to spend the summer with her and Poppy and Cassandra, how much I want Deanna and even Aloha to be there too. I hate this feeling of disappointment, as unfamiliar as if I'd slipped my bare feet into someone else's well-worn shoes.

"I'm sorry, Gigi." Fiona shakes her head and leans in close. "But this is serious. As serious as the most vomit-faced girl in the junior class getting up on stage at the Founder's Ball and making a tearjerker of a speech about how the Head Hottie I chose for next year is a total witch. How do you think that reflects on me, Gigi? Do you think I want that as my legacy when I graduate?

Do you think I want to be known as the Head Hottie that chose a little fascist to succeed her?"

She pauses for so long I'm wondering if it's not a rhetorical question. But when I open my mouth to answer, she whispers, "You went too far, Gigi."

"But . . . but I didn't . . . ," I stammer, "I didn't do anything different than what I usually do, the girl just freaked, she's a freak, Fiona, a total loser freak who—"

"The Network has already called an emergency meeting about your situation, Gigi," Fiona says firmly. "And it's been decided that you need to vacate the premises, effective immediately."

"And next year?" I ask weakly.

Fiona looks at me. "If all goes well, you'll come back to Swan's Lake and start your senior year as Head Hottie."

"Promise?"

"If you do what I say and leave Swan's Lake immediately, until we tell you it is safe to return."

I nod earnestly. "I will, I'll get out. I'll leave now."

"Good. And you can't talk to anyone, Gigi, not Deanna, not Aloha, not anybody," she says. "Understood?"

I shake my head. "Wait, what about my mom and dad?"

"What about them?"

"Well, they think I'm staying home all summer. Even if my mom's on a book tour, I can't just disappear on the night of the Founder's Ball and not talk to either of them for the whole summer. They'd freak."

"Yes," Fiona sighs, "I suppose you're right. There are rules about this sort of thing." She flips open her phone and proceeds to have a conversation with someone, I'm not sure who, which involves my dad's address at the hospital—which I didn't even know Fiona knew—and his surgery schedule, ending with, "Of course he'll believe you." She listens for a moment and then says flatly into the phone, "Permission denied. You are still under punishment. You'll just have to use your persuasion skills."

She ends the mysterious phone call without a good-bye, flipping her phone shut. "Well, that's settled, then."

I nod. "But where am I going?"

"Somewhere you won't be able to do any further damage to your own reputation, or that of the Hot Spot."

"But where?"

"That information is shared on a need-to-know basis, and you don't need to know. You'll find out when we get to the airport."

"Is it someplace bad?" I manage to squeak.

She makes a disapproving growling sound deep in her throat.

I search her face for some sort of friendliness. I will stop breathing and die a thousand deaths if Fiona Shay decides to hate me. She studies me for a long moment, and I try to hold her gaze, willing myself not to look sweaty and weepy and nauseous. A slow smile spreads across her face, like a ribbon unfurling in the wind.

"No, honey, it's not bad at all. In fact, I'm a little jealous of where you're going. And don't worry; when you get back to Swan's Lake at the end of the summer, everything will be the way it should be. You'll walk into school as Head Hottie and have the best year of your life."

Fiona's cell phone chirps. "What?" she says, slipping the phone under her curtain of black hair. She glares at me as she listens. "Got it. We are *go*," she sneers, "repeat, we are *go* for protective exile."

# CHAPTER SIX

**Earn Extra Credit in Summer School!
Classes in horticulture, HVAC, plumbing,
electrical work, and more!
See Ms. Carlisle for details.**

**(Remember, Ms. Cady loved a well-rounded Swan!)**

Exile sucks butt.

Call me naive, but I thought the Hot Spot would find it
in their charcoal hearts to send me somewhere fabulous. On
that late-night post-ball-massacre ride with Fiona to the airport,
the one spent signing and initialing the contract agreement
for protective exile, I was actually a little giddy with excitement. It's no secret that the Hot Spot Network has connections
the world over. I thought maybe with all those connections
they'd send me to hide away in a beachfront bungalow in a
small fishing village in Mexico, where I'd make nice with
the local boys and learn the secret for great guacamole from

my elderly neighbor, who would insist I call her *abuelita*.

But there would be no guacamole. There would be no moonlight rides with Pablo in the dinghy he borrowed from his best friend just to take the *gringa misteriosa* on a date.

Because they didn't send me to Mexico.

They sent me to Alaska.

They might as well have sent me straight to hell.

I work fifteen-hour days as a fish gutter on the slime line at Alaska Fisheries. I wear a plastic apron and goggles and gloves. My luggage was lost on the way here, so on my first day I had to trade a girl my Founder's Ball shoes for her extra pair of overalls. Someone else got my dress in exchange for two pairs of socks and a leaky set of rain boots. I sold my beaded clutch for enough money to buy a dusty pack of granny panties from the general store, a couple of white T-shirts, and a flannel shirt that I think the guy behind the counter used to wax his car.

Sometimes fish guts splatter on my face, and my face is so frozen I don't notice until my shift is over.

I sleep on a bunk bed with springs so worn my butt touches the floor when I lie down. I can't sit up once my bunk mate is in bed, or I'll scrape my head on the springs below her own sagging mattress. Three feet away from us is the other bunk. We take turns getting in and out of bed to avoid kicking one another in the face.

My roommates are college girls from Ohio. They squeal a lot, and giggle. They wear scrunchies and share with me the Milk Duds and Doritos their sorority sisters send in care packages. When I told them I was sixteen, they squealed and then sighed and tried to adopt me like a class hamster. In the Hottie Handbook there is a section Poppy read to us called "Dangerous Situations." It says if you are outnumbered, you must do what you have to in order to survive. That's what I'm doing. They feed me candy and ask me if I'm homesick, and I say, "A little," and they make cooing sounds at me. They like to braid my hair.

They also loan me fleece pajamas to wear to bed.

Fiona was dead serious about the communications blackout. I've heard only from my parents, who are very proud of me for "exploring the wilds of Alaska." I'm dying to call Deanna at the gymnastics camp where she's teaching all summer, but I'm afraid the Hot Spot would find out and I'd get in even more trouble than I'm already in. All I want is for this summer to be over, so that I can glide back into Swan's Lake in my rightful place as Head Hottie and bludgeon Daphne "Dog Face" Hall to death. Metaphorically speaking, of course. Head Hotties aren't allowed to commit actual violence, unless in self-defense.

I've gotten used to the routine here. Up at 6:00 a.m., on the slime line by 6:30 a.m. Break at ten, lunch at one. My roommates and I are on the same schedule, so at least I have someone to sit with during breaks and meals. I spent the first two days scouring the vending machines and general store for high-fiber foods and fresh vegetables, determined to keep the lithe body I'd worked so hard for. After three days I was starving and ended up doing things to a tray of microwave macaroni and cheese that would give most girls with skinny ankles nightmares.

I feel so far removed from my real life that I slip into a sort of netherworld of processed food and abbreviated hygiene rituals. In overalls and a flannel shirt I can hide from myself, plowing through the sort of delicious snack food that only comes pre-wrapped in cellophane: gooey cinnamon buns, cheese Danishes, and apple turnovers. Since my bag of makeup and beauty products never made it to Alaska, I spent the first three days trying to make do with what they had for sale at the general store: aerosol hair spray, electric-blue eye shadow, and cherry Chap Stick. But the extra five minutes of sleep I get when I skip the routine is too valuable, and I've ditched everything but the Chap Stick.

One day my roommates skip break for a conference call with their sorority sisters, and I'm left alone in the break room. There are a bunch of people there already, all the chairs at the long metal table filled except one. I mix two packets of powdered hot chocolate into a cup of hot water and sit down.

"You're still in high school, right?" I look up and see a girl with short, shaggy hair, the sort of carefully mussed hair used to signal a totally false look of lack of concern with her appearance.

I nod.

"Where are you from?" she asks. The table quiets. Apparently, a sixteen-year-old on work release is something interesting.

"I go to a small, progressive private school outside of Boston called Swan's—"

"Wait," a girl with slicked-back hair and fourteen earrings in her left ear says from the other end of the table, "*you* go to Swan's Lake?"

She catches me off guard. "You've heard of it?"

The girl laughs, slapping the table with both hands. "Heard of it?" She looks me up and down. I shift in my overalls and straighten my scrunchie. "My roommates and I at Blarkley were *obsessed* with it!"

Blarkley. Of course. One of those private co-ed schools with a huge endowment to pay for things like Olympic-size pools and bulk shipments of STD medication.

I look back at my hot chocolate.

"What's the big deal?" the girl with the aggressively unkempt hair asks.

Earring Girl laughs. "You don't even know! The place, Swan's Lake, is crazy! The girls there are, like, totally *obsessed* with their school. At graduation they freak out and scream and cry and pull out clumps of their hair and throw themselves against walls because they don't want to leave."

Everyone laughs a little and then looks at me.

I clear my throat. "That's not true."

"What? You guys aren't totally freaked-out in love with your school?"

"We have school spirit," I answer, trying to keep from throwing my hot chocolate in her face. "But we're not freaks."

"You totally are! Swan's Lake is where all the first-years have *duties*, right?"

I nod, sipping my hot chocolate even though it's hot enough to peel my tongue.

"Right! Because the place is, like, *falling* apart around you, and you can't afford to fix it." She looks straight at me. "My parents weren't interested in sending my sister and me where we'd have to clean to earn our keep. The overpriced tuition should be enough."

I look at her. She looks at me. Everyone looks at us. Finally I say, "I'm going to tell you what nobody else will."

She laughs, a nails-on-the-blackboard sound.

"People hate the sound of your voice. When you open your mouth, people flinch and then steel themselves for the rusted-nail shriek you call talking."

Earring Girl gulps, clearing her throat. "Shut up."

"When you get married and have children, your whole family will cringe when you laugh, when you sing 'Happy Birthday,' when you say 'I love you.' Eventually they will tune you out, and you will grow shriller to keep their attention. When you grow old, people won't even hear your words, they will just hear an old, unloved crow. Shrieking."

I get up and toss my hot chocolate in the trash, and as I'm walking out, I hear the girl with the shaggy-dog hair say, "And *that* is why I'm glad I'm not in high school."

I sleep most of the plane ride home from Alaska.

I turn on my phone as soon as we land. At least, I try to turn on my phone, but being in sleep mode for the past eight weeks has drained its battery of all life.

"DAD!" I yell when I see him in the waiting area. My dad turns and smiles, and I jump into his arms, almost knocking him over. "I'm so glad to see you!" I yell, hugging him harder. He laughs and puts me down. I feel the same giddy pride that I always do when my dad shows up in public wearing his scrubs, his hospital name tag clipped to his pocket.

"Let me look at you." He grins, his hands on my shoulders. "Overalls! How rustic! You look beautiful, honey. Alaska must have suited you."

I'm so happy to see him that I hug him again, and the phone clipped to his scrubs beeps. He answers it and smiles. "She's right here," he says, and hands me the phone.

"Is that my Girlie Bird?" my mom asks, and just hearing her voice, I can see her smile so clearly.

"It's me!" I yelp. "Where are you? When are you coming home?"

"Well, darling"—she sounds tired—"it's Monday, so it must be Tennessee, but we're on our way back to you. Just eight weeks and seven cities left."

"Good, I miss you!"

"I miss you, too. I've got to get on stage in a minute, let me talk to your dad again." I say good-bye and hand my dad the phone, staying close enough so I can hear him talk.

"She looks great. . . ." He hesitates for a moment before turning just slightly to quietly finish his sentence. "I think they fed her really well."

I turn to look at him when he says this, and he looks away, refusing to meet my gaze.

I look down to where my hands have found their usual position: laced in front of me, resting on my belly, my elbows propped comfortably on hips that I didn't have before this summer. *It's fine,* I tell myself. In the week before school starts I'll run every day; eat nothing but salad, nonfat yogurt, and whole-grain bread; and visit Jean-Claude's salon. By the first day of school I'll look like I never left.

My dad's off the phone with my mom. "So your suitcase is at home, you know that, right? Did you get another one in Alaska?" I shake my head, and we start toward the automatic doors leading to the parking garage. "The airline must have finally found it. They delivered it last night. It looks like you did okay, making do with what you found in Alaska. All ready for your first day of school?"

"You mean next Monday? Sure, I'll be ready."

"Gigi"—my dad wrinkles his brow—"the first day of school is today. Didn't you know that?"

"Today?" I ask, looking down at my overalls. "You're kidding, right?"

"Sorry, kiddo, today's the day."

"No . . . no, wait." I raise a hand, stopping him. "Dad, school starts next week. They sent me a letter and everything. It said school starts *next* Monday, not today."

"Honey, I'm sorry. You must have misread that letter. Don't worry, though. You can wash your face when you get to school."

"What's wrong with my face?" I ask, pressing my fingers to my cheeks as he walks ahead of me. He leads me to the oversize revolving door leading out into the parking garage.

*Oh my god, oh my god, oh my God.*

"Dad?"

"Hm?"

"Seriously, I can't go to school today."

"Gigi, it's your first day of senior year, you can't miss it."

"No, *Dad*, seriously."

My dad sighs and stops walking to face me. "Gigi, *seriously*, you're not missing your first day of school, and that's final."

I'm quiet as we get into the car. "Gigi," he says, and smiles at me. "You're applying to college this year, I just don't think it's a good idea to start the year with an attendance deficit."

"My application to Yale is practically finished, Dad," I argue. "I don't think I need to worry about missing one day of school."

I shove my phone into the charger.

"Gigi, I'm sorry," my dad says firmly, "but there is no room for negotiation on this."

I am wearing overalls. And a flannel shirt. And boots that most likely still have fish guts crammed into the soles. Not even with my bone structure is this a good look.

Once we're on the highway, my dad winks at me and says, "I know what you need."

"A girdle and a leg wax?"

"Nope." He winks again. "You need to affirm and confirm. You're just a little nervous about your first day of school."

"That's okay, Dad," I lie, "I affirmed on the plane ride home, like, a thousand times in a row."

"Aw, come on, Girlie Bird." My dad reaches over to smooth my hair. "Get into position and affirm away."

"Dad, really . . ."

"Come on . . . ," he coaxes.

I stifle a sigh. "Okay, sure." I pull my legs up and cross them, which for some reason is harder to do now than it was before. I get my arms into wing position, close my eyes, and concentrate. *I'm Gigi Lane and . . .* I get a cramp in my right leg. I adjust my position and start again. *I'm Gigi Lane and you wish . . .* Now there's a cramp in my other leg. I adjust again, but it's so uncomfortable that when I am finally through an *I'm Gigi Lane and you wish you were me*, my heart just isn't in it.

I drop my legs back to the floor. "You can actually just drop me off at the bottom of the hill, I can walk up." I don't tell him I'm planning on making a run for it as soon as he's out of sight. "I'm sure you have to get to surgery."

He glances at me as I stretch my legs. "No can do. I promised your mom I'd get a picture of you walking up your steps the first day."

"You can take it next week, she'll never know," I answer.

My dad looks at me. "That sounds a bit like lying, Gigi. I thought they were straight shooters up in Alaska."

"You're right, it was a dumb idea," I agree. "So, you can take a picture of me going up the stairs and then hightail it to the hospital, right?" I try to remember just how much of a drop it is over the side of the front steps to school. If I make the jump without breaking an ankle and get Deanna to take me to Jean-Claude's for an emergency intervention, I could be back to school by third period and make an entrance worthy of Head Hottie.

"Oh, and she wants one of you waving from inside the front door."

"Of course she does." I try to smile, but I think I might actually hurl.

# CHAPTER SEVEN

**Welcome Back, Swans!**
**Well, don't you all just look so pretty?**

**(That was a rhetorical question.)**

"Wow, that's quite a line," my dad says as we near Ms. Cady's statue at the bottom of the hill.

"It *is* a long line," I agree, sensing from his tone he is second-guessing his picture promise to my mom.

The line of cars up to the front doors of school snakes all the way down to the street, so my dad takes our place in line behind a blindingly white iceberg-size SUV. The windows are tinted a deep black, making the car look sort of like a snowman with a coal smile. There is a DON'T HAVE ANYTHING NICE TO SAY? SIT NEXT TO ME! sticker on the bumper.

"Oh no," I moan, recognizing the car as belonging to Beatrice

Linney's mom. *Crap, that's right, there's a couple other little Linneys.* Bethenny, that's the next oldest. She would be a first-year, so of course her parents are dropping her off her first day. I just hope her Vox Fox radar hasn't kicked in yet.

No such luck.

It takes just a few seconds, and soon I can see the silhouette of Bethenny Linney, in the backseat of the SUV, look over her shoulder as if she's a wolf that's caught a scent on the wind. She launches herself over the seat and is cupping her hands around her eyes, face pressed against the back glass, her sizable nose smooshed flat, as she tries to get a better look.

First-years are such dorks. I give a little wave, thinking, *Yes, that's right, it's Gigi Lane, the big, bad Head Hottie. Get a good look now before someone clues you in to the fact that you're supposed to avert your eyes.*

"Friend of yours?" my dad asks, and at first I think he's talking about Bethenny, but then I see him looking past me, out my window. I turn just in time to see the camera phone aimed straight at my face through the glass. The phone's owner has flipped it shut and started to walk away before I can even flash a smile. I can see now that it's Beatrice Linney.

My stomach twists tighter. Something very, very strange is going on.

Beatrice gives her sister a thumbs-up sign as she walks past their car, and a second later my phone vibrates with a text message. Relieved to see that it's actually working, I pick it up.

"Oh my GOD!" I scream, dropping the phone on the floor

and then scrambling to pick it up again. "What the hell is this?!"

"Language, Georgina!" my dad says loudly, the closest he comes to yelling. "What are you upset about?"

I can't even speak, I just hold the phone up to him with a shaky hand. On it is the *completely* unflattering picture Beatrice just sent with the subject line "TTOTS Breaking News: Gigi Lane Spotted!"

"What's TTOTS?" my dad asks.

I think for a second. "*The Trumpet of the Swan,*" I gasp.

"Oh. I didn't think they did things electronically. That's one of the reasons your mother was so excited about the journalism program here."

"They're not supposed to," I growl, "those Foxes are going to pay for—"

"The who?"

"No one." I snap my phone closed.

We've barely made any progress up the driveway when my dad glances past me out my window. "I think that hydrangea is waving at you."

I look out the car window and, sure enough, see the branch of one of the hydrangea bushes near Ms. Cady's statue frantically shaking and then bending down to expose for a split second the cherubic face of Deanna Jones.

"Deanna!"

The branch bends again. Deanna waves frantically.

"Get in the car!" I hiss.

The branch thunks Deanna in the chin as she lets go, then she takes a quick look around her and makes a wild-eyed dash for the car.

"Open the door!" she screams as she leaps across the sidewalk. I twist around, reach, and open the back door just as she launches herself off the curb and into the backseat of the car.

"Holy crap! I thought you'd never get here!" She gasps for air, leaning over the seat to hug me. "Never leave me again!"

My dad, ever the steady surgeon, says simply, "Good morning, Deanna, how was your summer?"

"Good morning, Dr. Bruce! Summer was great, the girls at gym camp were super adorable. I swear they get cuter every . . ." Deanna trails off, leaning between the front seats until she is staring me full in the face.

"I thought it was just a bad picture!" she gasps, holding up her phone, which is vibrating with multiple copies of the same horrid photo.

I press my hands to my face. "Oh God, I'm a monster!"

"No!" She shakes her head as if she's trying to convince herself, unzipping her bag and finding a small pouch of beauty products. "You look terrific! Healthy! Like you've been wrestling bears or something." She pulls out a premoistened cleansing cloth and goes for my face. I dodge, trying to get away from her, but the girl has freakish gymnast muscles and manages to pin me against the dashboard with her elbows and wipe down my whole face.

"Wait! Deanna, what the hell is going—"

My dad looks at me in shock. "Gigi!"

"Sorry, Dad. Deanna, what the *heck* is going on here?"

Deanna's voice is shrill. "You mean the fact that our whole world's gone to sh—dog poo?" She pauses, grimacing at the used cloth, now streaked with what looks like sludge. She pulls out another cloth, holding me still with one wiry arm, and goes for round two.

"That's exactly what I mean. Why would the Vox Foxes send out such a god-awful picture?"

"Oh, I don't know, Gigi!" Deanna shrills, reaching for her bag again. I hold up my hands, letting her know I surrender, and allow her to slather my face with moisturizer. She leans close as she works, and whispers, "Maybe because nobody thought you'd show your face here ever again!"

"What? Why?" I whisper back, racking my brain for what she's talking about.

Deanna looks at me in surprise, her mouth hanging open like the answer is so obvious she doesn't even know what to say. She scowls at something between my eyes and then starts plucking my eyebrows with her fingers.

"Ow!" I swat at her hands, rubbing the sore spot on my forehead.

"Trust me, you do not want to go into school looking like you have a woolly mammoth coming out of your forehead!" Deanna gives me a grim look and goes back to her bag. She glances at my dad and then mouths, *Do you really not know what's going on?*

"How would I know what's going on?" I whisper back. "I've been in exile! Wait a minute!" I say, noticing the familiar sweep-and-barrette of her bangs. "I thought you were growing your hair out!"

"Gigi, pay attention!" Deanna snaps. "My hair is the least of our worries! But since you mention it, our mortgage payments went up, so I'm back on the 'Tazz."

We're still close to the bottom of the hill, and the line of cars is barely moving. Deanna looks me up and down, and finally she sighs, "So . . . is that what you're wearing?"

I look at my overalls, realizing for the first time I'm about to be the first Hottie in history to walk into school sporting fish-scented farm wear.

My eyes brim with tears, and Deanna looks at my dad and says, "We'll get out here, Dr. Bruce."

"Take a picture for your mother!" my dad calls as he pulls out of line.

Two minutes later Deanna and I are back in the hydrangea, looking like we both lost at strip poker and are trying to regain our dignity by dressing as fast as possible. At first I try wearing her leggings, since she's got a miniskirt on over them. But Deanna is such a pip-squeak, the leggings barely stretch over my calves, even with Deanna holding the waist and me trying to bounce my way into them. "It's like trying to get a banana back in its peel," Deanna growls. "What the heck did they feed you up there?"

I ignore her question and hop up on my tiptoes, trying

to peek up to the front steps of school to see who is there, but the high stone walls of the staircase block my view. I don't even try Deanna's miniskirt, since it might not survive the trip over my thighs. We try just my flannel shirt with no pants but decide that's just asking to get expelled. Then Deanna Jones, America's Sweetheart and my hero, comes up with the answer.

"Perfect," she says, buttoning the last button on my flannel shirt, which is now around my waist, hung like a skirt, its arms wrapped tight around my middle. On top I wear one of the three stretchy shirts Deanna had layered on.

I look down, trying to size up the effect. "Does it look okay?" I ask.

Deanna looks at the outfit absently and says, "Maybe we should just skip school. No, wait. You've already been spotted. Running won't do you any good."

"Deanna Jones, you need to tell me what's going on right now."

"*Hello!*" she snaps. "Did you even read the latest memo?"

"Deanna! I didn't get any memos!"

"Wait, all summer? You haven't gotten anything from Aloha all summer?"

"How could Aloha send me a memo? I was in blackout all summer!"

"Gigi, she was our contact! The Network had her send us update memos all summer, but you never answered any of them."

"Because I never *got* them." I feel sick to my stomach. "All I got was a letter from school telling me school starts next week."

"Oh my God. Gigi, I don't know how to tell you this, but . . ." The first bell rings. "Oh, crap," she whispers. "I'm going to have rip this off like a Band-Aid." Then she raises her chin, looks me straight in the eye, and says, "You're out of the Hot Spot."

I fall over.

"What?" I ask from the ground. "What did you just say?" It's like I've lost control of all my muscles. I'm lucky I don't pee myself.

Deanna leans over me, blocking the sun with her head. "You're out. Both of us." She swallows. "And Aloha is in. She's Head Hot—"

"BUULLLSHIIIT!" I roar, jumping up. "You have *got* to be kidding me!"

I kick my way out of the stupid bush and start marching up the driveway, Deanna trotting along beside me, pulling my arm to make me stop, and then when she can't, picking sticks and pebbles out of my hair.

Out of the corners of rage-red eyes I can see my fellow students pressing their faces against car windows, pointing to me, mouths open in shock. *That's right, you tarts, I'm HERE!*

"Aloha!" I yell before I even get to the stairs, seeing her stupid face over the wall on the top landing. By the time I get to the foot of the front steps, I see they are crowded with Gizmos, Lacrockies, Art Stars, Greenies, Whompers, Bookish Girls,

Glossies. Everyone is there, even a few skittish first-years are peeking out the doors at the top of the stairs. And they all look happy to see me. Actually, as we get closer, it seems more like they are *hungry* to see me, because they are staring at me like I am the only food they've seen for days. I see one phrase repeated from one to the other: *Oh my God.* And it's not a good "Oh my God." It's not like when you find out your boobs went up a size; it's the kind of "Oh my God" that happens when you realize the side of your thong has snapped and its now wiggling it's way down your leg.

"I really wish you'd read those memos," Deanna whispers.

Aloha is staring down at me with what looks like detached amusement. God damn her, that's *my* look!

"Alooo-HA!" I scream, louder than I expected. For a brief, terrifying second I think I might actually be mad with rage and they might have to shoot me with a tranquilizer. "What the bloody devil is going on here?"

"Whoa," Aloha says calmly. "Gigi, please, calm down. We've been trying to reach you all summer. I didn't think you were even coming back to school."

"I've been in ALASKA!" I yell.

Aloha nods. "That must have been nice."

"It SUCKED! I smell like fish guts!"

Aloha sniffs the air. "You're right. You do."

Oh my God. I'm going to have a heart attack. My heart is going to explode into a ball of hot lava right here, and the first-years will have to clean up my gooey pieces with a spatula.

The crowd is still whispering. I hear one of them say, "I still don't think she gets it."

"Oh, I get it, all right," I growl, "but this bullshit is going to end right here, right now."

And it's like I can feel the superhuman strength of the wronged pulsing through me, turning my bones to steel, my blood to acid. I will take Aloha *down*.

"Gigi," Deanna whispers, "please, take it easy."

I take a deep breath, ready to scream Aloha off of the stairs, and then choke on that same breath a second later when Aloha says, "I believe you know my associates."

Heidi slips off the wall, pretty and perfect in her cheerleading uniform, and stands next to Aloha. No problem. I can verbally filet them both.

But then . . . then . . .

I think I actually black out for a second as Daphne "Dog Face" Hall steps into position beside Aloha.

Except she is a dog face no more. Everyone on the steps turns to look as Daphne smiles at me (dear God, her teeth have been straightened! *And* whitened!) and says, "Hello, Gigi."

"She's been beautified!" Deanna whispers. "I'd heard rumors, but I had no idea. . . ."

The shiny hair, the clear skin, the snug yet not slutty sweater, and the long, long, when the hell did she get such long, long legs? She's a goddamn stone-cold fox!

"You were in Alaska for the summer, isn't that right, Gigi?" Daphne asks, as if we're just two people having a conversation without most of the Swan's Lake student body listening in. My tongue swells in my mouth and then turns to ash. "They must have *great* food up there. But not a lot of beauty salons, I take it."

Laughter ripples up and down the stairs at her lame attempt at an insult. Beside her I see Aloha stiffen, knowing the insult was lame and yet needing to support her new BFF. She glances at me, waiting to see if I'll pounce. I open my mouth and a moth flies out. Metaphorically speaking. Aloha laughs, a little too loud. "Come on, ladies," Aloha says with a smirk, "let's go."

She turns and walks inside, Daphne close at her heels. I stare in silent horror at how cute her butt looks in her jeans. And her shoes. Dear God, just strike me dead now.

Heidi stays on the top step, smiling down at me. "I'll be just a minute," she says. "I have a little welcome present for Gigi."

I look at Deanna. *Please,* I try to tell her with my eyes, *please make it stop.* She looks at me, totally helpless.

"Ready? Okay!" Heidi yells, doing one of those robotic cheerleader nods, and all of a sudden it's like the rest of the Cheerleaders just *appear,* and then they are in formation behind her. In a single and terrifying movement the squad claps once in response and then jumps in the air, landing with legs apart, their hands on their hips, and evil-looking smiles on their faces.

And the crowd of kids on the steps knows what I am just realizing. I'm about to get cheered.

"Hey, girls!" Heidi yells in a singsong voice.

"Yeah, Heidi?" the girls sass back, their voices echoing off the bricks.

"Whatever happened to Gigi Lane?" Heidi chants, stepping slowly down the stairs.

"You mean that really evil girl that Daphne shamed?" the squad answers, following Heidi's slow strut down the steps.

"Whatever happened to that queen of mean?"

The crowd scoots, making room for Heidi to get by.

"You mean the one that ran away so she wouldn't be seen?"

There's a pause as Heidi reaches the bottom of the staircase and steps in front of us, her squad falling into formation behind her. She's standing so close I can smell the mint on her breath. She glances for a moment at Deanna and smirks.

All has gone quiet. The other kids on the stairs are frozen in anticipation. For a moment I think that maybe this is it, maybe Heidi will snap her fingers and break the spell, sending everyone on their way.

No such luck.

"I heard she was in rehab! I heard she changed her name! I heard she flunked the GED and ran away in shame!"

"I heard she was dead."

This comment comes from a familiar-looking, chubby-cheeked girl with frizzy double braids who is sitting on the bottom step, not two yards away from me. I recognize her as a junior, one of the Whompers: girls you see on the town common, beating each other with foam swords while wearing plastic armor and yelling things like "I smite you!" while pasty boys from Peyton do the same. I think it's the nerd equivalent of sex.

The Cheerleaders have gone quiet, and so has everyone else.

"Welcome back, Gigi," Heidi says, ruffling a pom-pom in my face. "You best stay the hell out of my way." And with that she turns on her heel, leading the rest of the Cheerleaders up the steps. Everyone else just sits there for a minute, staring at Deanna and me, until the second bell rings and they realize the show is over.

It's not until the last person disappears through the door that I realize I've been holding my breath. I let it out in a sour gush. I haven't even had time to brush my teeth.

"Ladies!" Ms. Carlisle steps out onto the landing, a too-tight gray polyester pantsuit hugging her in all the wrong places. "It's the first day of school, you don't want to be late now, do you?"

I finally find my voice. "No, Ms. Carlisle," we say in unison, starting up what now seems like a very long, very cold set of stairs.

It's Margot, sweet Do-Good Margot, that saves me from having to walk around in my flannel-shirt skirt all day. She wasn't out on the steps, since Do-Goods are wary of any sort of assembly that may involve bad language or sex jokes, but she is the only one still standing at her locker by the time Deanna and I get there. I haven't really said anything to Deanna. It feels like my whole body has grown a protective shell, and all I do is numbly murmur, "I texted Fiona. I'll tell you when I hear from her."

Deanna nods, and we move silently down the hall, looking for our lockers.

When Margot chirps, "Hey, Gigi," I flinch, wondering what fresh hell she has for me. "I thought you might . . ." She clears her throat. "I heard you came straight from the airport, and I thought you might want to borrow a skirt. We're the same size, but I always go a size up to avoid . . . well, you know. Here. I hope it's not too big." She hands me a neatly folded black skirt, and as she does, I see her glance down at my newly rounded thighs, clearing her throat. "Actually, maybe it will fit just fine."

I stare at the skirt; it's pleated, with creases neatly ironed into sharp, perfect angles. I press it to my chest. "Bless you, my child. Thank you."

Margot looks taken aback. "Of course. And if you guys need someplace to sit at lunch today . . ."

"I don't think that will be necessary." I hold the skirt up and feel a little better knowing that at least my ass will enjoy full coverage. "You've done enough for me for one day."

"Well, I've got to get to homeroom. I'm late!" She flushes at the danger.

It's strange how a personal crisis can you make you feel totally excused from the rules of school. Deanna skips homeroom and comes with me to the bathroom, and once I've put on Margot's skirt, I climb up on the wide window ledge next to Deanna. We kick our feet, letting our heels bounce on the wall.

Finally she speaks. "Fiona's the one that told me. She called me at gymnastics camp, said there'd been a change."

"I never should have let Aloha stay here alone this summer." I sigh. "I should have known better than to leave that snake around all these mice."

"It's not like they gave you a choice." Deanna shrugs. "Anyway, a couple weeks into the summer, Fiona called. I was actually excited." She gives a humorless laugh. "I missed you so much I was hoping maybe she'd heard from you. But she . . . she was still really pissed, Gigi, about Daphne, and the Founder's Ball. Seriously, that girl's language is *foul*. She said the Hot Spot Alumnae Network had a special meeting to discuss 'the incident'—that's what they kept calling it, 'the incident'—and the Network members were so disgusted with what had happened, and the fact that you hadn't responded to Aloha's memos all summer, that they wanted to eject all of us, sentence us to permanent exile."

"Permanent exile?" I gasp. "No one's been sentenced to permanent exile since—"

"Lydia Jarmush, I know."

"But wait, if we're all sentenced to permanent exile, why is Aloha prancing around like she's Head Hottie?"

"Because she *is* Head Hottie. I guess she cozied up to Fiona as soon as you were gone, convincing her that really she was the one that should be Head Hottie. She had gone through the training already, she said, and it would be a smooth transition for the school."

"She's a transfer student! She *can't* be Head Hottie!"

"Well, she is," Deanna says. "And Heidi and Daphne are her little sidekicks."

"And we're . . . what? Permanently exiled?"

"Well . . ." Deanna takes a breath. "You are."

"Just me?"

She nods. "The Network, in recognition of the whole America's Sweetheart thing, pardoned me."

"Right." I grit my teeth, trying not to be angry.

"But I'm out of the Hot Spot," she assures me. "For good. That's for sure."

The bell for the end of homeroom rings. "We should go." I jump off the window ledge and offer Deanna my shoulder so she can jump off onto her good leg. "Meet up for lunch?" I look at my phone. "That harlot Fiona better call me back. You'd think she'd have the backbone to tell me all this herself."

The day lasts for roughly sixteen million years. There is the humiliation of looking for a seat in each new class, all the empty chairs somehow reserved for a friend that never shows, until the professor takes curious pity on me and tells one of my fellow students to make room.

And there is lunch, where all activity stops the moment Deanna and I walk in, so much so that I know for sure we can't just walk out again. We have to keep our chins high and work our way through the hot buffet with everyone else.

Everyone else except for Aloha, Heidi, and Daphne, who are, I assume, reclining on chaise lounges in the DOS.

We stand at the front of the room, trying not to look like we're looking for seats, while scanning the room looking for seats.

"There's Margot." Deanna tries to sound chipper.

"I'd rather die," I answer. "I'm wearing her fat skirt, isn't that enough?"

Deanna looks at me. "Suck it up, Lane, and follow me."

I follow her to where Margot and the other Do-Goods are making room for us to sit. "Hi, Gigi," Margot says loudly, smiling at everyone who's watching, as if to say, *Nothing to see here, just me taking in the disgraced heathen.*

I mumble my hellos to Margot and the rest of her crew, and concentrate on my mac and cheese for the rest of lunch period.

Deanna offers to give me a ride home in the JFM, and my cell phone buzzes with a text as I'm getting in the car. "Finally!" I shout, seeing Fiona's name come up. I read the text and say, "She wants to have a conference call in twenty minutes. Can you come over?"

"Sure." Deanna shrugs. "Let's get this over with."


"So, girls, how was school today?" Fiona's voice, sarcastic as ever, spills out of the speakerphone in my mom's writing office.

"Awful?" Deanna finally offers, leaning toward the phone. I'm sitting in my mom's chair, and Deanna is perched, cross-legged, on the desk.

"I thought it might be," Fiona says tersely. "This has been, I hope you both know, a total disaster."

Deanna looks at me miserably. I wave my hand and mouth the words, *Don't worry about it.*

"Not since the disgraced Lydia Jarmush has the Hot Spot

been so humiliated by one of their own. You have totally—"

"So you're really going to do this?" I ask bluntly. "You're going to send me into permanent exile because some little dog-faced piece of crap girl threw a shit fit at the ball?"

Fiona's voice is maddeningly calm. "Yes, Gigi, we're really going to do this. Deanna, are you still there?"

"Yep."

"Have you given any more thought to our offer?"

I raise my eyebrows.

Deanna clears her throat. "A little. But I want to talk to Gigi about it first."

I look at Deanna. "What offer?"

"We've offered Deanna a secure place in the Cheerleaders. Head Cheerleader, actually. It's a good clique, Ms. Jones, you should really consider accepting."

I lean toward the phone, ready to play hardball. "What's included in the offer?"

"The usual," Fiona says. "Standing Saturday-night plans, a week at cheer camp over spring break, a new nickname—"

"We don't need new nicknames," I interrupt, winking at Deanna, letting her know I have this all under control. "Also, we'll take a pass on cheer camp, and we require private transportation to and from sporting events. We don't ride on buses."

"Now, wait just a minute, Gigi." I can hear Fiona pressing the phone closer to her face. "That offer is for Deanna, not for you."

My jaw drops. Deanna bites her lower lip and shrugs. Finally I sputter out, "Well, what am I supposed to do?"

"Frankly, the Network—"

I slam my hand on the desk next to the phone. "I want to talk to them."

"What?" Fiona laughs, shocked.

"I want to talk to them," I demand. "The Network. Whoever it is that's sending me into exile. I want to talk to them."

"You can't talk to them, Gigi. You can't even talk *about* them. You're going into exile—that means you're dead to the Network, and the Network has never existed for you. Got it?"

"Fine. If you won't put me in touch with them, I'll find them myself. I'm sure I can talk some sense—"

"You listen to me, Gigi." Fiona's voice takes on the same throaty growl it had after the Founder's Ball. "You have no idea who you're messing with."

I wiggle my eyebrows at Deanna, but she still looks a bit pale.

"The Network can *destroy* you, do you understand?" she asks. "You and everyone you love."

"Oh, come off it," I snap. "You're being melodramatic."

"We have people everywhere, Gigi. At the *New York Times*, where your mother's books are bestsellers and she's getting ready to be interviewed for yet another vanity piece that could very easily be turned into an exposé. We have people on the Licensing and Grievance Board of the American Society of Cosmetic Surgeons. Your father is currently in good standing, but that can change very, very quickly."

I look at Deanna, my confident smile faltering. She whispers, "Don't say anything else!"

"I would listen to your friend, Gigi," Fiona says. "Don't say anything else. Accept your punishment, and—"

"Severance." I smile, loving the way the word tastes on my lips.

Deanna waves her hands at me, mouthing, *Stop!*

There is a pause. "What?"

"If you want me to forget about you tarts, you owe me a severance package."

"A what?" Fiona's fake confused tone doesn't fool me.

"You're studying business and you haven't covered severance? What the hell kind of college are you going to? Sev-er-ance"—I pronounce it slowly. "It's what companies give executives when they kick them to the curb. For CEOs it's called the golden parachute. Usually several million dollars in cash and bonds, plus use of the company jet for life. That sort of thing."

"You want a golden parachute? From us? The people you completely humiliated?"

"You want to push this, Fiona?" I stand up and start pacing behind my mom's desk. Deanna hides behind her hands. "I'm agreeing to your terms. Happily. I will *happily* never think about the Hot Spot again. But you have to do right by me. I gave you a year of my life. You have to give me something in return."

"Hold the line," Fiona snaps. There is a click and then nothing on her end. Deanna looks at me questioningly and I shrug. A minute later Fiona comes back on the line.

"We've discussed it."

I look at Deanna, confused. "Wait, who's discussed it?"

"The Network. You didn't really think we were alone on this call, did you?"

"They're here? Listening in? HELP ME! YOU HAVE TO HELP ME!" I scream, leaning over the phone. "FIONA HAS LOST HER MIND!"

There is a long silence. "Are you done?" Fiona finally sighs. Defeated, I flop back into the chair.

"I swear, Gigi, sometimes I don't think you ever understood what the Hot Spot was really all about. The Network has discussed it, and we've decided that your request for severance is fair, considering the amount of time you put into rushing."

"So what's the severance? What are you giving me? Cash? A car?"

"You'll find out when you've completed your severance task."

"Wait . . . what? Are you kidding? You're kicking me out! I'm not doing any sort of *task* for you."

"That's your choice, Gigi. And in that case you will receive no severance."

I look at Deanna, fighting the urge to tear the phone out of the wall.

"What do I have to do?" I ask.

"There are two choices. Commit yourself to our service for a set period of time and receive your severance when that time is up."

I laugh. "Oh, that's funny! Be in your service? I'm Gigi Lane! I'm in no one's service but my own!"

"Okay, then," Fiona continues. "Your second option is to clear the cliques. Once you have been accepted into a clique, the severance will be yours."

"Clear the cliques?" I laugh. "Are you joking?"

"No. I'm not joking. You can clear the cliques or commit yourself to our service. The choice is yours."

"How do I know whatever it is you're offering would be worth it?" I huff.

"We're the Hot Spot, Gigi. Of course it will be worth it."

"And what if I don't do either? What if I just walk away?"

"We both know you won't do that. Oh, Gigi," Fiona says, "we could have had you excommunicated. Not even Deanna would be allowed to talk to you. Clearing the cliques to receive your severance is a very generous offer. And I advise you to take it. A girl like you is not meant to eat her lunch in the bathroom."

Deanna whispers, "Do it, Gigi. You'll just end up with the Cheerleaders, with me."

I sigh. "Fine. I'll do it."

"And you, Deanna? Will you accept the Cheerleaders offer?"

Deanna looks at me. I shrug. "Sure," she says, "I'll do it."

"I'm glad we've gotten this all settled. Now. Gigi. You are hereby permanently exiled from the Hot Spot. If anyone asks me or any other Hot Spot alum if we know you, we will say no. If we see you when we are at Swan's Lake, we will ignore you. And if we hear that you have talked about the Hot Spot, we will come after you, and you will regret ever saying our name. Is that understood?"

I glare at the phone.

"It is not a rhetorical question. Do you understand the details of your exile?"

"Yes," I hiss, leaning forward so my mouth is right up against the microphone.

"Good. Your permanent exile begins now." And then Fiona is gone, and Deanna and I are staring at the phone, listening to the dial tone.

"So that's that," Deanna says.

"So that's that," I repeat, clicking end call. "I should call her back and tell her exactly what I think of her new Hot Spot."

The doorbell rings when Deanna and I walk downstairs. It's the postman, with a letter sent certified mail.

This letter is to serve as formal notification of your ejection from the Hot Spot. You are forth-with forbidden to use the words "the Hot Spot" in conversation, including conversations with others, with yourself (a.k.a. talking to yourself), with animals (stuffed or living), with plants (silk or real), with photographs, and with other animate or inanimate objects. Note: Silent prayer to whatever higher power you choose cannot be monitored and is therefore allowed. This does *not* include confessions; priests are people too and are therefore included as animate objects. Mention of the Hot Spot is also forbidden in written form,

including diaries; blogs; websites; letters; tattoos;
memoirs; short stories; novels; magazine articles
(print or online); T-shirts, hats, and other apparel;
banners; skywriting; scraping words into sand
with a stick, finger, or toe; and rubbing words into
steamed-up mirrors or windows.

"They like the drama, don't they?" I ask Deanna, showing her the letter.

Deanna lets out a huge sigh. "I have to go to the mall. Want to come?"

Going to the mall for Deanna isn't like going to the mall for most people. It's more like a job, but much more annoying than working in the food court.

"Where do you want to hit first?" We're standing in front of a backlit map and directory of stores, and I read off Deanna's usual go-tos. "Foot Locker? Pretty Girl Jewelry Company? Or—"

"No way, dude! We're getting you new clothes first." She waves her hands in front of my body like she's tracing my curves. "We've got to dress your new va-va-va-voom!"

"I have Margot's fat skirt and my overalls." I shrug. "What else do I need?"

Deanna points her finger very close to my nose. "Gigi Lane, so help me, if you become one of those body-hating curvy girls, I'm going to go Killer Pixie on your head."

I sigh. In my mom's book *Love Your Feathers, No Matter the*

*Weather: The Girlie Bird's Guide to Loving the Skin You're In*, she talks about trying on clothes without looking at the sizing—just keep going a size up until you find what looks best on you.

I look at my translucent reflection in the smudged Plexiglas covering the mall directory. I need a haircut and a manicure and a serious fashion intervention. You know that nightmare when you walk into school and realize you're in your underwear? That used to be my *favorite* dream, the kind that I would wake up from and then bury my head in the pillow, hoping to get back to that feeling of exhilaration. Because in my version of the dream, everyone looks at me—my face free of makeup, my hair windblown, my whole *being* glowing with a sort of almost-naked wild beauty that shows the world that it's not about nail polish, lip gloss, and next season's jeans. I don't need any of those accoutrements. In the dream I say my affirmation out loud to my classmates, "I'm Gigi Lane and you wish you were me," and they nod and murmur their agreement, "Yes, yes, we do wish we were you." And then, most times, I rise up over them and fire shoots out of my mouth.

But now, as I stare at my distorted reflection in the warped Plexiglas, my affirmation comes out as a question in my mind. *I'm Gigi Lane and you wish you were me?*

"Actually, Deanna," I say, trying to smile. "I think I'm just going to shop online and pay for overnight shipping."

"Fine, be that way." Deanna shrugs. "But what about beauty stuff? You *love* beauty stuff, and you don't need to take your pants off to try it on."

The thought does cheer me up a bit. "Are you sure? We can do your Razzmatazz stuff first. . . ."

"Nah, let's go buy some beauty junkity junk," she says with a wink. "I think we need to address your . . ." She looks at me for a second, trying to decide on a word, and settles on, "Situation."

"Okay." I nod, trying to convince myself. "Beauty stuff will be fun. Just like old times, right?"

"Right!" she squeals, grabbing my hand and leading me toward the absolute mall mecca of beauty products: Sephora.

We work our way from one end of the store to the other, dropping deliciously shiny boxes containing little tubs of various creams into a shopping basket. But as the basket gets heavier, so does my mood.

"Icing on the cake," I blurt out as Deanna drops tubs of lip gloss into my basket.

"What?" she asks, holding an open sample of cream blush next to my cheek, before pulling a closed package off the shelf and adding it to the basket. She reaches for a compact of eye shadows, and I touch her wrist, stopping her.

"Deanna," I say, pouting, "I think I'm having an identity crisis. I mean, if I'm not Head Hottie, who am I?"

"Um . . . you're Gigi Lane?"

"Of *course* I'm Gigi Lane!" I say, more crossly than I intended. "And that's no small consolation, but it's like I'm the only one that knows what that means anymore!"

"So . . . ," Deanna ventures, "it's not you having an identity crisis, it's everyone else?"

I'm almost moved to tears by her understanding. "Exactly!"

Deanna half laughs, half groans. "Oh, Gigi, I really missed you and your . . . special philosophies."

"Well, I'll tell you what, Deanna," I declare, invigorated by her sensitivity to my situation, "I'm going to make you proud. Just like my mom says in her book *Molt: The Girlie Bird's Guide to Shedding Her Feathers and Starting Anew*, I'm going to be the best darn Cheerleader Swan's Lake has ever seen."

"Yeah!" Deanna pumps her fist in the air. "Let's celebrate with snacks!"

We walk a little bit after our trip to the food court, but then have to sit down on a bench.

"Wow, Gigi," Deanna groans, "popularity and gymnastics kept us away from so much good food for so long."

My stomach rumbles. I burp and then clasp my hand to my mouth.

"Are you about to be accidentally bulimic?" Deanna gasps.

I close my eyes, taking a deep breath through my nose. Finally I take my hand away. "False alarm," I say, "I'm okay."

"Good." She stands up and stretches. "The mall's closing soon. I should get to work."

"You actually have room in your stomach?"

Deanna shrugs. "Sure."

She slips off the barrette that holds her signature pointed bangs in place, then pulls a bottle of bright green liquid out of her bag. Its label reads RAZZMATAZZ ENERGY ELIXIR. She opens it and takes a swig. I'm used to what comes next, but it's still hard not to burst out laughing.

"Wow," she says loudly, "Razzmatazz energy drink sure gives me the get-up-and-go when I need to get up and go!" She takes another gulp. "This stuff is great!"

The mall is emptying out, but there are still a fair number of people around. They glance in our direction, some of them recognizing Deanna, some of them not. When she first started working the malls, she would be mobbed before she even took her first sip. Now the attention is a little more . . . subdued. It takes a few minutes, but eventually she gathers enough of a crowd for me to snap a picture to send back to the Razzmatazz folks as "proof of performance."

# CHAPTER EIGHT

**New Year, New You?**
**Looks like some have blossomed into**
**Swans, and some have gone back to being**
**ugly ducklings.**

**(Boo hoo.)**

"I guess there *is* something sort of prosaically charming about being a cheerleader," I call to Deanna from the little cove of lockers where I am getting changed the next day, my first day of practice. "It's kind of cute," I continue. "Like we're living in the 1950s or something. All in all, it won't be a bad way to spend my senior year, especially considering the undoubtedly extremely generous severance package the Hot Spot will give me once I'm officially a Cheerleader." I walk out into the sink area to check out my outfit. I frown at the skirt, whose hem is below my knees, and roll it up at the waist. Better. "Cheerleaders are my people, you know? Fit, beautiful, talented. Oh . . . hi," I falter, stopping short when I see Simone sitting on the bench across from the sinks, holding a clipboard and watching me. *I'm Gigi Lane and you wish you were me.* There. That's better. "Where'd Deanna go?"

Simone looks at me for a long moment before answering. She clears her throat. "Because you and Deanna have a preexisting relationship, it was decided that she should not be the one to supervise your week with us."

"This is high school," I remind her, remembering Simone's part in my Cheerleaders' "welcome" yesterday. "It's all preexisting relationships."

"That may be so," she says, standing up, "but this is not something you get to decide. I'll be supervising your tryouts, not Deanna."

"Whatever. So how'd you get this gig? Why do you get to supervise?"

"I volunteered," Simone replies crisply, clipboard held to her chest.

"Why?" I ask, standing in front of her. "Are you moonlighting for the Vox Foxes? Is that what your little clipboard is for?" I give the clipboard a tap. "For taking notes for your big news story?"

Simone looks at me for another long moment. Then she lowers the clipboard, pulls the pen out of the clip, and jots something down, before pressing the clipboard back to her chest.

I smile. "You got pen on your uniform. You should have let it dry first."

She glances down, moving the clipboard just an inch so that she can see. Then she looks back up and glares.

"Gotcha." I smile.

For a second it looks like Simone is going to do what people usually do when they think better of confronting me: drop her eyes, mumble, and then avoid me. But she doesn't drop her eyes. She looks right at me. "Why didn't you bring me to London?"

My jaw drops. I just look at her for a second before going over to the sinks. "Are you serious?" I watch her in the mirror. I pull the elastic out and let my hair fall over my shoulders. "You seriously want to have this conversation?"

"Yes. I do."

I pull my hair back, working it into the standard cheerleader ponytail. "God, Simone, that was, like, seven years ago. You're really still upset over something that happened in fifth grade?"

She doesn't answer. She just raises her eyebrows and taps the clipboard with the pen.

I snort. "Fine. I could only bring two people. So I brought Deanna and Aloha. You shouldn't have been all that surprised. Everyone knew they were the ones I'd end up taking."

"'End up' being the operative words," Simone says. "You told me I could go too."

I shrug, turning around to face her. I lean back on a sink. "I told a lot of people that."

She gapes at me. "But why would you do that if you knew who you were really going to pick?"

I shrug again. "Because it was fun. Everyone falling all over themselves to be nice to me. You gave me that heart locket your grandmother gave you."

"Which you then *lost*."

"Well, you shouldn't have given it to me if you knew you would want it back."

"And you shouldn't have taken it if you knew you weren't going to bring me to London. I got in *so* much trouble for losing that locket, Gigi."

"Yeah, I remember. My mom let your mom come over and search my room. She went through my underwear drawer."

"And then you told everyone my mom was a panty sniffer!"

"Simone, that was years ago! Kid stuff, you know. Joking around."

"Well . . . jokes hurt, Gigi." She looks down at her clipboard, and I wonder if she's going to start crying.

"I'm sorry, okay?" I finally snap. "I'll get you a new locket."

"You can't. It was an antique, brought over from England by my great-grandparents."

I sigh. "Simone, have you ever heard of Buddha?"

"*Yes*," she answers. "Why?"

"Well, if you've heard of Buddha, you might know that he was totally against being attached to objects. You don't own objects, objects own you."

"What exactly is your point?"

"My point is that the locket was just an object. A thing. It wasn't your actual grandmother, or your great-grandmother. It doesn't matter who has the locket, it's not like you lose the love for your family if you lose the locket."

"But I didn't lose the locket. *You* did."

"Simone," I sigh, "pay attention. The locket doesn't matter! I just hope that our . . . *preexisting* relationship won't have an effect on my rushing the Cheerleaders."

She looks taken aback for a second, surprised at the turn in conversation. *Ha,* I think, *I've got her.*

"Because if it affects your decision, I think it's only fair that someone else supervise. Are you able, Simone, to be fair and unbiased, despite that little misunderstanding all those years ago? Or am I going to have to call Fiona Shay at Yale and tell her that you aren't fit for the job?" I step closer to her and whisper, "You have no idea the things she could do to you, Simone. You do not want to disappoint her."

"You seem to have come out all right." She smirks at me.

"I'm Gigi Lane," I purr with a smile, "I *always* come out all right."

"I'm fit for it," Simone grumbles. "But I'm not going easy on you, Gigi. You have to try out, just like everyone else."

"Everyone else" turns out to be a bunch of first-years hoping to get on the JV team. They had part of their tryouts before school started, and now, as luck would have it, they are having a week's worth of practice with the varsity squad to see if they make the team, just like me. Oh, goody.

Deanna takes her place as captain at the front of the squad, and Simone lines up beside me, her clipboard in hand. I give her my most winning smile. She frowns, picks up the clipboard, and writes something down. I lose the smile.

"On the floor, ladies. Legs apart, stretch forward." I look at

Deanna. She's successfully managed to send her feet north and south, and is currently reaching far east with both hands. I've managed only to scratch the dry skin on my kneecaps.

Beside me, Simone succeeds in laying her body totally flat on the floor between her split legs *and* makes another note on her stupid clipboard.

All popular girls look good in shorts and are naturals at things like beach volleyball and tennis. And cheerleading. Or so I thought. It is occurring to me that I might be wrong. Because these girls, these *cheerleaders*, are some sort of freakish superhumans with Silly Putty instead of muscles, and overcooked linguini instead of bones. For forty-five minutes Deanna leads us in a series of increasingly ridiculous stretches, bends, splits, and other contortions that send my thong right up my butt.

Simone has covered one side of the paper on her clipboard with notes and is halfway down the other when Deanna jumps up, claps her hands, and says, "Good job, everybody!"

"Oh, thank *God!*" I cry, standing up, my legs watery and unsure beneath me. "Can we go get doughnuts now?" I ask Deanna. "Because I did not consume enough calories to support a workout like that."

There is some scattered laughter. I look at the first-year in too-short shorts standing next to me. "What?"

"Um, practice hasn't started yet?" she yips and yaps in typical first-year question-speak. "That was just the warm-up?"

Hasn't *started* yet? If memory serves, cheerleading practice in grade school consisted of doing a couple somersaults and eating Sour Patch Kids while we waited for our moms to pick us up.

The first-years gather around me like flies on a dropped hot dog. They look at me, full in the face, their upper lips a little curled. "Yeah, we still have to, like, practice?" one of them pipes in, standing on her tiptoes as she speaks.

"Hey." A girl with her auburn hair pulled into a classy chignon at the base of her neck moves herself into my line of vision, until I'm looking down into her adorably and irrevocably freckle-covered face. "Weren't you supposed to be super popular this year?"

"Aren't you a little young to be wearing that much eyeliner?" I shoot back. "This is high school, not a cabaret."

I hear the click of Simone's pen and turn around to see her scribbling something down. "Oh, come on!" I hiss at her. "They're swarming!"

Simone smirks happily and writes something else.

Another first-year, this one most obviously a future Glossy on account of her beautiful face and slobbery lips. "I heard you got deported."

I flinch at the drop of spittle that flies out of her mouth. "Listen, you little . . ."

*Click.* Simone watches me, her head poised.

"You little moppets." I pat the closest one on the head, even though she's almost as tall as me. "I'm on what they refer to as a journey of self-discovery. Have you read my mom's books?"

The first-years look nervously at one another, just now realizing this may have been required reading.

"Have your *moms* read my mom's books?" I sigh.

They nod eagerly, cheeping and chirping, "Yes-yes-yes!"

"Well," I say, smiling at them, always happy to spread The Word of the Bird, "I'm doing what is referred to as meeting my tweet."

"My mom has that T-shirt," Slobbery Lips offers. "She sleeps in it."

"How nice for her," I continue. "As I was saying. I'm on a journey of self-discovery."

The redheaded little minx perks up. "So, you discovered you're a total loser?"

Her friends pale and gasp, their wide eyes focusing on me.

I feel a familiar heat crawling up the back of my neck. I've never verbally crucified a first-year; their tender flesh couldn't take it. But now words tinged with venom are clamoring behind my teeth, knocking for space to be the first ones out. I bite down, glancing at Simone's poised pen.

Deanna saves me from committing social infanticide by doing a double handspring into the center of our little circle and saying, "All right, let's do some clapping!"

I let out a sigh of relief as the first-years clap for Deanna.

Clapping. *This* I can handle.

And I do handle it—for the first two minutes, anyway—and then, with Simone taking notes, I'm told to partner with the redheaded devilette so she can "bring me up to date on clap dynamics."

I think she knows she dodged a bit of a bullet, but she is still flushed with pleasure at getting to instruct me. "No, Gigi, like this!" *Clap, clap!*

I nod, starting to sweat a little. "Got it." *Clap, clap.*

The redheaded fire starter looks over at her friends and giggles. "No, no, no, but almost, try it again." *Clap, clap!*

I wipe the sweat from my brow with my shoulder. "Right." *Clap, clap.*

*Click.* Simone's pen scribbles across the page. Deanna comes over to help.

"All right, Gigi, you've almost got it. It's *clap, clap! Clap, clap, clap!*"

I repeat exactly what she just did. The redheaded girl looks on, grimacing at my hands.

Deanna nods encouragingly. "You're so close! It's—"

"Deanna! I'm doing the exact same thing as you!" It's rude, but I clap right in her face, almost yelling, "*Clap, clap, clap!*" as I do it.

Deanna crosses her arms over her chest, waits for me to finish, and says nothing. She just raises her hands and claps right back at me, a rhythm that is, now that I think of it, totally different from what I just did. Then she raises one eyebrow in her signature look, one that is both an invitation and a warning.

"Don't you get all Killer Pixie gymnastics diva on me," I huff.

"I knew you when you thought French-kissing meant kissing a boy on both cheeks."

Deanna laughs. "You're such a wanker, now try it again."

But before she can continue her clap lesson, everyone turns to where Aloha, Heidi, and Daphne are walking into the gym, crossing to sit on the bleachers directly behind Deanna and me.

"*Hi, Gigi!*" Daphne stage-whispers. "How's it going? I really miss our little meetings!" Then, in her regular voice, for all to hear, she continues, "Gigi used to make me miss class so she could give me *life lessons.*" Aloha snorts, and Heidi breaks into a silent, ugly laugh. "Right, Gigi? Remember? You would corner me in the girls' bathroom and breathe all over me and tell me the reason nobody but the Art Stars liked me was because I was . . . what did you call me? A troll?"

I refuse to acknowledge her, choosing instead to look at Deanna, who, while looking a little sorry for me, looks more like she wants to say, *I told you so.* Someone, either Heidi or Aloha, whispers something to Daphne. It sounds like firm encouragement.

"I *said,*" Daphne says louder, "what was it you used to call me?"

"Troll." I turn, leveling my glare. "I called you a *troll.*"

"Right!" Daphne exclaims with a truly winning smile that doesn't reach her eyes. "Troll. Well"—she stands up and spins around—"I just wanted you to know that I took *all* of your beauty advice. But you know what they say. . . ." The flat smile is back, and she looks me up and down. It's like my ass gets bigger just from her looking at me. "Those who can't do, teach."

The rest of the team looks from me to Daphne and back to me again.

Deanna claps. "Cheerleaders, continue with your clapping!"

The team halfheartedly goes through the motions, watching us the whole time.

Aloha surveys the team. "Do you all know who we are?" she asks loudly.

There are nervous glances, a collective holding of breath.

"I *said* . . ." Aloha steps into the center of the group. Heidi and Daphne exchange glances of excitement. Aloha is almost yelling now. "Do you all know who we are?"

I see the redheaded first-year gulp, glancing at her friends, who furiously shake their heads at her. *Don't do it!* one of them mouths. *It's a trick!* But the redhead doesn't listen. She raises her chin, glances at me, and says, "You're the Hot Spot."

Aloha's eyes widen along with her smile. She nods. "That's right. We're the Hot Spot."

"Are you crazy?!" someone yells. Oh wait, it's me. I shove through the crowd, my heart pounding, until I am standing in front of Aloha. "You *know* you're never supposed to use those words in mixed company!" I turn to glare at the redheaded first-year, who takes a step back. "And *you* better watch your mouth, little Swan, because you have *no idea* the sort of people you're dealing with." I turn back to Aloha. "Keeping your big mouth shut is rule number one, you idiot! Even you know that!"

"Rule number one?" Aloha asks. "You mean the first rule in the Hottie Handbook?"

I almost throw up on her shoes. Talking about the Hottie Handbook is even more verboten than taking about the Hot Spot. All around me the Cheerleaders, especially the first-years, are standing as still as possible, not wanting to make a noise lest they break the magic spell.

"Aloha," Deanna murmurs quietly, "you're really not supposed to—"

"Shut up, Dear Heart," Heidi hisses at her, to a chorus of gasps. *Nobody* talks to Deanna like that, though I can tell from the evil look on Heidi's face that she has been waiting a long time to do just that. Deanna slowly raises her eyebrow. The first-years drop their jaws and prepare to witness a cheerleading beat-down.

Heidi snorts and feigns a shudder. "Ooooh! Are you going to go *Killer Pixie* on me?"

"You'd better hope I don't," Deanna whispers, stepping closer to Heidi. "Because I'd have no problem busting my other knee kicking your butt."

"Enough with the Cheerleader smackdown," Aloha snaps at them, quieting the first-years' excited titters. "Gigi, how would you know what's in the Hottie Handbook? You've never actually read it, have you?"

I don't answer her. I can feel Daphne standing next to me, and it's like my right side is convulsing with cringes, just knowing she's so close. Out of the corner of my eye I catch her lean just slightly toward me. "I've read it," she whispers. I close my eyes, my neck bending so that the ear she whispers in almost touches my shoulder, as if I could physically block out the sound. "You wouldn't believe it, Gigi. The things in that book," she adds with a groan, "would blow your mind."

Deanna saves me, grabbing my arm and pulling me toward her. "We have a practice to finish, if you ladies don't mind."

Aloha considers.

"Look," Deanna reasons. "We get it, okay? You're the new *you-know-whos*. You've got us shaking in our bobby socks. Can we just take the drama down a notch so that we can finish practice?"

Aloha scoffs, but Deanna interrupts her before she can speak. "Aloha," she says quietly. "Seriously. It's the first week of school. Isn't it a little early for a reign of terror?"

"Fine," Aloha agrees, walking back to the bleachers. "We'll just sit and watch. Except I think Heidi should lead this practice. . . ." She winks at Heidi, who breaks into an evil smile. "For old time's sake."

"That tart hurt my feelings!" I whine to Deanna with a wet sniff, half pouting, half laughing, as we wait by the front steps for her mom to pick us up after practice. My stupid car is in the stupid shop.

"You have feelings?" Deanna laughs.

"Yes, feelings of pure, unadulterated rage," I growl. "Heidi totally humiliated me.

"Come on, Lane, buck up!" Deanna says, socking me in the arm. "It wasn't that bad."

"Deanna," I cry, "she didn't even let me finish practice! It was humiliating! Making me pick up all the water bottles by the bleachers, and I kept dropping them on the way to the equipment room, and then I kicked that one into the basketball team practice, and then *they* just kept kicking it, and finally they had to stop practicing so I could pick it up. The whole thing *sucked*."

"Life as a mere mortal does suck, doesn't it?"

I shrug, taking a shuddering breath, trying to calm myself. "It does seem to be a dubious start to my life as a civilian."

"You'll hardly be a civilian. Cheerleaders are top tier."

Deanna is balanced on the curb like it's a balance beam, stepping through the routine she did at the Olympic trials.

"It still feels like a long way to fall. What'd you think of it?" I ask.

"Of what?" Deanna asks, holding one leg straight up to her ear. "Practice?"

I nod, stepping behind her on the curb and trying to copy what she does.

"I thought the *you-know-whos* little show of force was more like a show of farce. Last year's *you-know-whos* never had time for that kind of thing, even the first week of school." She jumps off the curb and I follow, parroting her wave to the invisible crowd. "Let's go through the routine from today."

"What's the use?" I sigh. "They're just going to keep me on

136

the bench once I get accepted, and parade me out once in a while to wave at the crowd."

"I'm team captain. No best friend of mine is going to warm a bench," Deanna declares, kicking at my ankles until my feet are spread far enough apart. "Good. Now just do what I do."

I laugh. "Those are exactly the words you said to me when we were little kids, right before I realized you were *way* out of my league at the Little Tumblers Gymnastics School."

"You were really good at somersaults. Now watch."

She goes thoroughly through the cheer routine from today. I try to watch her but get bored and sit down on the bottom step, tugging my skirt so that the backs of my thighs don't touch the stone. "Are you sure your mom's coming?"

"Sure I'm sure," she says, stopping the cheer and moving into a gymnastics routine. "And unless you want to spend our senior year having our only access to a car be the Jones Family Minivan every other Saturday night, you need to get your car fixed. Did you really give Daphne *life lessons?*"

"Sort of?"

"I never knew that."

I shrug. "It was just kind of a hobby."

Deanna stands in front of me, her hands on her hips. "It sounds mean."

I shrug again, trying to meet her stare.

"That's not you, Gigi," Deanna says. "Being that mean to someone, that's not really who you are."

I snort. "What? I'm really a brassy blonde with a heart of gold?"

"You *do* need a dye job," Deanna says, kicking lightly at my shoe.

I automatically touch my hair. She's right. I'm in dire need of a mud pack and highlights.

"I just mean that your whole mean-girl thing is just an act." Deanna pauses. "Right?"

I think about this for a moment. "Well," I muse, "there *is* a performative aspect to my . . ." I hestitate, trying to find the right word. "To my role here at Swan's Lake."

Deanna looks at me, puzzled. "And what role is that?"

I shrug. "Peacekeeper?"

Deanna bursts out laughing.

"What?" I ask, laughing a little myself. "It's true! Deanna, no one wants to say it out loud, but without people like you and me to tell them where exactly they belong in the whole"—I flutter my hands—"social hierarchy, this school would self-destruct."

Deanna's still laughing. "So it's for their own good?"

"Precisely!"

"Gigi," Deanna groans, "sometimes I think you bought your own hype."

I wink at her. "It was an easy sell."

"Good afternoon, ladies."

We both look up to see Ms. Carlisle walking down the front steps of the school. She's frumpy as ever, today wearing a mud brown skirt and an itchy-looking sweater. "Practicing your cheerleading routine?"

We both nod. She smiles, and I try not to flinch. It's like she actually *painted* on those coffee stains. "That's nice. I heard you were both"—she clears her throat—"trying that on for size. Have you two thought about where you're going to apply for college?"

"A little," Deanna says. "I'm looking at sports medicine programs."

"Yale," I say.

"Oh, Yale!" Ms. Carlisle says, her voice so breathless it almost seems fake. "How *wonderful* for you! I'm sure you'll be very happy there. If you get in."

"Excuse me?" I ask, my jaw dropping. "Of *course* I'm going to get in."

She ignores me and turns to Deanna. "And sports medicine sounds like a wonderful option for America's Pixie Sweetheart!" She claps her hands. "Oh, goody, goody gumdrops!"

We're saved by Deanna's mom pulling up in the JFM. We say a quick good-bye and hurry into the minivan.

"Okay, you cannot tell me she wasn't just making fun of us to our faces," I insist as soon as I get in the car. "There has to be a law against that."

"She's just a little awkward," Deanna says, leaning over to kiss her mom on the cheek. "God, would you look at her car? Now, that's just sad."

Her mom and I follow Deanna's gaze to where Ms. Carlisle

is yanking on the door handle of a decrepit station wagon, its back bumper hanging like a lopsided smile.

Her mom purses her lips and shakes her head. "Bad cars happen to the best of us, girls."

Deanna laughs and pats the dashboard as her mom starts driving. "The Jones Family Minivan is *not* a bad car, Mom!" She leans over to her mom and bats her eyelashes, quoting the commercial she and her mom appeared in for the JFM. "'It's our chariot of dreams!'"

Her mom laughs and glances at me in the rearview mirror. "Gigi, how was your summer? I was so surprised to hear you went to Alaska!"

"To be honest, it was a serious lapse of judgment on my part, Mrs. J.," I answer. "I didn't really understand what I was agreeing to when I signed up. It was kind of a dark time in my life that I'd rather not discuss."

She glances back at me in concern. "Why, were you hurt? Did something happen?"

"Oh, no, Mrs. J.," I assure her. "The abuse was strictly fishy in nature. I was taken in by a pack of sorority sisters from Ohio that looked out for my basic needs."

Deanna picks up a pair of swim goggles from the crap holder between the seats. "Were you at the pool?" she asks her mom.

"Yep, and I'm starving. Open the glove compartment and get me a snack, would you?"

Deanna groans, "Mom, you don't have to eat these." She opens up the glove compartment and pulls out a Champion Bar, scowling at it before handing it to her mom. The Champion Bar people were another one of Deanna's sponsors. They were going to pay Deanna a million dollars and a lifetime supply of granola bars for being their spokesperson at the Olympics. When she got hurt, they canceled the contract. Deanna's lawyers tried to fight it, since Deanna and her mom had gone way into debt for her training, planning on paying it back with the sponsorship. The lawyers lost. Well, almost lost. They did manage to get the lifetime supply of Champion Bars, though the company gave them to Deanna all at once. She and her mom have been trying to eat through them ever since.

"Can't we just donate them to charity?" Deanna asks.

"They're expired, you know that," her mom scolds, biting hard into a bar and grimacing. "Someone could get sick. Then how would you feel? Gigi, do you want one?" her mom asks, grinning at me in the rearview mirror, granola stuck in her teeth.

"Sure." I reach for the bar that Deanna reluctantly holds out, and she opens one of her own. We have our usual contest to see who can eat through the most before having to throw it out the window. Deanna's mom usually wins, eating through about a quarter of it, though once I ate through a whole one. I didn't poop for five days.

I manage three bites before stuffing the remainder back in the wrapper. Deanna makes it only two. Mrs. Jones takes five bites, but one doesn't count because she has to spit it back out.

"So, Gigi," Mrs. Jones mumbles, sucking granola bits out of her teeth, "how are the college applications coming?"

"Well . . . ," I hesitate, considering that fact that I haven't *really* put much thought into college applications since I got home. "I hear Yale is looking for nontraditional summer experiences, so I'm hoping that serving out my sentence in Alaska will be of some benefit to my personal statement."

"Oh," she says, nodding, "that makes sense." She winks at Deanna. "I bet they'll get a real kick out of you being a gymnastics coach for the past three summers. That's pretty special, right?"

"Mom." Deanna shifts in her seat.

"What? It *is* special. Not many people can say they've done that. You could have coached future Olympic—"

"Mom!" Deanna groans, her eyes brimming with tears. "Seriously, just stop it. I'm a camp counselor, that's it. None of those girls are going to the Olympics. And neither am I, so just drop it."

I realize I'm watching in the rearview mirror as Mrs. Jones's eyes tear up, and I look away. When I look back, she's reached over and squeezed Deanna's hand. Neither of them says anything until we get to my house. Then they both say a friendly but wet good-bye.

I miss my mom.

The rest of the week is a blur of pulled muscles and pom-poms, an interminable countdown to my severance and my new career as a Cheerleader.

On Wednesday I'm officially "off the floor" and on water

bottle duty, my fingers growing numb as I fill bottle after bottle with frigid water from the water fountain, tuning out both the discomfort and the sound of the Cheerleaders by imagining what my severance might be. Travel? Stocks? Diamonds? A horse? I glance up at the windowed doors leading out of the gym and watch as Daphne, Aloha, and Heidi walk by, pausing outside the doors with their backs to me, talking heatedly, each of them pointing in a different direction. Aloha throws up her hands in frustration, then focuses her glare on Daphne, reaching out to yank—none too lightly—on her hair and hiss something at her. The water overflows the bottle I'm filling, splashing onto my shoes, so I jump back, and when I look back up, Aloha is standing in the window smirking at me and giving me the finger.

On Thursday, Heidi comes back to practice and makes me dig the Spirit Stallion mascot costume out of the supply room. Of course it's weird that our school is called Swan's Lake, but our sports mascot is a stallion. It's a recent development. Seven years ago the Swan's Lake trustees decided our school should go coed. No one was really worried that it would actually happen, because they'd tried a bunch of times before and the outcry from alumnae—and the threats of pulling donations—was too loud to ignore. This most recent time the trustees hired an advertising company to "brand" the school. The Spirit Stallion thing came around because the ad agency worried that Swan's Lake was too "feminine" to attract male students.

I think it was the press conference that did it. The Head Hottie that year was Phillipa Jones, and she gave this amazing speech while holding up the head of the stallion costume by its forelock, like she had just chopped off the head in battle. She ended with, "You can keep your boys, but I think we'll keep the horse."

It was glorious.

By the time Friday rolls around, I am prancing around the gym with the deceptively heavy foam horse head planted firmly on my shoulders while the girls cheer, "We are the Stallions, NEIGH!!!"

On the way home after practice I chatter on nervously to Deanna. It was my last tryout practice today, which means that tonight or tomorrow morning I'll get my official acceptance from the Cheerleaders, and then my severance from the Hot Spot. Deanna tries to keep my mind off the wait by shuffling through *Get Psyched, Volume VI: Know the Taste of Your Enemy's Heart.*

"Oooh, this is a classic," she says, and a second later the opening strains of Bikini Kill's "Suck My Left One" come screeching through the stereo.

I wake up with a sugar hangover. Not only did the concession stand guy at the movie theater give us free refills on cherry Coke ("Dear Heart! No way!"), but he threw in a jumbo-size box each of Raisinets and Jujubes. We decided to go for a double feature, and laughed and joked our butts off through the first movie (a silly romantic comedy starring that actress with a snaggletooth), but by the end of the second movie (a wartime love story with lots of looooong silences and floppy male frontal nudity) we were both sugar-crashing hard, yawning and groaning, and finally falling asleep, Deanna's head on my shoulder, my own head flung back against the seat, which is why I think I was snoring so loud.

Snug in my own bed the next morning, I wake up long enough to roll over and luxuriate in the fact that I am sleeping between clean, fresh sheets and not in a damp and stinky sleeping bag in Alaska. I spread my limbs, reaching out to find the spots not warmed by my body, and slip back into a happy doze.

In my dream a sweet little bird has landed on my windowsill and is singing a special song just for me.

"Hello, little bird!" I coo, crouching in front of my window, the sun warm on my face. "Are you a subconscious message from my mother, the bestselling author of the Girlie Bird self-help books, which have helped over twenty million people find their true heart's song?"

The bird tweets and then wags its little bird tail.

"Well," I say, patting its little feathered head, "you tell my mother that her little Gigi Bird is doing just great, and that she's a Cheerleader now!"

"I'm afraid you are mistaken," the bird says with Darth Vader's voice.

"Wh-what?" I ask. The brilliant blue sky is muddying, like someone has taken a stick and stirred up the muck above, leaving it swirling and gray.

"You are mistaken," Darth Vader bird says again, turning to look over its bird shoulder behind it. "See for yourself."

I look out the window and see Cheerleaders flying toward

me through the blackening sky, flaming pom-poms in their fists. Their mouths are gaping black holes too big for their faces, from which they scream, "R-E-J-E-C-T!"

I wake up with a yelp, jump out of bed, and scramble to my window, tearing open the curtains and squinting at the bright morning sun. I frantically scan first the blue sky and then the yard, its lush green punctuated with the first fallen leaves of fall. My heart stops trying to break through my chest, my breath slowing to normal, as I see that both sky and yard are empty.

But then . . .

I hear it.

Oh, the horror! I clutch at my chest as the sound grows louder, I try to tear my eyes away from the street, but my whole body has been fossilized, and all I can do is stare in mute terror as a caravan of convertibles stops in front of our driveway gate.

"R-E-J-E-C-T, that is what you are, Gigi, a reject, a reject! You are a reject! Wooh!"

They cheer as they spill out of their cars, scrambling up the wrought-iron gate and backflipping into the yard like an invading army. They sprawl out on the lawn, spelling the word "REJECT" with their bodies. It's the first-years from tryouts that add the exclamation points.

They leave as quickly as they came, still cheering as they get back into their cars and drive away. When I'm sure they've gone, I go out on the front lawn in my bare feet and scuff up the grass with my toes, erasing the imprint of their bodies and that awful, terrible word.

When Deanna answers the phone, she doesn't say anything. We just sit there listening to each other's breath until I ask quietly, "Did Simone want you to come with them to my house?"

"I'm captain. I outrank her. I said I wouldn't go," Deanna answers. She lets out a huge sigh. "I really thought you had a chance, Gigi."

I gulp, beginning another long silence. She finally murmurs, "So I guess this means you'll . . ."

I groan. "Be Head Glossy. God, I can't believe it's come to this. I really felt like a Cheerleader, you know?"

"I know you did," Deanna comforts me, "and you would have been great. But you'll be a great Glossy, too."

I sigh. "I know you're right, it's just that having to redefine myself as the leader of yet another clique is exhausting."

# CHAPTER NINE

**Fascinating, Isn't It?**
**Like a car wreck, you just can't look away.**

**(And why would you want to?**
**The carnage is so pretty.)**

Deanna has to cheer at a game Saturday night, and I don't start rushing the Glossies until Monday, so I'm left in a sort of cliqueless netherworld for the weekend. Saturday night finds me eating take-out Chinese in my Alaska overalls and listening to a voice mail message from Veronica, head of the Glossies.

"Gigi, it's Veronica. We're not in the habit of taking castoffs from the Cheerleaders. But . . . as a special favor to Aloha, we're letting you rush."

"*Letting* me rush," I grumble, erasing the message. Glossies are the discount irregular cashmere sweaters of Swan's Lake. The girls you think are *so pretty* until you see them up close. Gummy smiles. Freakishly long arms. Saliva that gathers in the corners of their mouths when they get excited. Each of them is stricken with one singular trait that keeps them from a true saturation of beauty. They will forever be "almost beautiful" or, worse, "beautiful in spite of." Of course, most will go through some sort of self-love phase, usually led by my mom's book *We Can't All Be Swans: The Girlie Bird's Guide to Being an Ugly Duckling*, at the end of which they will practice phrases like "I'm beautiful not *in spite* of my freakishly short neck, but *because* of it!"

One look in my closet on Monday morning makes it obvious that I really should have gone shopping. Since Cheerleaders wear their uniforms at all times, I didn't have to worry about dressing for school at all last week. My jeans and skirts from last year look harrowingly narrow as I flick through the hangers, and I spend a good amount of time standing in front of the mirror looking at my newly round butt and lamenting the fact that I am going to have to exercise it right out of existence without the help of daily cheerleading practice.

I manage to squeeze into a pair of fat-day jeans and find a flowing peasant blouse that nicely covers up the fact that my stomach now hangs over the waist of my jeans in the sort of muffin top you see in "Before" pictures on late-night infomercials for motorized sit-up machines.

Veronica, the junior-year Glossy in charge of my rush, is waiting for me on the front steps, sitting just slightly right of center.

"Do you guys always sit out here?" I ask, sitting next to her. "I never noticed you before."

She snorts. "Only every single day, Gigi."

"You always get here this early?" It's barely seven, and the first-years, including my redheaded friend from cheerleading tryouts, are scampering up the steps for duties.

"We don't want to miss anything," Veronica says. "And we don't want anyone to miss *us*."

Veronica leans back and rests her shoulders on the step behind her, her oversize sunglasses covering up her own particular Glossy irregularity—crazy bulging eyes. The kind of eyes that look perfectly normal until their owner gets upset or excited, and then her eyelids pull all the way back and you can see the full circles of her irises and the round slopes of her eyeballs sucking back into her head.

I lean back too, mostly because I think the button on my jeans might make a run for it. I slip on my sunglasses, rest my elbows on the step behind me, suck in my stomach, and swear on a stack of imaginary Bibles that tomorrow I'm going to start eating healthy again.

Veronica has that stupid clipboard in her lap.

"So, Gigi," she begins, clicking the pen. "I think you're familiar with the sort of things us Glossies find important."

"Hmmm?"

"Are you listening to me?" Veronica asks, narrowing her eyes. "Because people are going to be here soon."

"Yes. I'm listening. The things you find important in a Glossy."

"Right. Can I help you?" Veronica pushes her sunglasses up

on top of her head and scowls at someone behind me. I turn around and see Beatrice Linney, the photographer of that awful, hateful first-day-of-school picture.

"Hey, Gigi." She clears her throat nervously. I debate throwing my shoe at her head. But if there's one thing I understand, it's that a clique has to do its job. Beatrice was only being a Vox Fox when she took that picture of me, and it helped her break the biggest story of the year.

"Hey, Beatrice." I make peace with a forgiving smile. "How's the scoop business?"

Beatrice sits down next to me, and Veronica practically starts vibrating with hatred. Hotties and the Vox Foxes are allies. Vox Foxes and Glossies are sworn enemies, due to the fact that the Glossies are pretty much totally absent from any and all issues of the *Trumpet of the Swan*. Vox Foxes have as little patience as I do for the antics of bit players. I'd rather read about the Gizmos breaking into NASA's computer (again) than an article detailing the bland adventures of the Glossies.

And on the rare occasion that a Glossy does something that's actually worthy of coverage, the *Trumpet* chooses to stick to its policy of "All the news that people actually care about." Which is why last year, when that Glossy whose name no one remembers rescued an old lady from a burning building, the headline of the *Trumpet* read SLOW NEWS DAY, NOTHING TO REPORT on top of an entirely blank piece of paper.

"We're busy, Beatrice," Veronica snaps, adjusting her sunglasses on top of her head. Then she thinks for a minute.

Seriously, I can actually see the wheels turning behind her too-big eyes. "Unless you want a story. I'll give you an exclusive. 'Gigi Lane Rushes the Glossies, the Inside Story from Veronica Herself.'"

Veronica smiles, hopeful eyes bulging.

"Nah," Beatrice says without hesitation. "I think we'll pass on the exclusive. See you later, Gigi, I've got to go stake out the dining hall."

"Later, Beatrice."

Veronica stews for a full minute after Beatrice goes inside, gripping the edge of the clipboard so tightly that the veins on the backs of her hands rise up like river lines on a map. Finally she takes a breath and growls, "I hope you're aware that Glossies *do* have body mass index guidelines, and I have to say you're looking a little—"

I interrupt her. "You know I can get you into the *Trumpet*, right?"

"Thick around the middle," she finishes with a smirk. "And yes, I am aware of your former . . . allegiances."

I ignore her comment about my newfound curves. "Then why make me rush?" I ask. "Just let me in and I'll get Beatrice to do a weekly style segment on you guys."

"Bribery will not work for you."

I laugh. "Bribery works for everyone."

"Well, not this time. You have to rush. For the full week. Those are the rules."

I push up my sunglasses and smile at her. "Aw, Veronica.

You just want to put me through the ringer a little bit, don't you?" I drop my sunglasses back down. "Fine by me. Do your worst. You know by next week we'll be BFFs."

Veronica shakes her head. "You really believe that, Gigi? Do you really believe that any clique really wants to take you in?"

"Um . . . *yes?*" I ask, though I have to admit I'm a little flustered by her tone. I rush through a few quick *I'm Gigi Lane*s until I've collected myself.

"Well, you can believe what you want," Veronica snickers, "but you're not exactly Swan's Lake's most wanted."

"Oh, look," I say, pointing, my voice shriller than expected. "There's Jen. She's a Glossy, right? Hi, Jen!" I call to the girl walking up the school driveway. She's got great hair, but she's way too tall for her face. It's like her face stopped growing before the rest of her did. So she's totally hot on paper—six two, blond hair, athletic—but with a baby's face. She has tiny teeth, too.

Jen climbs the steps.

"Won't you sit down?" I ask, glancing at the empty space beside me.

"Sure," Jen answers, sitting next to Veronica. Okay, maybe a baby face doesn't equal a baby brain, because with the look she and Veronica are both giving me, it's obvious they're onto my plan of Glossy domination. There's no way I could take up with any clique and not make myself its boss. Except the Cheerleaders, because being their boss means being double-jointed. Which I am not.

"We have a Head Glossy, Gigi. If we take you in, it will be strictly into a nonleadership roll," Veronica says firmly.

I sigh. "Whatever. Where's that girl that sits with you guys all the time? The one that's really cute except for that one over-size nostril? I want to see what happens when she sneezes."

The steps are filling up now, and I notice that the Gloss-ies are uniformly ignored by pretty much everyone. My skin prickles at the thought of being ignored for the rest of my senior year. The lower tiers don't pay us any mind, and Aloha, Daphne, and Heidi certainly don't give us a second glance on their way up to the top of the steps. Even the Cheerleaders breeze right on by to sit directly below the Hot Spot. I turn and watch Deanna sit, teasingly pinching Simone on her arm when she sees me.

"Gigi!" Deanna calls, jumping up. "I didn't even see you there!"

"Well," I say, trying to smile, "here I am!"

Deanna starts down the steps toward us, but the bell rings and she gives me a helpless look as everyone stands and starts to head into school.

"You get used to it," Veronica offers, standing up and shrug-ging. "Everyone has this sort of hysterical blindness when it comes to Glossies. The Do-Goods are our closest allies, but of course they don't spend time on the front steps. Especially now that they have to take turns in the nurse's office handing out Band-Aids and tampons."

"Why are they doing that?"

Veronica shrugs. "The nurse quit or something. So they need volunteers."

• • •

154

The only thing more humiliating than rushing a clique that nobody cares about is getting rejected by a clique nobody cares about. All week I sit with the Glossies on the steps, eat with them at lunch, and try not to bang my head on any nearby hard surface in order to knock myself unconscious.

It's like they speak beige.

I told myself again and again that once I was in the Glossies I could shake things up a bit, put some *va-va-va-voom* into their lukewarm lives.

Veronica calls me with the "unfortunate news" Friday after school, her stupid droning voice drilling into my ear. I hang up on her and am on my way into the kitchen for some caramel swirl ice cream therapy.

"Deanna!" I whine when I call her two minutes later, my mouth full of caramel swirl. "I'm a Glossy reject!"

She is appropriately shocked and comes over after practice to cheer me up.

"This sucks, Deanna!" I moan from under the couch cushions, where I cocooned myself after seeing how cute Deanna looked in her cheerleading uniform. "What am I going to do?"

Deanna pats the cushion over my face. "Oh, you'll come out okay, Gigi, you always do."

"No, I won't!" I wail, pushing off the cushion and sitting up, a few nacho chips falling off my Alaska overalls as I do. After shoehorning myself into jeans all week for the craptastic Glossies, it was a relief to get back into my overalls. "I'm destined to roam the halls, rejected and alone, like some Cursed

Unaffiliated. I should have just done whatever their stupid, evil severance task was. It has to have been better than this."

"Don't be silly, there are, like, a zillion more cliques for you to try!" Deanna dusts nacho crumbs off the couch and into her hand. She drops them into the empty ice cream carton on the coffee table.

I pull my hair out of its scrunchie, a good-bye present from my roommates in Alaska. "Did you see Daphne 'Dog Face' Hall wearing vintage Jordache jeans yesterday?"

"No, I didn't notice."

"Her stupid, fat butt was stuffed in there so tight I bet they'd split if she farted."

"Gigi . . . ," Deanna groans.

"What?"

"Just . . . that's not a very sisterly thing to say."

I pout. "She also tripped me when I was running down the hall trying to get to lunch before they sold out of minipizzas. I got a rug burn!" I hold up my palms for Deanna to see. "I swear it's like they never spend any time in the DOS just so they can torture me." I kick off the rest of the cushions and stand up. A small hailstorm of chip crumbs fall to the floor. "Deanna, look at me," I whisper, looking down at my overalls, my unwashed hair, my wool socks. "*This* is what sisterhood has done for me."

Deanna laughs. "Gigi, it's been two weeks! I know you feel like you've gone through some crazy transformation, but I hate to break it to you—you look exactly the same! Get a facial and a haircut and you'll be good to go."

"The transformation isn't about overalls and split ends," I say, shaking my head, "it's about *my heart.*"

"Okay, drama queen. Can we just pay-per-view a movie on cable and stop this pity party?"

I shrug. "I guess."

"Good." Deanna plops down on the couch. "And tomorrow before practice I'll go shopping with you."

"Why bother? I like my overalls." I sit down next to her, pulling a cushion into my lap. "They're like wearing a hug."

"Oh, come on, don't you want some cute tracksuits for next week?"

"Next week?"

"The Lacrockies, silly! If you want in with them, you *need* at least twelve velour tracksuits." She playfully pokes me and tries to lure me with, "They have elastic waistbands!"

The phone call from the Lacrockies comes the next morning when I'm in the shower.

"Gigi. It's Darlene, field hockey cocaptain. You're with us next week. Practice is Monday after school. I don't tolerate wusses on my team, Gigi. You might break a nail. You might break a kneecap. Wear a sports bra—no one needs to see your knockers knocking."

# CHAPTER TEN

## Need Guidance?
## Read a book!

**(Headmistress Carlisle will no longer
offer office hours for college counseling.
If you're not smart enough to get into college
on your own, you don't deserve to go.)**

*Aahh.* There is something so perfectly fall-like about being out on
the field, the cheers and shouts from my teammates punctuating
the chilly air. The thick groves of trees that surround our school
and its athletic fields are morphing from deep greens to oranges
and reds and golds, and the air has a delicious crispness to it. Every
breath is like biting into an apple. Today, my first day of practice,
is a uniformed scrimmage, and in our skirts and long-sleeved polo
shirts, with our flushed cheeks and strong thighs, we could be
doing a photo shoot for a Ralph Lauren ad. *These* are my people,
these strong young women with their rowdy camaraderie.

"KILL! KILL! KILL!"

I am hyperventilating behind a Hannibal Lecter face mask while a vaguely familiar girl attempts to score a goal not by shooting the ball around me, but by knocking me over, stepping on my head, and then tapping the ball into the goal to a chorus of cheers from her—and my own—teammates.

She doesn't step on me before she walks away, but she does squat down and whisper, "Hey, Gigi, remember in seventh grade when you told everybody I took a big number two in the bathroom and then didn't wash my hands?"

In my weakened state all I can do is nod. I do remember that. It was funny. People started calling her—

"Poop Hands. They called me Poop Hands, Gigi. Nobody would touch me for years. *Years*, Gigi, and people wouldn't even let me borrow a pencil."

"I'm sorry?" I offer, though it seems a bit unfair for her to be attacking me this way, for something that happens in the normal state of play of school-chum relations. All's fair in love and junior high, right?

"It's like, even if people knew it wasn't true, even two years later, it still grossed them out to think that *these* hands . . ." She holds up her two wide palms, and I try not to grimace. Even if I was the one that made up that rumor, something like that sticks in your head, you know? And it would have been disgusting if it had been true. "That these hands might be a public health risk."

And with that she sticks one hand under my face mask and presses her palm firmly into my face. I try to scream, and her thumb slips into my mouth, which I think surprises us both. We both freeze for a moment, her salty thumb lying across the smooth damp of my tongue, her thumb knuckle bumping against my teeth.

"Aggawagga!" I scream, and she yanks out her thumb, herself screaming, "Don't bite, please don't bite!"

She holds her slobbery thumb up in front her, I prop myself up on my elbows, and we both stare at it.

"Gross," I finally say, turning my head to spit.

"Truly." She grimaces, wiping her thumb on her plaid skirt and standing up. I stay lying on the ground, paralyzed by the fact that I just sucked her thumb.

"We're, like"—her eyes roll up, as if she's looking at a math problem inside her forehead—"halfway to even."

I nod. The grass tickles my neck. "Okay."

Poop Hands smells her thumb. "I didn't think girls like you ate Cheetos."

I prop myself up on my elbows and spit again, shrugging. "I'm kind of going through something."

"Hmph." Poop Hands stares down at me, twists her mouth like she's trying to tie a cherry stem into a knot.

From the other end of the field the coach blows the whistle. "Good job, everybody! Let's call it a day."

Poop Hands looks at me for a moment more before trotting away. I flop back on the grass, the cool air no longer crisp, but damp and chilly, working its way through my uniform and under my skin.

"Good job, team!" I finally call to the empty field.

By the time I limp my way out of the locker room, cursing the lack of hot water in the showers, the school is almost empty.

As of Thursday I am officially off the field, handing out water from the bench, when Deanna plops down beside me. She's in her cheerleading uniform, a snug Swan's Lake hoodie zipped up to her chin.

"Holy crap," I say, "you look freaking adorable!"

"Thanks." She blushes, shaking her head when I offer a bottle of water. "We just got the sweatshirts in. Good thing, too. They still haven't turned the heat on in the gym yet. How's it going out here?"

"Well. Let's see. I suck at field hockey, my mouth was sullied, the girls keep spitting water at me, and the coach made me hand wash everyone's shin guards with a toothbrush the other day."

"Ouch," Deanna laughs, "that's rough."

I shrug. "Whatever. You know that girl Poop Hands?"

"Becca?"

"I guess. I'm thinking about making her my second in command once I'm Head Lacrockie."

"That's cool. Why are you choosing her?"

I purse my lips and stare off into the distance. "We shared something. Duck."

"Wha—"

I put a hand on the back of her head and push, so we're both sitting with our noses to our knees as Poop Hands trots by and aims a stream of spit right where our heads just were.

"All I can say," I continue when she's a safe distance away, "is the Hot Spot's stupid severance package better be worth this torture. It better be, like, my own spaceship or a map to the fountain of youth. Anyway, how is cheerleading?"

"Really fun, actually, except the Hot Spot kicked us out of the gym for the afternoon."

"Why would they do that?"

Deanna shrugs. "They're doing it to all the cliques. I think it's their way of laying claim to the entire school. You know, we still need someone to dress up in the stallion costume. . . ."

I laugh. "I really don't think things are that dire, but thanks."

My cell phone rings. It's my mom.

"Gigi! You are a hard girl to get a hold of! How are things?"

"Hi, Mom!" I say, waving to Deanna as she leaves. "I'm *great*. Did Daddy tell you I've taken up the sporting life?"

"He did!" my mom crows. "That's why I was calling! I'm just so proud of you."

"Lane!" the coach bellows. "No cell phones on the field!"

"Mom, I'm sorry, but I have to go. The coach, she's really running me ragged."

My mom sucks in a happy gasp. "They only do that if they think you're really good! I'm so glad you've found your flock!"

Later, when I'm searching in the weeds next to the field

where Coach kicked my cell phone, I think about what my mom said. She was obviously referencing her book *Birds of a Feather: Finding a Flock to Call Your Own*. I don't really remember the details, since I read it while watching *Celebrity Bingo*, but the gist of it was basically "Whatever you're doing, be the best at it."

Do I *really* just want to coast through the year never getting off the bench?

It's time to take the Gigi Lane sports machine out for a test-drive.

"I'm ready to go in, Coach," I tell her the next day at practice. My black velour tracksuit glints onyx in the fall sun.

"What the hell," Coach says with a shrug, "it might be good for a laugh."

Before she even blows the whistle, I'm charging down the field, stick held high, knocking into girls left and right. I am on fire!

I'm vaguely aware of people cheering me on, screaming my name. I blaze down the field to the goal and hit that ball so hard it actually knocks the face mask off that bucktoothed girl Mena Denver.

"Yeah!" I yell, raising my fists in the air. For extra effect I try to break the stick over my knee, but the thing is solid, so I just whip it across the field instead.

Well, the good news is Mena now has a reason to get her teeth fixed, which, honestly, she should have had the prerogative to do herself. I did think it was a little rude of her to spit blood on my dad's business card when I tried to slip it into her hand as she was getting loaded into the ambulance. If that's the way she wants to be, then maybe she deserves a little scarring.

The Lacrockies' rejection comes later that day. It's written on a field hockey ball, and it's shot right into our front door by the vengeful and heavily bandaged Mena Denver, whom I then see run like hell down the street with three other Lacrockies in matching tracksuits, bounding away like deer.

"That'll leave a mark." I suck my teeth, running my hand over the circular indentation in the door. I read the letter, scoffing aloud. "'Unfit for sportsmanship'? I'm Gigi Lane! I'm fit for whatever the hell I choose!"

Up in my room I rummage through the bottom drawer of my dresser until I find a folded-up piece of notebook paper near the bottom. I sit on my bed and unfold it flat in front of me. It's the flow chart Deanna, Aloha, and I made as first-years, when we were first figuring out how things worked at Swan's Lake. I ruefully trace my finger around the box at the top that says, in Deanna's bubbly writing, "The you know whos." I follow the boxes down past the Cheerleaders and the Glossies, below the Lacrockies.

"Great," I grumble, poking the words "The Mr. T.'s" so hard the paper rips a little.

Deanna and the other Cheerleaders are cheering at a chess match Friday night and have an all-day practice on Saturday, so she can't come over to cheer me up about the fact that I am going to have to be the Head Mr. T., otherwise known as the Queen of the Drama Queens.

I'll need some royal garb, so on Saturday I head to the mall, determined to dress my *instrument* in clothing worthy of an ingénue's stage debut. Unfortunately, my instrument seems to have expanded to proportions that will only be housed by clothing in sizes I didn't even know they made for people that weren't pregnant, or perhaps conjoined to a twin and forced to cram four legs and a supersize rear into one pair of pants.

Since I'm not the sort of Swan that wastes time hating her body, I shed no tears over the pile of dresses that lay slain at my feet. I instead call out to the shop girl and request a slimming ensemble of all black; the sort of thing worn by actors in those horrific plays where they speak gibberish and expect you to clap.

My dad finally has a break from his overnight shifts, and I surprise him by asking if he wants to go out to dinner. My mom's going to be home in a few weeks, which means our sodium binge is going to have to end soon, since she went the way of the nutrition freak when she wrote her cookbook *Feeding Your Flock: The Girlie Bird's Guide to Keeping Your Family Healthy Through Quality Foods.* My dad and I decide on the International House of Pancakes.

"I'm glad to see you're taking an interest in sports," he says, taking an enormous bite of pancakes. "And cheerleading."

"Cheerleading's a sport," I correct, polishing off a sausage.

"Well, it takes place when sports are going on, so I guess

you could call it that. But in that case, drinking beer could be considered a sport too."

"Don't be crude," I say. "Look at this bruise!" I hoist my leg up on the table, narrowly missing his pancakes, and show him the fading yellowish bruise on my ankle that I got from dropping the stallion head on my foot. "See, you don't get that from a nonsport."

"Hmm." He squints, putting on his glasses and looking more closely. "Very impressive."

"Thank you. But that's nothing, look what happened during field hockey!"

He's even more impressed with the field hockey bruise I got trying to break my stick over my knee. "So you're on the team now?"

I stuff another minisausage in my mouth. "Not exactly. I'm not sure if it's my sport."

"Hmmm." He eyes my empty plate. "What do you think your sport is, then?"

"Not sure if it *is* a sport," I say, my fingers crawling close to where half a biscuit sits on the edge of his plate. "I think I'm going to try out for a play."

"A play?" He hands me the biscuit. "Wow. That is going to look great on your college applications."

"Oh, yeah!" I force a laugh after I say it, not wanting my dad to realize that I sort of forgot about college.

"And speaking of, your mom and I are giving you the dining room."

"You're giving me the dining room?"

"For your home base. I know you have most of the work for your applications done already, but this way you can really spread out all of the brochures and applications and files. Really decide where you want to apply."

"Great." I try to fake a smile. It's not that I don't want to go to college, it's just that last year I saw girls whose hair—seriously—fell out from the stress. There was a lot of emotional snacking going on, and when Fiona's parents called her at school to tell her she'd gotten her acceptance letter, she stood up in the cafeteria and screamed with her fists raised, skinny legs quivering. It was not attractive. It was also not attractive when Cassandra *didn't* get into Yale. She missed three days of school, and until she got her acceptance from Dartmouth, she stopped showering.

My parents and I did everything we were supposed to last year. We toured schools, met with admissions officials, narrowed my list of fifty schools down to fifteen. And the plan was that this year I would just dive right back in, starting on my applications, asking teachers early for reference letters before any of my classmates could get to them.

And I'll do all that. Really, I will. Once I figure out where I stand, socially speaking.

My dad looks at his watch. "I bet your mom's done with her seminar by now. Let's invite her over for dessert." He puts his phone on the table, dials the number, and presses speaker.

"I am so glad to hear from you," she says when she picks up the phone. "Am I on speaker? Is my Girlie Bird there?"

"I'm here, Mom. How was your day?"

"Tiring. They messed up the conference room reservations and my assistant had a fit, so I ended up being late to my own seminar because I had to calm her down. What are you two doing?"

"We're out to dinner."

"Am I in time for dessert?"

"Yep."

"Oh, good! Hold on, I'm getting a pack of Oreos from the minibar."

I don't do a lot of talking during our dessert date, but that's okay. I like listening to my mom's stories of the road, and to my dad talking about his patients. More than that, though, I like hearing them talk to each other. It reminds me of being asleep in the backseat of the car on the long rides to Nana's house, and dozing on and off to their conversations.

"What play are you trying out for?" my mom asks.

"Not sure," I answer, pulling out the itinerary. "It's some sort of free-form improv and the tryouts will actually be drama exercises."

"Oooh! Tell me how they are, maybe I'll do them in my seminars."

"Okay."

"I'm off to bed. We have an early flight tomorrow. At least we're heading in your general direction. Seven more days and I'll be home."

"Hey, Mom?" I ask, picking up the phone and taking it off speaker.

"What's up?" she asks.

"It's just me now," I say, turning in the booth so that my dad can't hear me. "I was wondering . . . has your affirmation ever stopped working for you?"

"Well, darling, you know I've had the same affirmation for twenty years, and it hasn't failed me yet! You'll know when you find the right one. When you do, it will feel like coming home for the first time."

"Oh," I sigh. "Okay, thanks."

# CHAPTER ELEVEN

## Think the First Floor Bathroom Stinks? Then don't use it!

**(Honestly, you would think with the way Swans parade around here like they're the smartest thing since sliced bread, this solution would be obvious.)**

I lie on the wooden stage floor, curled into a tight ball, my eyes closed.

"You're an . . . atom?" This first suggestion comes from Lauren, the leader of the Mr. T,'s, who is in charge of my tryouts.

I don't move.

"Um, you're a rolled-up armadillo?" someone else says.

I curl tighter. To be honest with you, I probably should have thought of what I was going to be before I volunteered and curled up on the floor, but in the heat of the moment I had to hope something would just come to me. Would you believe they're not even building a set for this play? It's "minimalist," which means there will be no starry sky or mountaintops for me to act my heart out in front of. I hear the pen click, and Lauren scribbles something down on her clipboard.

"Don't imitate, Gigi," comes Mr. T.'s soft drama-teacher voice, "*be*."

Right. Be. What am I being? *Beeeeeee*. I am a bee. I am a dead bumblebee, swatted down by a picnic goer, and I am now a dead little bee ball.

"Remember, you must be something alive."

I open one eye and glare at him. He smiles and nods encouragingly. I close my eyes again. Who am I? *I'm Gigi Lane and you wish you were me.* I sigh, my affirmation doing nothing to help.

*Okay, Gigi. Concentrate. Who are you? Who are you? Whooooo are yooooooou?* I am an owl. I am a *living* owl, a beautiful owl knocked from the nest she had so carefully built and tended to, kicked to the ground by an evil, dog-faced owl who . . .

Oh, God.

Tell me they did not just hear that.

Why, oh why, oh why, did I let my dad make me huevos rancheros for breakfast? And why, oh why, did I ask for extra beans?

My stomach rumbles again. I curl more tightly.

"Good," Mr. T. purrs, "I can see you're onto something. Go with it, Gigi, see where it takes you."

There is a long silence before another suggestion from the class. "You're one of those bugs that curls up into a ball?"

"You're an atom?"

"Do we really have to guess? I mean, she's been down there for ten minutes."

"Yes, you have to guess," Mr. T. says. "Gigi, remember to *be*, that will make it easier for us."

Oh, for the love of all things holy. The rumble is moving south. Please no. Please, no, no, no, no. I order myself not to fart. *Do. Not. Pass. Gas.* I imagine my butt cheeks are an impenetrable vise that not even a squeak of air can escape.

"You're an apple?"

"A pear?"

A pear! As in pear-shaped? I may have put on a few pounds, but I am *certainly* not pear-shaped! A thin whip of a girl! The accidental fruity insult distracts me so much that by the time I remember what I'm doing, the rumble is dangerously close to blowing my cover.

I think of my mom's book *If You Want to Be a Bird, Zen Be a Bird! The Girlie Bird's Guide to Meditation.*

I am in the moment. I am in the moment. And in this moment I am clenching so tightly that all sound has disappeared and I am a perfection of Zen mastery, willing my body to do as I order. *Obey! OBEY!* I shriek in my mind.

I panic, having no idea what the last suggestion offered by the class was, but I jump up, hoping my shout of "That's it!" will cover up the gross bleat that has just escaped my pants. "You got it!" I say to no one in particular. "You totally guessed what I was."

My classmates look at one another in ashen-faced horror.

Did they hear? No. Those aren't the faces of kids that just heard their former teen queen toot. Those are faces of something else. Shock?

"What?" I ask in confusion.

"Gigi has to pee!" Lauren says, grabbing my arm and dragging me off the stage and out into the hall. "Holy moly, Gigi, how could you say something like that?"

"Well, excuse me for having beans for breakfast!"

"What?"

I eye her carefully. "Wait, what are you talking about?"

"I'm talking about the fact that you just insulted Mr. T. in a way that . . . that . . . ," she stammers, her mouth hanging open. "I cannot even *begin* to fathom how one person could be so cruel!"

"Wait!" I cry, starting to get freaked out. "What did I say? Please, tell me what I said!"

She looks at me in shock. "You agreed with him when he said his acting exercise was about as successful as the 1983 Broadway opening of *The Moose Murders*!"

"Um . . ." I clear my throat helplessly. "I don't really know what exactly you're referring to."

She narrows her eyes at me. "The *Moose Murders* is the Broadway flop that all other flops are judged against. It is universally acknowledged to be the floppiest flop that ever flopped. And that's what you just compared Mr. T.'s acting exercise to."

"I really didn't mean to—"

"He's really sensitive, you know. He *cries* in class, like, all the time if our performances are good. I knew you were mean, Gigi, but not that mean. Not so cruel as to pick on the theater teacher, for Christ's sake! He's an artist! He's fragile!" she shrieks, pronouncing "fragile" with three syllables. She gulps a breath. "And what the hell is that smell!"

"I don't smell anything." I shrug, trying to breathe through my mouth.

"Look," Lauren sighs, after taking a few steps backward, "me and the class have been talking."

"No, no wait, but it's only Wednesday. . . ."

"I know, and you're welcome to come to rehearsals for the rest of the week. We do appreciate the fact that you're actually trying. You surprised us, really. But . . ." She looks genuinely sorry. Then again, she is an actor. "We think your spirit is a little too . . . cruel . . . for this production. People are going to be getting really raw, really real, and they're just not comfortable doing that in front of you. They don't want you judging them. But you're totally welcome to be our prop master, not as a Mr. T., but as a volunteer."

"*Prop* master? What about master master?"

"What?"

I shake my head and close my eyes, trying to gather my thoughts. I think about affirming but then get a better idea. I open my eyes as fast as I can and give a rueful laugh that's so full of volume and scorn she *has* to see I'm made for the stage. "Brahahahahaha!" I roar.

She takes a step back. I take a step forward, my pointer finger inches from her face. "You think you can get on without me? Fine! I've been spurned before. But I never thought it would be by you." I shake my head. "Of all people, Lauren."

"Lisa."

"What?"

"My name is Lisa."

"Wait. Really?"

She actually laughs, but not exactly in a mean way, which gives me hope. "*Yes*, my name is Lisa. Gigi, you're really a piece of work. I would *love* to play you on stage."

"Wow," I gasp, truly touched. "That's so flattering!"

She nods, studying me. "I mean, you're so out of touch with reality it's like a gold mine for an actor."

"Laur—" I interrupt myself. "Lisa, can't you reconsider? If I were in Drama Club, you could study me all year long and then do a Gigi Lane monologue for your auditions in college!"

"Gigi, you've never even spoken to me before this week," Lauren-Lisa says flatly. "Unless it was to make fun of me."

"Why would I make fun of you?" I ask.

"You seriously don't remember?" she persists, grabbing her boobs like she's going to shoot them at my head.

*Wait a minute*, I think. "Oh my God, you're Honkers!" I yell, hitting her lightly on the shoulder. "Wow, how the heck are you? I always wondered what happened to you! Didn't you, like, drop out or something?"

She just stares at me for a second. "No, I didn't drop out! The only thing that happened to me was everyone else got boobs, so you and your little posse of sadists finally left me alone!"

"Oh, that makes sense," I reason, nodding. "I bet these C cups really took the pressure off you!" I wink, giving my own rack a squeeze. "So, come on. You're not really going to reject me, are you? I'm Gigi Lane. I think I really could be of use to you guys."

She bites her lip and shakes her head. "Sorry."

"Wait!" My stomach suddenly drops as I realize that I really, truly am about to get rejected from the Mr. T.'s, a clique that I really, truly never cared anything about until now. But now I see a year of theatrical camaraderie, of perhaps finding that my true heart's song is really a show tune, slipping through my fingers right along with my Hot Spot severance. "I don't need to be the *master* of anything. I'll just sit to the side of the stage and not say a word. Please, just don't reject me." I try to work up some tears and am shocked—shocked!—at how quickly they come.

"I'm sorry, Gigi," she murmurs, resting a hand on my shoulder. "We're going to have to let you go."

"You don't want me?" I say with a hiccup, my face crumpling. A hot sob slips its way up my throat and out of my mouth. "Does *nobody* want me?"

Lauren-Lisa winces, and I know this must be devastating for her—to see the person she most looks up to in the world showing her tender underbelly. I turn away from her and cover my face with my hands, ducking my head.

"Oh, Gigi . . . ," she soothes, stooping down to try and see up into my face. "I wish . . ."

I peek at her through my fingers, hoping for a reversal of fortune, but the moment is ruined when we hear a familiar voice. "Oh, for fart's sake, is she *crying*?" I drop my hands to see Aloha and Heidi at the far end of the hall doubled over laughing. Heidi's dropped her pom-poms on the floor, and she's hunched over in a fit of laughter, her cheerleader skirt bunched up in her fists against her stomach in a truly unladylike way. Aloha's screeching laugh echoes down the hall. "What's wrong, Gigi? No role for you in this year's production of *The Bitches of Eastwick*?"

I wipe my tear-slicked palms on my leotard and turn away, only to see Daphne coming out of the theater room. She stops when our eyes meet, and I raise my chin, swallowing back tears. Lauren-Lisa stands beside me, crossing her arms over her chest. "This is a private meeting," she sneers. "No Art Star turncoats allowed."

Daphne looks past us to Aloha and Heidi, who are making a big production out of composing themselves from their apparently devastating fit of laughter. "They're clearing out now," she calls down to them.

"We need the theater room for a few minutes," Daphne mumbles.

"Why?" Lauren-Lisa demands. "You guys have your *top secret* hideout, why do you need our room?"

Daphne miserably looks behind us to where Aloha and Heidi are clomping their way down the hall, and sighs. "We just do."

"Is there a problem?" Aloha asks, stepping right in front of me and then looking at Lauren-Lisa. "Hooters? Is there a problem?"

Lauren-Lisa shakes her head. "No problem."

"Good!" Heidi squeals, shaking her pom-poms. "Let's go, then."

Aloha smirks at me. "Doing some emotional eating, Gigi?" She pokes me in my stomach. "You're filling out the leotard really well."

She turns on her heel and walks away. She passes Daphne and snarls, "You need to address your hair situation, pronto."

Daphne flinches.

The Mr. T.'s send a mime with my rejection letter on Friday afternoon. He shoves it into my hands when I open the door and says, "You ought to be ashamed. Mr. T. helped me find my inner mime."

"I thought you weren't supposed to talk."

He mimes me a one-fingered salute in response. Classy. I close the door behind him, my stomach lurching at the thought of my popularity free fall. *Severance*, I tell myself, *the severance will make it all worthwhile.*

# CHAPTER TWELVE

**Think the School Newspaper
Has a Bad Attitude This Year?
We don't care.**

**(Stick THAT in your trumpet and blow!)**

"We call it live-action role-playing, or LARP," Fred, the rather nice though pimple-faced boy from the public high school tells me as he helps to fasten my helmet. It's chilly for October, and it feels like winter is just waiting patiently to swallow us whole. We're in a field of high grass by the town dump, readying ourselves for what I guess should be described as battle. At the other end of the field is the only other member of the Intramural LARP Society to show up today—a junior, Fred says. Fine by me; if they can't bother to show up, I'm glad I didn't bother to brush my hair.

I spent the weekend numbing myself to the fact that the

bottom of the social barrel was coming at me, fast. I could stop. I *should* stop. I should just opt out of the whole matrix and find a way to live a life of parallel popularity—all of the accoutrements, but none of the on-campus perks. If a popular girl roars and no one flinches, is she still popular?

I want my severance. I *need* my severance. I need the tangible proof that I was almost part of the most spectacular clique Swan's Lake has ever known. I need proof that I almost mattered.

"I think you'd better run," Fred says, tightening my helmet for me. Usually I wouldn't let someone with such unfortunate early male-pattern baldness touch me, but he seems nice enough.

"Why?"

He looks down the long field. "That's Farah."

"Who?"

He shakes his head.

"Wait, Farah Soon?" The girl from the front steps on the first day of school who thought I might as well be dead. "We were in Outdoor Girls together."

"Exactly."

What does he know about Outdoor Girls? What do I know about Outdoor Girls? It was so long ago that I was kicked out.

"Oh dear." Fred winces, backing away from me as Farah gets closer. I can almost make out her face now but still can't hear what she's screaming. Outdoor Girls, Outdoor Girls, what in the world did I get kicked out for? Wow, she is really moving. I can almost make out her words.

"Die, you patch-stealing wench!"

Oh right, that was it. Maybe I *should* run. I turn and start trotting away, catching the foam sword that Fred tosses me. It's really hard to run in fake armor. Farah catches up to me in no time, and even though I turn to face her with arms raised in surrender, she clocks me on the head with her foam sword.

"Ow! Stop it!"

"Die, you wench!" She hits me again.

"That really hurts!" I yelp, trying to duck her blows.

"You ruined my life!" she screams, raising her sword for what might actually be a deathblow.

I block with my own sword, forcing hers to the ground. "I'm really sorry about that whole Fire Builders Patch thing," I say calmly, her sword still pinned to the ground. "I really didn't know it meant that much to you."

"I was kicked out!" she yells, dropping her sword and headbutting me in the stomach.

"Ooof," I groan, trying to remove her head from my abdomen. "I know you were, but . . ." I get her in a headlock, though I try not to hold on too tightly. "I really thought that using gasoline wasn't cheating. Plus, you didn't really argue. . . ."

She manages to reach behind me and give me a wedgie, forcing me to release her. As she drags me backward through the field, she yells, "I did too argue, but you didn't listen! And you said you'd be my friend if I let you cheat! And then you totally ditched me, so I had zero friends!"

"I'm really sorry."

"They made me turn in my sash!"

"That seems harsh."

"It was!" She pouts, releasing my now-stretched-beyond-recognition underwear. She plops down in the grass, gasping for breath, pulling a familiar-looking clipboard out from behind her armor and marking something down. "It was really, really harsh and it totally ruined my life."

A moment later Fred comes walking up. He looks down at Farah. "Okay?"

She nods, breathless. "Oh yeah, I'm great."

"Are you okay?" he asks me.

"Sure," I say with a shrug, trying to dewedgify myself. "I actually think I might have deserved that."

Farah smiles and flops back onto the grass. "This is, like, the best day of my entire life!" After a moment she props herself up on her elbow. "Can I ask you something?"

"Sure." I sit down next to her.

"How were you ever friends with Aloha?"

"It was a marriage of convenience," I answer. "I never really liked her, but she's too good-looking to keep at arm's length."

"Keep your friends close and your enemies closer?" Fred asks.

"Exactly!" I smile, glad to be understood. "And obviously I made the right decision in pulling her into my fold, even if I did get burned in the end. Imagine what would have happened if she had gone rogue sooner?" I shudder. "She could have *ruined* junior high."

"So are you still not allowed to talk about the H—"

"No." I hold up my hand. "And you shouldn't either. Rules are rules, even if they are being enforced by wicked witches."

"Do you think Daphne even likes them?" Farah continues. "The girl's an Art Star, through and through. She's just not evil like Aloha, or out of her freaking mind like Heidi. Do you think she likes them?"

"The thing is," I explain, "when you get to that level of popularity, it's not really a matter of liking your friends. It's more about . . ."

"A marriage of convenience?" Fred offers.

"Exactly!"

It's the next day that I discover that Aloha and Daphne are having marital trouble, so to speak.

"I thought I told you to buy some new jeans," I hear Aloha say as I open the door to the bathroom. I don't open the door all the way—I let it close until it is open just a crack.

"I did."

I peek through the crack, and in the mirror I see Daphne and Aloha standing by the sink, Aloha roughly pulling Daphne's hair into a sleek ponytail.

"I can tell a bargain when I see one," Aloha says, finishing Daphne's ponytail and glaring at her jeans. "Were they on sale?"

Daphne shrugs. "They're the ones you told me to get."

"No, I told you to get them in indigo. There's a reason the light-wash ones are on sale, and it's because they're fugly."

"But I can't—"

Aloha leans close to Daphne. "What? You can't *what*? Afford them? I'll tell you what you can't afford. You can't afford to be out of the Hot Spot. You think your precious little Art Stars would take you back after what we did to them? Face it, Daphne, without us you'd be *nothing*." Aloha leans back and grins. "Besides, you don't really want to leave us, do you?"

Daphne shakes her head.

"I didn't think so."

I let the door close before I can see anything more, a cold, sick feeling sinking into my stomach.

I thought maybe since I'd given Farah the best day of her entire life, and since for the rest of the week she and I actually became pretty good at sparring with each other, and since I had her over after school so we could tailor our armor together, I might have some chance of getting an offer from the Whompers.

Their rejection comes wrapped around an arrow with a suction cup on the end that is firmly planted to my bedroom window with a *shunk* sound.

# CHAPTER THIRTEEN

**Yes, Yes, It's All Very Sad.
The librarian has quit.**

**(Get over it.)**

"I don't mean to be rude, but what exactly is it that you do all day while the rest of the Swan's Lake student body is in class?"

Lara, leader of the Deeks, leans back in her sagging lawn chair and smiles. "This."

"Oh," I say, adjusting my perch on my own lounger. "I see."

My week with the Deeks has started, and though I was dreading a senior year spent chock-full of petty theft and truancy, I have found myself happily mistaken. From what I can see, being a delinquent means sitting in the unused courtyard behind the wood shop and discussing soil pH levels. The courtyard is tucked beneath a windowless wall, hidden from view by a tall fence thick with vines. I always assumed it was a cracked slab of concrete overrun with weeds and strewn with garbage, the sort of place vermin call home. But this morning, when I pushed through the heavy metal door to the courtyard, I found myself standing in a small, cheerful garden.

I found four of my fellow delinquents gathered under a lattice-topped pagoda enjoying the warmth of the late-fall day.

"We use the eastern turret in the off-season," Lara explains, "but we don't move house until well after the first frost."

I'm wearing what I thought was the standard uniform for a delinquent, at least the ones with any fashion sense: black leather motorcycle jacket over a tight white T-shirt with the sleeves cut off, dangerously high heels, and a pair of very snug—very, very snug—jeans. I'm finding myself wishing I'd worn my Alaska overalls, since these Deeks seem much more salt-of-the-earth than danger-to-society.

"I don't want to be rude," I say, leaning forward, "but are you all on parole or something? I just don't understand this good behavior."

"We're on a crime hiatus," Lara explains after exchanging a glance with Isabelle, who seems to be her second in command. The other two Deeks haven't said a word since I arrived. They lie back in their chairs, wearing sunglasses and headphones, feet occasionally twitching in their sleep.

"Hiatus?" I press. "So you're not on the lam? In hiding? Under house arrest?"

Lara and Isabelle exchange another glance, and I notice the

other two Deeks have stopped twitching their feet and seem to be paying close attention despite their headphones.

"Can we be honest with you?" Lara finally asks.

"Of course!"

"The Deeks are . . ." She searches for the right word. "Defunct."

"Defunct?" I repeat, not sure I heard correctly.

"We're all legacies," Isabelle explains, "younger sisters to older Swans that were in the Deeks, so we were funneled into this clique whether we had criminal tendencies or not. It's been *years* since a Deek has actually broken the law. Even our older sisters partook in nothing more than occasionally foul language and lying about their age to get the children's rate at Funland."

"I mean, have you seen the recidivism rates for kids that do time in juvie?" Lara sniffs. "I'm just not interested in being a part of our nation's overcrowded prison problem. Plus, with a college diploma I'm likely to earn over a million dollars more in my lifetime than without one."

"Wait, let me understand this." I try to make sense of it. "You're not criminals?"

"Nope," Lara says, shaking her head, "we just got stuck in a clique we can't get out of."

"But you're always skipping class!"

She lowers her voice. "Carlisle lets us take most of our classes as independent studies anyway. Our GPAs are all between three point seven and four point oh. This courtyard has been in the

Deek family for years; it's the reason we all score so high on our environmental biology independent studies."

"So if I become a Deek," I realize aloud, "I'll spend the rest of the year—"

"Studying. And doing community service."

"Well, sign me up!" I laugh, slapping my knee.

"Okay, then," Lara says, "no sense in keeping up the facade."

And with that, the Deeks, those hardened criminals of high school, pull out their textbooks and quiz one another on world history.

I actually really liked hanging out with the Deeks; I got a ton of studying done, and they seemed to really appreciate it when I brought them all copies of my mom's book *Meet Your Tweet*. "For next year," I told them, "to help you figure out who you really are, if you're not fake rabble-rousers."

It stings when the rejection letter comes, even with the handwritten note from Lara telling me to look her up once we get to Yale.

# CHAPTER FOURTEEN

**Why Has the Trumpet's Voice Changed?
Puberty.**

**(It happens to the best of us.)**

It does not go well with the Gizmos, though it does give them occasion to pat themselves on the back for being such devoted followers of the credo "Back up (your files) or die."

They let me know of my rejection by "blipping" my house. They somehow hack into every electronic system we have, and at the exact same moment all the lamps shut off, the phone rings, the microwave beeps, the alarm goes off, the AC turns on, and the garage door opens.

A second later everything goes back to normal. Everything, that is, except for my heart.

# CHAPTER FIFTEEN

**All Art Classes Will Now Be Independent
Studies in Papier-Mâché and Decoupage.
Bring your newspapers, magazines, and glue.**

(And please stop whining about
the lack of art supplies and art teachers.
It's getting very annoying.)

On a Monday morning several weeks later I lie on the floor of
my closet staring up at the racks of clothes that trace the path
of my destruction.

A dress made out of my old Hello Kitty pillowcase for the
Art Stars, who, it turns out, only wanted to make art about
being abandoned by Daphne. Apparently, she and the rest of
the Hot Spot wreaked havoc by dousing everyone's papier-mâché
projects with water, turning them into mush. "We're not even
supposed to work with papier-mâché this year, but our oil paint
order hasn't come in yet. It kills us to see her stomping around

in her stupid indigo jeans." Then they let me help make a collage about their pain.

Next to the pillowcase dress is the only thing I could think of wearing for my week with the Do-Goods—a fitted, but not too fitted, Life is good T-shirt. Apparently, the Do-Goods have been doing double do-good duty, comforting an endless parade of girls who burst into the bathroom crying after being verbally filleted by Aloha or Heidi or sometimes even Daphne.

Stuffed in a corner behind my whomper shield is a pair of hemp underwear, my fashion concession for the Greenies. There is also my getup from my thoroughly confusing week with the Vox Foxes—a 1920s newsboy cap, knickers, and long socks that proved to fit my frame more easily than the standard Vox Fox vamp attire. The entire week Beatrice kept giving me peculiar looks and saying things like, "You *really* don't know where we get our headlines?"

She didn't let me attend any private meetings, she just kept me stationed in the dining room so I could get people's comments on the increasingly disgusting food served at lunch.

My rejection came in the form of a *Trumpet of the Swan* special edition delivered, mercifully, only to me. There were no articles, just one headline that read:

GIGI LANE:

THE CLEARING OF THE CLIQUES CONTINUES

(Good luck, Gigi!)

A beret and black scarf from my week with the Bookish Girls. I sigh, thinking of the sad look Rebecca gave me when she rejected me. "We really did appreciate you referencing the beat poets of the 1960s with your wardrobe. But I'm sorry, you just don't fit in with us."

I stare at the ceiling. I have no idea even what to wear today. What in God's name does one wear for the single most humiliating day of your life? *Severance,* I tell myself. *Just get through this week, and severance will be yours.*

I sit up and yawn. *I'm Gigi Lane,* I think. I yawn again. "Ugh, why even bother."

*Why even bother is right,* I think later that morning, my carefully washed, toned, and made-up face completely ignored by every single person I pass by on my way up the front steps and into school. I haven't worn makeup in weeks, and to think I trotted out my brush skills for *this?* I should have just worn a bag over my head and been done with it.

"Gigi!" I jump at the sound of my name and see Deanna rushing toward me. I'm so relieved to see her, to see that she *sees me,* that I almost cry out. She pulls me into a hug. "I've been trying to call you! Are you okay?"

I shrug. "I've been better. Just trying to get through the week, you know?"

She nods. "I know. It'll be over soon, and then you'll get that sweet severance, right?" She pinches me lightly on the side and then tries to cover her shock at just how much chub she actually grabs.

"Right!" I chirp, trying to sound happy.

"Well"—she looks over her shoulder to where the Cheer-leaders are gathering—"I've got to go."

I nod. "I'll talk to you later."

"Okay, call me tonight and tell me how it goes!"

My week with the Cursed Unaffiliated has me in tears the first day. Seriously, these are the saddest little social orphans you will *ever* meet. That is, *if* you actually meet one. They are those girls that you don't notice unless you trip over one of them while walking backward and calling sassy insults to your girlfriends. And once you fall over them, it's like they disappear in a *poof* of unpopularity.

And they don't even hang out together—that's what kills me! They have no leader, they're just this totally flat, listless organization. I find one of them, Brynn, in our allotted meeting place before school. She's right where she said she would be, in the never-used bathroom on the third floor, last stall.

"Hey, Gigi." Brynn glances up at me. She's sitting on the toilet, lid down and pants up (thank God), doing her homework. The clipboard is propped up on the toilet paper roll holder.

"Hi, Brynn." I lean against the stall door. "Why don't you do your homework in the library?"

"They're not open yet."

"Oh."

"And I can't do my homework at my house because my mom is off her meds and I have to keep an eye on her while my dad goes to work the night shift."

"Oh," is all I can say.

"So . . ." She motions to the bathroom stall. "This is basically it. The Cursed Unaffiliateds don't really hang out together. I honestly don't even know how many of us there are. It could be just me. That's how it feels sometimes." She looks at me, focusing on my eyes. "Sometimes I think that I want to scream, just to have people hear me. And then I wonder if I'm screaming already." She shudders and then shrugs. "Anyway, I have detention at lunch—I was wrongfully accused—not that we'd sit together anyway. You can probably find space in the library or maybe the upstairs bathroom."

"Are you all right?" the postman asks as I sign the receipt for the Cursed Unaffiliated's rejection letter.

"Fine," I answer.

"Are you going farming later?" he asks, his voice cheery.

I look at him questioningly.

"Your overalls . . . never mind. Have a good day."

"Thanks," I mumble. "You too."

I don't bother brushing off the dead leaves on the wicker chair before I sit down. In the cold the cushion has hardened, and it chafes my ankles as I pull my feet under me. A hard wind blows, scraping more leaves up the porch, where they swirl against the open front door, some of them fluttering inside. I tuck my hands inside my overalls, just two fingers out to rip open the letter.

The last line of the Cursed Unaffiliated's rejection letter is like a stiletto to the heart. "You get used to it," the letter says, and I realize the Cursed Unaffiliateds are right. Over the past weeks my heart has hardened, a shell of bone leaving just enough room for my heart to barely beat. I lay my head against the back of the wicker chair and listen to the wind and the leaves and the jailed beat of my heart.

"You don't have the necessary melancholy to be a Cursed Unaffiliated." Please! I should write them back the "jailed beat of my heart" thing. That's the sort of bunk they live for. Oh, woe is me, my heart's in jail, I'm slowly turning to stone, nobody likes me, everybody hates me, might as well eat some worms.

From inside I hear my cell phone ring. I kick most of the leaves out of the front hall and shut the door behind me. I switch on the lights, impressed that I sat on the chair long enough for it to grow dark around me and for my fingers to turn a splotchy red. If that's not true melancholy, I don't know what is.

I should have just let the phone go to voice mail.

"Gigi? It's Beatrice Linney."

"Oh. Hey, Beatrice," I say. I flop forward over the back of the couch, my butt in the air, my face buried in the cushions. "I thought you might be calling."

"I just heard. I know I'm supposed to stay objective, but I have to say I'm really sorry about the way things have ended up for you. Swan's Lake isn't the school it used to be. It's like we're falling apart, the building and the students."

"Mm-hmm."

"Gigi, I hate to bother you in your hour of need, but I'm going to have to ask for a statement."

"A what?"

"A quote. Your side of the story. About . . . about being rejected by all the cliques."

I groan.

"What was that? Can you repeat that, please? How does it feel to be rejected by the Cursed Unaffiliated? What does that even make you?"

I stand up, my head swimming from being upside down. "A free agent." I sigh into the phone. "And yes, you can quote me on that." I hang up before she can ask another question. My phone rings again before I can put it down. I look at the number and sigh. I debate just letting it go to voice mail, but I know I have to get this over with.

"Hello?"

"Gigi, this is Fiona Shay. I am calling to inform you that you have failed your severance task and will therefore not receive your severance. Once again, please remember that—"

"I hope you're happy," I say.

"Once again, please remember—"

"They're destroying the school, you know."

Fiona sighs impatiently. "I have no time for your high school drama, Lane. Just let me get through this. Please remember that—"

"And it's all your fault. You could have stopped it—"

"Gigi, I don't know what you're talking about. Please-remember-that-you-are-permanently-exiled-from-theHotSpot andyoucan'ttalkaboutuseverGood-bye!"

She hangs up.

I wish you could listen to the dial tone on a cell phone after someone hangs up, instead of that digital *click* sound. That'd be much more dramatic than lying here with a silent phone pressed against my ear, my legs dangling over the back of the couch, my head hanging almost to the floor. I know that I should call Deanna, though she can probably guess what happened already.

You know that saying "Misery loves company"? It's total bullshit. I'm miserable and I don't want company, especially not Deanna. How could I even face her? She's a Cheerleader and I'm a . . . a nothing. I'm starting to think maybe it really is better that I stop talking to her, especially at school. I can't take her down with me. Even if she is top tier, it's not guaranteed that the Hot Spot's rampage will spare her. It's for her own good.

All the blood rushing to my head is making me loopy. I listen to the silence of my house and then yell, "It's Friday night! Woo-hoo! Par-*tay!*" My voice sounds nasally. "Gigi Lane is in the house!"

I realize what I'm about to do before I do it. Gooseflesh ripples up and down my arms as I take a deep breath and then scream as loud as I can, "I'm Gigi Lane and you wish you were me!"

There. It's done. The words ring in my ears, their power gone by the simple act of screaming them out loud. I don't need that affirmation anymore. It didn't work.

A familiar, media-ready voice floats in from the front hall. "Well, that's not exactly grammatically correct, but it's a good start!"

I fall off the couch.

"Where's my little Girlie Bird?"

My mother's home.

My mom spends her first day home from her tour in her pajamas. It reminds me of those documentaries or behind-the-scenes videos of movie stars, where even when they are out of their makeup and costumes and contact lenses, even when they are wearing eyeglasses and a messy ponytail, there is something undeniably glamorous about them. You can tell they're special even if they're wearing sweatpants and eating Wheaties. That's how my mom is, and that's how I used to think I was.

When I come downstairs Saturday morning, she is sitting in the windowed breakfast nook in the kitchen, sipping coffee out of a big mug and reading the paper, her feet up on a chair and her reading glasses perched almost on the tip of her nose. There's something polished about her, even first thing in the morning, and it feels like I'm looking at a candid black-and-white photo of a talk show host, or maybe a senator, instead of a real, live person, instead of my mother.

"Good morning, sunshine," she says, looking at me and smiling. "Aren't you a beautiful sight for sore eyes. Is your stomach feeling any better?"

I begged off the welcome-home dinner with my mom and dad last night, complaining of cramps and sneaking a can of Coke and a bag of Funyuns up to my room to hide out for the night.

I give a nervous laugh in response and bury my head in the refrigerator, pretending to look for the milk.

I have always felt like my popularity was a good balance to my mom's fame, like they set each other off really well. I loved the reaction I got when I was introduced to people at my mom's book parties and things like that. When I was younger, I'd go for a precociously polite effect, but once you pass a certain age, precociousness just looks like arrogance, so later I opted for youthful yet polished enthusiasm balanced with a beyond-my-years maturity. "It's a pleasure to meet you," I'd say, shaking someone's hand, "my mom's told me so much about you." And whoever it was that I'd just been introduced to would raise his or her eyebrows at my mom and say, "You've got a lovely daughter." And my mom *has* to have a lovely daughter, you know?

But now that the bottom has dropped out of my social stronghold, it feels like I have no weight to balance against my mom's sort of staggering fame. I pour myself a bowl of cereal and sit down at the table with my mom. She smiles at me again, pulls out the Fashion section, and slides it toward me.

"Thanks." I smile, glad she knows it's my favorite section, and then notice that she's on the front page.

"I was so tired when they took that picture." She laughs. "The makeup artist had to shellac the concealer on."

The article is called "Fly Away Home: A Girlie Bird Gets Ready to Land."

"Wait, what?" I wrinkle my brow, reading the headline again. "'Ready to land'? What's that mean?"

"I know, it's a good line. I wish I'd thought of it myself, actually."

"But what does it mean?"

"Oh, it's just about this being my last tour."

I look back to the article, surprised at the tears stinging my eyes: "After ten years on the road the acclaimed author of the Girlie Bird self-help books is ready to call it quits."

"You're quitting? I didn't know that."

"No, I'm not quitting. I'm just not going to travel as much. It's gotten to be too much. The whole quitting thing was Barry's idea." Barry is my mom's PR guy, the one who gets my mom on talk shows and profiled in Sunday magazines. "He thinks it will up the interest."

"So, you're not quitting."

"No, not technically."

I look at her, and she holds my gaze for a moment before sighing.

"It's a publicity stunt, Gigi. I'm not proud of it, but that's the business I'm in. I have no plans to retire, but Barry thinks I may have reached media saturation too soon. He's afraid the public will turn on me, so the plan is to pretend to quit while I'm ahead, and then come back due to popular demand."

"But you didn't even tell me you were going to fake-retire."

"I'm sorry, honey, it's just something we've been working on, nothing was really settled yet."

I hold up the paper. "This looks pretty settled."

"Well, we let them break the story. Aren't you glad I'll be home more?"

"Of course I'm glad you'll be home!" I lie, not wanting her here to witness my total social annihilation. "I just wish you had told me. What, did you think I'd leak the top secret story of your fake retirement?"

"No," she says calmly, "I did not think you would leak the top secret story of my fake retirement." In my mom's book *Hold Firm to That Worm: The Girlie Bird's Guide to Social Combat*, she recommends that if someone is sarcastic to you, you should just repeat back to them what they've said in a totally neutral tone of voice.

I hate it when she uses the Bird on me.

She looks at me for a long moment before continuing. "You have just been very hard to get a hold of for the past few months."

"I've been busy," I snap ruefully.

"With what?" she asks.

"Life?" I sigh.

She studies me. "You're an adolescent," she finally says, nodding to herself.

"Excuse me?"

"Oh, sweetie, I didn't mean to sound so clinical. It's just that it's basic child development. You seem to be going through some sort of adolescent phase."

"*Child* development?"

It's like she doesn't even hear me, even though she's staring right at me. "Have you been meeting your tweet?"

I consider. Since she has actually heard my tweet affirmation and didn't seem that impressed, I guess that answer is, "No."

She nods. "And have you been holding firm to that worm?"

Most definitely not. "No."

"Of course not." I can't tell if she's mad or excited. "And you and your dad, you've been loading up on all of the unhealthy foods on the 'Rotten Worm' list from *Feeding Your Flock*, am I right?"

I don't know how to answer that, since I don't want to get my dad in trouble. "Umm . . ."

My mom taps her fingers on the table, still nodding. "Interesting. Very interesting. Now," she says, "tell me about school."

I lie through my teeth.

# CHAPTER SIXTEEN

**It's Come to Our Attention That Swans Have Stopped Reading the *Trumpet*. Suit yourselves.**

**(But you may want to spread the word that we now require you to sign your name next to each daily issue. And if you don't sign, you don't pass.)**

I don't return Deanna's calls all weekend. That's the first step. I've broken up with enough friends to know that the immediate and total communication blackout is the only way to go. You've got to rip off the Band-Aid, make the breakup so immediate and complete that they wonder if they were ever friends with you in the first place. You have to make it so that after just a few days they look at you in the dining hall and see a stranger.

It's really the compassionate way to do things. Friendship euthanasia.

Deanna "Dear Heart" Jones has been through enough in her

life not to have to worry about a newly branded loser like me pulling down her social market value. I failed her, and it kills me. Honestly, it just kills me. Of course my own social implosion has its sting, but I'll recover. I mean, I *am* still Gigi Lane. Even if nobody in her right mind wants to be me at the moment. Including myself.

But Deanna . . . I just don't know if she could recover from a free fall like the one I've had. Sure, she bounced back from "the moment that shocked the world," but that was gymnastics. This is high school! Deanna will be doing follow-up "America's Sweetheart: Where Is She Now?" interviews with *Sports Illustrated* until the day she dies. If she goes down in high school, no one will care where she's gone.

My parents spend most of their time together all weekend, which is good because I'm avoiding them. I read up on the chances of getting into Yale if I drop out of school and take the GED. Not good, unless I can come with a mitigating circumstance better than social crucifixion. I look into homeschooling, too, but that would require telling my parents what's going on, which would involve them talking to Ms. Carlisle.

The last thing I need is adults trying to sort out my life.

I spend a lot of the weekend lying on my bed, staring at the ceiling and trying to figure out where I went wrong.

I can remember the exact moment I became popular.

It was in second grade. Up until then our grade had been a pretty flat organization. That was before Aloha, when Deanna was still in school with us full-time. Popularity just wasn't on our radar yet, but I remember feeling like all of the other girls were always looking at us, clamoring to sit next to us on "our" bench at recess. Then one of the other girls, Simone or someone like that, brought her older cousin into school one day. She was from the city, and even though she was just a year older than us, a third grader, she dressed like a little adult. Not in a creepy kid-in-a-beauty-pageant kind of way, but in a sophisticated kind of way. You could tell she was enjoying being an outsider, and when she sat down with us at lunch, she started with the questions. "Which of you has a boyfriend?" Ummmm . . . none of us? "What do you do on a Saturday night?" Sleepovers? And then she asked, "Which of you is the most popular?" When I think about it now, the girl was obviously some sort of rabble-rouser, but when she asked the popularity question, everyone got kind of quiet and looked sheepishly at one another. I remember thinking, *Someone should say something, someone should just speak up.* I knew it was important, that moment. And so I said, "I am," and everyone looked at me, and I could tell a few of them, like Heidi, wanted to argue, but the visiting city cousin looked so satisfied with the answer that they all kept quiet.

It just made so much sense to me. Like when you're at a birthday party and there's one cupcake left and everyone's too shy to take it. Once you reach out and grab it, they all look at you with such jealousy, not because you have the cupcake, but because you had the guts to take it. That's all I did. I reached out and grabbed the popularity cupcake because it was there for the taking.

And as soon as I had it, there were girls who tried to take it away.

I'm not going to be one of those whiners that complains about how hard it is to be at the top, but I will say that it takes a certain amount of work. And I was *good* at it. I was so good at popularity, and that's why Fiona wanted me in the Hot Spot. She said she admired the way I balanced my barbed tongue with acts of kindness, like rescuing that first-year who got stuck while vacuuming out a heating duct.

I know what kind of target I'm going to be when I go to school on Monday. I'll be what the Hot Spot want—something pretty and shiny they can squash under their kitten heels.

So I just have to erase the bull's-eye from my forehead.

"Time to disappear, Gigi Lane," I say to my reflection, "time to say good-bye."

I mean that figuratively, of course, because no one with my sense of self-worth and bone structure would do something as vulgar as off herself because some tarts were about to play demolition derby with her reputation.

I'm just going into a sort of hiding, is all.

I start with my bathroom vanity, pulling out and throwing away every hydrating mask, pore refiner, and exfoliating scrub I can find. I dump the powdered blotting papers, tinted moisturizer, mascara, and twelve tubes of lip gloss. I get rid of my hair mousse, styling lotion, and finishing cream.

When I've emptied the vanity, I move on to the shower, tossing the body scrubs, polishes, and exfoliating cleansers that are lined up neat and pretty on the shower shelf. When I'm done, the small plastic trash can is full, and its heft feels good in my hands. I leave myself only a bar of soap, a bottle of shampoo, and a bottle of conditioner. At the back of my vanity, stuck with a glob of toothpaste to the shelf, I find my scrunchie and pull my hair back up into a ponytail.

There. I look . . . pretty. But plain. Like one of those girls that are nice to look at, but not so nice they're threatening. From now on I'll be scrunchie girl. Harmless, boring scrunchie girl. I won't wear makeup other than Chap Stick. People will describe me by saying, "You know, Gigi Lane. She's sort of pretty . . . wears her hair back in a scrunchie all the time."

I'm done. I'm out of the game. I concede, I give up, I surrender my lip gloss. I'm going to go from persona non grata to persona non. If they want a pretty girl to slap down, they can look somewhere else.

I'm taking a vow. A vow of unpopularity. An exile from everyone and everything. For the good of myself and the people that love me. Namely, Deanna Jones. Everyone knows that the wrath of the Hot Spot scalds whoever is closest to the target. I won't let Deanna get burned. I won't.

# CHAPTER SEVENTEEN

**Did You Know That Swans Are Actually Filthy, Vile Creatures?**
**But they are so pretty, aren't they?**

**(Most evil things are.)**

You know, if somebody had told me being unpopular could be this fun, I would have given up my hair dryer ages ago. What all those whiners who say being unpopular set them up for a lifetime of failure are crabbing about, I have no idea.

Check out my schedule!

| | |
|---|---|
| **7:00 a.m.**<br>**Wake up** | That's right, I no longer get up at six to primp and polish. I just roll out of bed. Sometimes I don't even wash my face. |
| **8:15 a.m.**<br>**–3:25 p.m.**<br>**School** | You would not believe the things you see when you're invisible! First of all, the |

teachers, who I have honestly never paid much mind to, are *totally freaking out*. Apparently there have been some sort of budget cuts, and they are forever trying to get time with Ms. Carlisle to "discuss." And Ms. Carlisle is just not around. Nobody ever knows where she is! I mean, she shows up at school in the morning, then disappears into her office for almost the whole day, and whichever poor first-year is assigned to front office duty has to sit outside her office and duck spit as the teachers yell at her.

**3:30 p.m.**
**Go home**

Nap. I nap a lot. Sometimes I fall asleep on the couch in front of afternoon TV and wake up at five, when the evening news comes on. Napping is interrupted only by snacking. Or by going online (and snacking).

**2:00 a.m.**
**Go to sleep**

This late-night bedtime may be why all I can do in the morning is roll out of bed, but what happens is I'll start watching TV or playing games online, and then I look up and it's already tomorrow. Sleeping in my clothes helps, though I have been sure to brush away whatever crumbs have gathered. The other day I woke up with a Cheeto stuck to my cheek, and I didn't even notice till my dad picked it off.

It's a good life, for the first couple of weeks at least. But after my second weekend of snack food and sleep and dodging Deanna's phone calls, my mom greets me when I walk through the front door Monday after school by asking, "Are you ready?"

I look longingly at the couch. "For what?"

"College," she states firmly, leading me into the dining room, with its empty file folders, unused Post-Its, and highlighters. With her hands still on my shoulders, she sits me down in the chair at the head of the table. "You were on a great schedule last year, Gigi, and I've let you rest up from the summer, but it is time for you to get back on track."

"Don't you have a book tour to go on?" I groan.

"Wow," my mom says, her mouth gaping, "you are really in the throes of it! Fascinating!"

"Of what?"

My mom doesn't answer, she just plants me at the dining room table in front of my laptop, sits next to me with a pad of paper and pen, and says, "Begin."

"Begin *what*?"

"Gigi, you have to get started on your college applications."

"Get started? But I'm applying early decision to Yale. . . ."

"I no longer think that's a good idea."

"Why?"

"Because Yale's early decision applications were due last week."

"Oh."

"Exactly. Ms. Carlisle and I have discussed it and—"

"You guys discussed me? Gross!"

"It's not gross, Gigi, we care about you. And I have to say that if you had spent the summer the way you were supposed to, and if you had petitioned to be president of *any* of the student organizations on campus, if you had done any of the things we talked about, then early decision to Yale would have been a viable option. But now . . ." She pauses. "You need to go online and request new brochures from your backup schools."

"We have those brochures from last year. Plus, for most places I can just fill out a master application online and check off where I want it sent. And also, brochures are a waste of paper."

"Humor your mother," she says, making a note on her pad. "Watching you receive college catalogs in the mail as a senior in high school is something I have looked forward to since the day you were born. Yes, really," she persists, interrupting my interruption.

"Fine, I'll request the brochures." I know it will take ten minutes at the most, and then I can get back to the TV.

"And then I want you to look again at the personal essay options for each school and start brainstorming."

I swallow back a yawn and mumble, "Fine."

"And I'll want to see a list of ten new ideas for essays that you and I can narrow down tomorrow evening."

I drag myself through these tasks like a stick through mud. It is just so . . . tedious. Point and click and yawn. I work down my list, discovering after the first couple that I can bypass most of the content on each site by making a beeline for the "More

Information" links. It takes me just a half hour, and I now have twelve catalogs winging their way to me through my best friends, the United States Postal Service.

The essay question list takes longer.

A lot longer.

By the time my mom starts dinner, I'm only halfway through the list. It wouldn't be so bad if I hadn't had to skip my nap. I'm fuzzy headed and cranky, and these essay questions are going to take forever.

"Luckily" for me, according to my mom, Thanksgiving break is in two weeks, so I'll have plenty of time to work on my applications. My mom spends most of those weeks with me at the dining room table. While I suffer away on my laptop, she writes longhand on a legal pad. When I ask, she says she's just scribbling down some ideas for a new book.

I used to love it when my mom and I were study buddies. She thought snacks were intrinsic to good work, and every once in a while we'd take breaks to read each other what we were writing. I heard snippets of her first five books that way, before I gave up studying at home for studying alone in my room or with Deanna.

Now, though, my mom's presence is like putting my last nerve through a cheese grater. She just *sits* there and watches me bite my nails, or she scribbles on her stupid notepad and then watches some more. It is driving me batty.

Finally, on Wednesday, she lets us quit early so we can get everything ready for tomorrow's Thanksgiving dinner. Then she lets it slip that she invited Deanna and her mother for dinner tomorrow, "like always."

"Wait, what?" I ask, trying to remember the last time I talked to Deanna. "You invited them?"

"Of course I did. You know they don't have any family close by. They always come over for Thanksgiving dinner."

I am filled with a sense of . . . guilt? Dread? Guilty dread? I really did a hatchet job on my breakup with Deanna, walking away when she tried to talk to me in the halls, ignoring her phone calls, avoiding her at all costs. How am I going to do that with her sitting at my dining room table?

Deanna and her mom come over around two the next day, and they leave around four, which is about five hours earlier than past years. I can understand why, dinner *was* a little awkward. I talked to Deanna, I realized it would be rude not to, but I talked to her like I had never met her before. Like she was a foreign exchange student. It just would have been too cruel to reestablish our old rapport and then have to incinerate it again come Monday.

"I'll take first shift on the dishes," I said as soon as I'd crammed my last bite into my mouth, taking my plate and going into the kitchen. I caught my parents exchanging a look with Mrs. Jones. Out of the corner of my eye I saw Deanna look down at her plate and shake her head. As I scraped the plates and put them in the dishwasher, I heard Deanna and her mom leaving. "Tell Gigi we said good-bye."

The front door isn't even closed before both of my parents

are in the kitchen, arms in warrior stance (crossed over chest for Mom, on hips for Dad).

"Georgina Lane, what in the world has gotten into you?"

"Adolescence?" I offer. This answer doesn't seem to please even my mom.

Later that night, after my parents' disappointment has been made abundantly clear, I sneak out of the house and go over to Deanna's. Max the security guard waves me through as usual, but I don't pull into Deanna's driveway. Instead I drive past, around the corner, and then park. I watch from a distance until all of the lights in her house turn off, and then I sneak up to the front door and leave a book on the doormat.

It's *Anne of Green Gables*, which is all about these girls that call each other their "bosom friends." It is why it was Deanna's and my favorite when we were younger, and we spent a long time calling each other "breast friends," since we knew that's what the word "bosom" really meant, and since the same summer we read the book, we each sprouted our very own A cups.

I'm hoping when she sees the book, she'll see it for the message of hope that it is. Breast friends forever, which is what our matching BFF necklaces we bought each other for Christmas that year really stand for.

# CHAPTER EIGHTEEN

**None of You Are All That Pretty.
You know that, right?**

**(Just checking.)**

Have you ever wondered what hopelessly unpopular kids do with
themselves all day? Me neither. I think I had some sort of vague
notion that it involved skittering out from hiding places when
no one was looking, and then skittering right back in at the first
sound of footsteps.

I spend a while looking for the Cursed Unaffiliateds I met
when I was clearing the cliques, but it's obvious they don't want
to be found. While I'm looking, I do catch Aloha, Daphne, and
Heidi in the Founder's Path between classes. I don't see them
until it's too late, and they stop whatever evil it is they are doing
when I walk by. They lean against the wall and watch me pass.

I debate starting my search for the DOS again, but I think finding it would only depress me. I don't want to know what I'm missing. I don't even want to know that the Hot Spot exists. The feeling is mutual, I think, because even though Aloha seems to be in the halls as much as I am between classes, she avoids me faster than I can avoid her. I can understand. No one wants to look her own worst nightmare in the eyes. It might crack Aloha's stone heart right down the middle.

Daphne seems to be faring a little better with Aloha. I enjoy watching her strut down the halls in outfits that burn whatever Aloha's wearing at the stake. We avoid each other for the most part. I think we both feel exhausted at the thought of having to confront each other, since there really isn't a playbook for a Hot Spotter confronting someone who was rejected by the Cursed Unaffiliated. Picking on me would be worse than picking on a poor, orphaned dyslexic.

Heidi just seems like she's gone off the deep end. She still wears her cheerleading uniform every day, even though she stopped going to practice and games. She's become fond of kicking the walls everywhere she goes, cheering under her breath.

For my part, I sink into a kind of pleasant numbness.

I read my mom's book *Flying Solo: The Girlie Bird's Guide to Being Alone*. In it she says, "Take this time to get yourself in shape: mind, body, and spirit."

I concentrate on "mind" first, since my grades have been circling the drain. I finish my college applications, including the one for Yale, writing a personal statement I call "Finding Myself in the Wilds of Alaska."

For "body" I don't have a whole lot of choices. School-sanctioned sports are obviously out of the question. So I start running a few days a week after school and once a weekend.

"Spirit" brings me back to the question, what do hopelessly unpopular kids *do* with themselves all day? I mean, I assume they have some sort of inner life, hopes and dreams, that sort of thing. To find out, I hit the bookstore at the mall and clear out their section of young adult books.

I tell you, it is like coming home for the first time. *These* are my people. These forlorn main characters, these rejected, self-hating protagonists with their crushing secrets, doomed loves, and tiny flickers of hope.

The first thing that becomes abundantly clear is that I need a hobby. Every unpopular girl has a secret talent. They are writers, artists, secret masters of the art of origami. This makes sense because I've learned that if you have no friends, you have plenty of time for things like color-coordinating your sock drawer. What a lot of these girls have in common is *the notebook*. They carry it with them at all times, stuffed in their backpack, hidden under their bed when they sleep. It's like each one has her own personal Hottie Handbook that she never has to give up, and she never has to share. I buy an old-fashioned composition book with a mottled black and white cover at the general store, and I immediately vow to take it everywhere with me and record my innermost thoughts through poetry.

*Oh woe is me,*
*I have to pee*
*But cannot get to the potty.*
*If I don't go now,*
*My bladder will pow!*
*And that'll be the end of this Hottie.*

After a second I cross out the word "Hottie," digging my pen into the paper and running it back and forth until the word is hidden under an almost solid rectangle of black.

I try prose poetry too.

> I am the flower, dying behind the brick wall
> you pass by each day on your way to school.
> Yesterday, you spit out your gum, and it landed
> on my last petal. It's okay, I will hold it for
> you here, next to my heart.

I also learn through my research that unpopular girls usually eat alone in the bathroom or library, crying into their sandwiches. Usually these girls are in stall bathrooms, with ugly metal doors, leaky faucets, and cracked tile floors. Once again I thank my lucky stars I go to Swan's Lake. Sure, we have your standard sort of restrooms, with metal stalls and soap dispensers, but lucky for me, Swan's Lake is all about tradition, and our traditions are all about Ms. Cady.

Her suite sits on the fourth floor, untouched except for an

occasional first-year cleaning. At first I want to eat in her room, sitting on her brass four-poster bed, but I'm too afraid someone will walk in. If I'm in the bathroom, I can hear someone open the bedroom door, and it will give me a moment to hide.

I know, eating lunch anywhere near a toilet is unappetizing, unless you're bulimic, and then it's just convenient. But the toilet in this bathroom is tucked into a corner, almost an afterthought to the main events: a claw-foot bathtub, a giant fuzzy rug, a pedestal sink, and a lady's vanity complete with oversize lightbulbs. So I spend many a happy lunch period sitting on the cushioned vanity chair, my feet propped up on the bathtub, reading and eating.

One day, though, I get to the bathroom and find it locked. I jiggle the handle and then stop, realizing someone else might be in there. I admit I'm a little grossed out by someone actually going to the bathroom in my private dining room. I take my hand from the doorknob, wipe it off on my shirt, and make my way to unpopular-girl hangout number two: the library.

Supposedly, a librarian from the giant New York Public Library in New York City came to visit the Swan's Lake library once and said, "Wow, we've got nothing on you." She was right; the library at Swan's Lake is absolutely magnificent, and not in spite of the "darkness, with shafts of light illuminating swirling constellations of dust," written about in that toilet paper volume *The Guide to New England Private Schools*. The darkness, and the dust, actually make this place better. Homier, I think.

There are aisles and aisles of wooden shelves filled with books, each one marked with a copper plate stamped with that aisle's Dewey decimal contents. The floor is wooden, like most of Swan's Lake, and creaky, though thanks to a donation from a "mystery alum" (which we all know means a former Hottie), there are Oriental rugs of the highest quality lining most of the rows, and old brass lamps with arms with multiple elbows hang off many shelves. You turn on the lamp and extend the arm until it shines where you need to look.

The one thing that stupid review has right is that the place is a labyrinth, with aisles that don't run from one end of the hall to the other, but instead make turns of various angles, sometimes doubling back on themselves, sometimes leading to a dead end. It's in one of these dead ends that I end up taking my lunch. It's an amazing space. Down a long, long aisle and into what is basically a tiny room walled in by bookshelves and carpeted with a worn but beautiful rug. There are a couple of the extending lamps and, even better, a skylight casting a mottled (it is quite dirty) patch of light right in the middle of the rug. I sit with my back to a bookshelf, my legs extended and crossed at the ankles, and happily eat my sandwich and work on my poetry.

I hear other people in there sometimes, finding a quiet place in the stacks to gossip. Sometimes I'll listen in, trying to make out their words, but most times I'll just pop in another Cheeto and take a nap.

This is how winter and spring pass: a warm and cozy blur of books and sandwiches and running through the cold air until my cheeks sting, and finally, an acceptance letter from Yale.

I kind of underestimated how much I'd miss Deanna, so for the past several months I've been operating undercover as the stallion mascot. I usually sneak into the locker room once the game has already started.

Then one day: "Don't you even care anymore?"

I look up from my ham and cheese to see a familiar girl standing at the entrance to my little library cave.

"What?" I ask, swallowing a mouthful.

The girl nervously tugs at the end of her long red ponytail before crossing her arms tightly over her chest. She steps closer, scanning the books on the shelves.

"This is where you've been hiding?" she asks.

"I'm not hiding," I correct. "I'm eating lunch. Carrot stick?"

She shakes her head. "No thanks." She goes back to looking at the shelves. "Oh, hey!" I smile, finally recognizing her. "You're that first-year from cheerleading tryouts!"

She smiles a little and nods. "I was really hoping you would get on the team. It would have been fun to cheer with the famous Gigi Lane."

I sigh in understanding. "I know it would have been lovely for you. But the Cheerleaders are still a great clique for you to be involved in, even on a junior level."

She nods, like she's trying to convince herself I'm right.

"Are you okay?" I ask, noticing a certain degree of wetness in her eyes.

"I just thought high school would be different," she says.

I pat the rug next to me, and she plops down. "How so?

Swan's Lake is ranked the eighth-best nonparochial, non-residential school in the country. It doesn't get much better than this."

The girl takes a shuddering breath. "It's just . . ." She looks at me. "You know how when you're an ugly duckling at the baby school, even something like having to do duties once you're a first-year sounds exciting?"

I laugh. "I couldn't wait to be handed a mop."

The girl nods earnestly. "Exactly! And it was great, at first, but now that all the sophomores are rushing the Hot Spot—"

I raise my hand to stop her. "Please, show some respect for the past and future of Swan's Lake and use the term 'the you know whos.' The current regime may have eviscerated decades of tradition, but this school and its traditions will stand long after Aloha and her minions have removed their stench from these halls."

"Oooohkay," she says, starting over, "now that all the sophomores are rushing the *you know whos* . . ."

"I'm . . . I'm sorry," I stammer, "my brain must be muddled from its recent lack of stimulating conversation. Did you just say the sophomores were rushing the you know whos?"

She looks at me in confusion. "You didn't know? Don't you read the *Trumpet*?"

I shake my head. "Not lately. It seems like it's gone downhill."

"Aloha and Heidi and Daphne are holding an open rush for the Hot Spot. Almost all the sophomores are rushing, and the juniors, too. So there's no one to supervise us during duties, and we don't have the keys to the supply closet."

"Is that why dust bunnies keep hopping into my lunch bag?" I ask, staring where my lunch bag lies on the rug, surrounded by a thick layer of unvacuumed dust.

She nods. "It's been going on for a couple of weeks now, and it's awful. Plus, it seems like the whole school is just falling apart around us. It's like nobody cares about Swan's Lake, or Ms. Cady, anymore." A fat tear rolls down her cheek and falls into her lap. She sniffs. "It's just different from what I thought it'd be."

I sigh. "You want me to supervise you guys for Duties?"

"Well," she says, looking at her hands, "I was kind of hoping you would take down the Hot Spot and make Swan's Lake what it used to be."

I laugh and pat her on the head. "You're sweet, but no. I only have a few months left here, and I'm not going to waste my time on those tarts. But I sure as heck can school you little ones on the right way to dust the Ms. Cady portraits. Let's see, today's Friday, so have every first-year that's available outside the front doors at seven a.m. Monday morning."

It's like walking into a monkey house. I've been so wrapped up in my own pleasant ennui, my poetry, my books, and my snacks that I haven't even noticed what has happened to my school. I get there at six Monday morning, planning to inventory the cleaning supplies so I can have Ms. Carlisle put in an order for anything we need. I expect just the staff to be here this early, but I'm wrong.

School is already in session.

A couple of girls—they look to be sophomores—almost knock me down as I'm walking through the door from the student parking lot. They run past me, toward the steps to the basement. "We have no time!" one of them screeches.

They disappear down the steps, leaving me leaning against the door, my heart pounding. "What in the world?" I mumble aloud, stepping into the senior hall. There have to be ten girls on their hands and knees, their ears pressed to the carpet as they peer underneath each and every locker.

"What are you doing here?"

I swing around to see Daphne approach, a wide-eyed and slightly frantic look on her face.

"Duties," I answer. "What are you doing here?"

"I'm rush supervisor this morning." She raises her chin. "And you're not authorized to be here."

"I don't care about your *rush*, Daphne. I just want our school to not be a garbage heap." I look at her, waiting for a response.

"You . . . you can't . . . ," she stammers, her voice shaking a little. "Aloha will—"

"Nice pants." I smirk.

"What?" she asks, confused.

"Your pants. I thought they would fit, they seemed like your size."

She looks down at her clothing. "You?"

I shrug. "I had some extra money from gutting fish this summer, so I thought I'd throw you a bone and help you out in the wardrobe department."

"But why?"

I shrug again. "Because I like to see Aloha squirm."

Daphne beams and says quietly, "Me too."

"Good." I walk away but call back over my shoulder, "We're going to be vacuuming this hallway in an hour, so your girls better move out of the way."

It takes two weeks of double duties for Swan's Lake to get back to at least a modicum of decency. I help the first-years wax the floors, scrub the front steps, and weed the cook's garden. We beat out the rugs, dust every bookshelf in the library, and get back to a daily schedule of mopping the floors in the restrooms and dining hall, skipping the rest room of the first floor, since it seems like it's a health risk. I try to get a meeting with Ms. Carlisle to discuss our cleaning supply needs, but she just disappears into her office at eight a.m. and doesn't even come out to pee.

Meanwhile, the rest of the student body seems to be engulfed in the flames of Hot Spot hysteria. At any given moment a dozen or so Hopefuls are dashing through the halls, their beige tunics (Aloha's idea, I'm sure) rippling, on their way to some fresh hell of the Hot Spot's doing. And Aloha, Heidi, and Daphne are omnipresent, even more so than before, hissing orders, tripping Hopefuls as they run. I swear they don't have anything better to do with their time.

• • •

I have some time Friday after school before I have to don the stallion for tonight's basketball game, so I go to the library to check the dusting job the first-years did. I smile when I get to the little cave of bookshelves I used to call my own. It's only been a couple weeks since I spent time here, but it looks so much smaller now. I tilt my head to the side, catching the title of a book on the bottom shelf that I liked to lean against when I ate my lunch.

It's called *The History of Private Secondary Education in the Northeast*, and I sit cross-legged on the floor, pulling it into my lap. I flip through the chapters, each one focused on a private school I hate. When I get to the chapter on Swan's Lake, I smile and scan the pages. Most of it I know already, how Ms. Cady was a suffragette, an abolitionist, a stunt pilot. How for years no one in Swan's Lake even knew there was a school up on the hill, because Ms. Cady knew the townspeople would disapprove of her teaching biology and calculus and boxing to young ladies. The girls came from all over New England, sent in secret by their families, who would tell their neighbors that their daughters had been sent to "Great-Aunt Gertrude's" to help out while she recovered from a stroke.

I lean closer over the book when I see a section called "The Benevolent Sisters of Swan's Lake."

> Students at Swan's Lake are well known
> for their devotion to their school. Since its
> inception there has been a watchtower of

sorts, a select and secret group of girls who act as the protectors of their beloved school.

"The Hot Spot" I whisper, and pull the book closer.

> These girls call themselves the Benevolent Sisterhood of Swan's Lake and have taken it upon themselves to anonymously and kindly intervene when they see one of their "sisters" is not upholding the honor of Swan's Lake. These interventions usually involve a written request slipped into a girl's desk, reading something along the lines of "You will write out our school song twenty-five times. Leave it in your desk when you are done. We are watching. Yours in sisterhood, The Benevolent."

"No way!" I say aloud as I shut the book. "'Anonymously and kindly'? That does *not* sound like the Hot Spot." I bring the book up to the front desk at the library to check it out and stop short when I see Headmistress Carlisle behind the librarian's desk.

"Where's the librarian?" I ask.

Ms. Carlisle shakes her head sadly. "Budget cuts, I'm afraid, my dear. What do you have here?" She smiles at me with crooked lipstick. I hand her the book, trying not to grimace at her face. "Very interesting," she says, glancing at the title.

"It is," I agree heartily. "They have a lot of information about Swan's Lake in there."

"Do they really?" she asks absently. "How interesting."

"Umm . . . right. It is."

"I heard you got into Yale. You must be thrilled."

"Yep."

"I'm sure that was due to Swan's Lake and our exemplary education." The way she says it is like acid burning through her words. Sarcasm? About Swan's Lake? From the headmistress?

"I'm sure it was," I agree pointedly. "Our school is the eighth-best nonparochial, nonresidential . . ." I stop talking. "Did you just roll your eyes?"

"What? No, don't be silly. It's just these new contacts."

"You're wearing glasses."

"Yes, well, that would explain why they're not working, wouldn't it?"

She slides the book across the counter to me, but when I try to pick it up, she's still holding it. "You do love your school, don't you?"

"Of course."

"Such a shame."

"What do you mean?"

"Nothing." She lets go of the book. I start to walk away but turn back to ask, "Ms. Carlisle, have you ever heard of the Benevolent Sisterhood of Swan's Lake?"

"No, never," she says flatly. "Enjoy your weekend."

# CHAPTER NINETEEN

**Blah, Blah, Blah.
Do you Swans ever stop squawking?**

(I mean, really!)

"Dude!"

I gasp, caught red-handed, and quickly stick the horse head on my head.

"Gigi." Deanna laughs, sitting down next to me on the bench in the locker room. "I know it's you, you dork."

Crappers. This is not going to be pretty.

I take the stallion head off and rest it in my lap, keeping my eyes on its tangled mane as I work out a knot with my fingers. "I didn't realize anyone would be here."

Deanna nudges me with her shoulder. "I knew it was you. In the costume. I knew it was you."

I venture a glance, and one look at her valentine face just melts my heart. How I've missed her! "You did?" I ask.

"Totally! I can spot the Gigi strut-strut from a mile away!"

I smile but say nothing, picking up the flat brush and working it through the stallion's mane. I count the number of weeks we have until school is out. Six. Six more weeks of ignoring Deanna, and then comes the Founder's Ball and graduation, and then we can be friends. . . .

"I'm really sorry, Gigi."

"For what?" I ask, surprised.

"For not clearing the cliques with you."

"Why would you clear the cliques?" I say with a shrug. "You had a spot with the Cheerleaders."

"I know," she groans, "but I totally abandoned you in your time of need, just so I could be the top of a pyramid. It just threw me for a loop when you didn't make Cheerleader—"

"You and me both, sister."

"I didn't know what to do, I should have stuck by you. No wonder you're furious with me."

"What the heck are you talking about?" I ask, hefting the horse head off my lap and placing it next to me on the bench. "I'm not mad at you at all."

"If you're not mad at me then why are you avoiding me?" She sniffs.

Sometimes when my dad asks a question my mom thinks is really, really stupid, she will just ask the question back to him. That's usually enough for him to realize he's being an idiot. "Well, why do you think I'm avoiding you?" I respond patiently.

Deanna takes a deep breath. "Because you hate me."

"Oh my God, are you on crack?" I yell, jumping up. *"Hate you?* Did you not get my secret message? You're my breast friend, for God's sake!"

"Gigi, what are you talking about?" Deanna cries, looking both relieved and confused. "Wait! Breast friend? Are you talking about *Anne of Green Gables*?"

"Of course I'm talking about *Anne of Green Gables*! Why the hell else would I use the word 'breast' in a sentence? You know I prefer to use to the word 'boob.' Didn't you get my package?"

"Oh my GOD!" she screeches, jumping up and hugging me. "That was from you?!"

"Of course it was from me! Honestly, Deanna," I sigh, "sometimes I think you're not even paying attention."

"So you're not mad at me?" she says with a gasp, squeezing my hand.

"No, you freak. I was doing the same thing you'd do for me if the roles were reversed."

She looks at me blankly.

I speak slowly, waiting for her to catch on. "Distance yourself from me until graduation, when we could go back to being best friends."

"Why would I do that?"

"Deanna, have I taught you nothing about high school? Unpopularity sticks like dog poo on a shoe. And until I get out of this place and go to college, I'm dog poo. And you're the shoe. You don't want to be stuck trying to scrape me off on a curb, because the stink will say with you, and everything you've worked so hard for will go down the drain because of me. So I'm taking the high road. I'm taking a bullet for the team, and I'm keeping my distance from my best friend until graduation. I *promised* you that high school would be the best years of your life, and I'm delivering on my promise."

Deanna stares at me for a long time. Then she says, "You are such a fricking idiot."

"Deanna—" I start, but she cuts me off.

"Do you really think I give a crap about being a Cheerleader?"

"Um . . . yes?"

"Well, I don't. Sure, I care about being on a team, about seeing how far I can push myself, but the popularity stuff? That means *nothing* to me." Her voice is quivering.

"Gigi, your friendship saved my life."

I have literally nothing to say to this, so it's a good thing Deanna keeps talking.

"Do you remember that day?"

I nod. There's no question as to what day she's talking about. I know it's not the day we got into, or kicked out of, the Hot Spot. I know she's talking about the day the whole world saw her gymnastics career come to an end.

"Well, there's something I've never told you." She takes a deep breath. "It wasn't an accident."

And just like that, I know it's true. I remember that day as clearly as if it were happening right now, in front of my eyes.

The day of the competition Deanna was just *on fire*. Toward the end of the day she had only one event left: the balance beam. At that point everyone pretty much knew she was on her way to the Olympics. The beam was her best event, and there was no doubt that she was going to knock it out of the park. In her sparkly leotard, the sharp point of her bangs settling on her forehead, she raised her arms and readied herself before jumping onto the beam. She was flawless. If you'd held out your hand and blocked out the balance beam, you wouldn't have believed she was doing those flips and tumbles on a skinny piece of wood. My stomach flipped and turned with every move, and then my mom squeezed my hand, and I knew Deanna was about to do her dismount, cementing her place on the Olympic team. She steadied herself on the far end of the beam, holding her arms straight down to her sides. Even though other people were performing in other parts of the stadium, every eye was on Deanna. She stared down the balance beam, and I saw her chest heaving with heavy breath. I noticed something then, something that I forgot about until this moment, sitting with Deanna in the girls' locker room.

"You blew the landing," I gasp.

She nods.

She raised her arms up over her head, and I could see her muscles tense, ready for a powerful run down the narrow beam. And she . . . flinched. Or faltered. Or I don't know what, but for a split second her whole countenance changed, moving from rigid to what looked like someone being held up by puppet strings, but then a heartbeat later it was gone, and she was powering down the beam, planting her hands firmly down and flipping, twisting her body up and off the beam, and landing. . . .

I lean forward, pressing my palms against the cement floor of the locker room, my stomach lurching with the memory of Deanna's right knee snapping the wrong way under the full weight of her landing. Gooseflesh is rippling up my neck and down my arms, a metallic taste is in the back of my throat. They said it was one of the worst moments in sports history, recorded live and played again and again and again for the whole world to see.

It was the sound that got me. Sure, seeing her knee . . . it was awful. But what was worse was the gasp that ripped out all the air in the stadium, filling people's lungs so that they could scream it out a second later. The screams were short, just a burst of horrified shrieks, but their sound was horrible. Even the commentators. There were three of them, and two of them screamed, and one of them yelled, like he was calling out to her, "Oh, Dear Heart!"

"I didn't really mean to do it," Deanna says, laying a hand lightly on the small of my back. "It was just an idea that sort of flickered through my mind right before my dismount. I know better than to think things like that. I know how it can mess with your mind."

I sit back up. "Think things like what?"

"Like that my mom and I would be better off if I wasn't competing. We were going broke from it, that's why we had to stay with you for the competition. We couldn't afford a room of our own. And even though everyone kept saying that with sponsorships we would have enough to pay back our debts and still have a lot left over, I just didn't believe it. That stuff only happens if you're in the top two, *maybe* if you're in the top three. And if we spent all that money on training and I went to the Olympics and bombed . . . where would that leave my mom and me? With nothing. That's what I thought about, up on the beam. I made myself put it out of my mind, I made myself unthink it, but it was too late. I knew it, when I was in the air, I knew that those negative thoughts had worked their way into my muscles and bones, and that I wasn't going to stick the landing."

I am speechless. And then I think of the stupidest thing in the world to say, so I blurt out, "We could have loaned you money."

"It wasn't just the money!" she says loudly. "It was the fact that we were away from home all the time. And my nana was sick and my mom never got to see her. And that my mom could never even go on dates, and that she gave up her job for me and I know she missed it so, so much. She was missing out on *everything*. And so was I. But then I screwed it up. I don't know how I ever thought me not competing would make things better for us. We're more broke than ever. And then Nana died. And now my mom is dating this bucktoothed guy from the pool. I mean, who has buckteeth anymore?" she asks loudly. "If he can't afford braces, I don't want him dating my mom."

"I didn't know she was dating someone."

"They're just 'friends.'" Deanna scowls. "He's all right, I guess. I just didn't think about how much it would bother me to see her getting all glossed up to go out on a date with him. Anyway," she sighs, "after the accident, when I was in the hospital and you came to see me, I . . . I almost had my mom send you away."

"Why?" I ask, hurt.

"I was scared you wouldn't want to be friends with me anymore."

"Why on earth would you think that?"

"Gigi, I'd seen you drop friends for getting a bad haircut. I had just gone from being America's Sweetheart to being a great big nobody. I didn't think you'd want me around anymore."

"Well," I sigh. "I can see why you would think that. Heidi's seventh-grade haircut *was* shockingly bad and made her look like a chipmunk, but that is hardly the same thing as accidentally on purpose ending a gymnastics career. Bad haircuts are easily avoidable if one goes to a quality salon and communicates with one's stylist. Emotional breakdowns due to a lifetime of pressure to be the best"—I pat her good knee—"are a little more difficult to dodge."

Deanna beams. "You convinced me to come back to Swan's Lake, even though I just wanted to hide out at home and be homeschooled. You told me high school would be the most fun I've ever had in my entire life. And you were right." She laughs.

"I mean, until you ditched me. And you're done ditching me, right?"

I open my mouth to object.

"Gigi, I don't give a crap about my reputation. I just give a crap about my friendship with you."

"Oh, Deanna!" I cry, hugging her. "You're my breast friend forever! Of *course* we can be friends again!"

She hugs me back, laughing and crying at the same time. She gives a final squeeze, glancing at the clock and saying, "Let's continue the love fest later. I should get going. I need to get home before I come back for the game, and I forgot my bag in here. Oh! Do you want to come home with me?"

"That's all right," I answer, pulling the stallion head back into my lap. "I have to finish this up."

Deanna opens a locker and then slams it shut again. I look up from the horse head. She's leaning against the locker she just opened, her mouth an odd O shape.

"What?" I ask.

"I opened the wrong locker," she breathes, her face breaking into a huge, mischievous smile. She opens it again, and I recognize Heidi's book bag hanging on a hook inside the locker. The bag is hanging awkwardly, open and gaping, the edge of a black leather-bound book sticking out of the top.

"Holy crap!" I jump up, sending the horse head to the floor. "Is that what I think it is?"

Deanna's got her fingers to her mouth, a giggle already hissing from her lips. "Should we . . . ?"

"Yes, we should!" I whisper loudly, jumping up and reaching out toward the Hottie Handbook. I freeze midgrab, though, when we both hear the locker room door swing open. Deanna motions frantically for me to sit back down. She quickly and silently closes Heidi's locker and opens her own. We hear Heidi hurrying down the aisle, muttering, "Oh shit, shit, shit, shit, shit, shi—" She freezes when she rounds the corner and sees us, and she looks immediately to her closed locker. Her face is pale and tear streaked. When she sees us, she narrows her eyes and growls, "What are you two doing here?"

"Oh, hey, Heidi." Deanna smiles wanly, pulling out her bag and closing her locker. "Just getting my stuff."

I don't say anything, I just hold up the stallion head I'm brushing.

Heidi looks again at her locker, and I can tell she's afraid to open it with us there, in case we see the handbook, but she obviously can't just leave it in her locker. *Poor Heidi,* I laugh to myself, *this is a pickle, isn't it?*

"Are you walking back out?" Deanna asks Heidi pleasantly. "I'll walk out with you."

"I just need"—Heidi swallows—"to get my bag."

"Oh, sorry." Deanna hurries out of the way. Heidi looks at Deanna for a second, like she's trying to decide something, and then looks at me, but I act like I'm too busy detangling the stallion mane to look back. I do see her out of the corner of my eye, pressing her body almost against the locker door as she opens it, reaching her arm in and zipping up her bag before bringing it out and slinging it over her shoulder.

"Let's go," she orders, slamming the locker shut. "And I should have known you were the one in that stupid horse suit, Lane. You look like an idiot out there." She turns on her heel and walks away, leaving Deanna to wink at me and mouth, *No, you don't!*

When the locker room door clicks shut behind them, I let out a huge sigh. I didn't even realize I'd been holding my breath.

"Holy crow," I whisper.

I never thought I'd see the Hottie Handbook again. But for a sweet split second it was there, right in front of me, and it's like the moment I saw it, my heart started beating out a different rhythm, one I thought I'd forgotten. A heartbeat of pure *want* that lilted and tapped to the tune of our school song.

That book was supposed to be mine. Its weight was supposed to become familiar in my hands. I was supposed to be its protector, and I was supposed to read from it to a new group of Hottie Hopefuls, and I was supposed to write down the names of next year's Hot Spot in its pages. I was supposed to record everything that happened this year; I was supposed to write its newest chapter.

*Stop it, Gigi,* I tell myself, willing my heart to return to its rhythm of the girl who wants nothing, who needs no one. I yank the brush through the stallion's mane so hard a clump of hair rips out.

Deanna picks up her phone the fourth time I call her. I've stayed at school, eating the dinner I brought in Ms. Cady's room.

When Deanna finally picks up her phone, I'm lying fully clothed in the empty claw-foot bathtub, the Stallion costume laid out on the fuzzy bath mat beside me.

"Deanna!" I say, sitting myself upright.

"Oh, hi, Mom!" she purrs. "I'm just hanging out with Heidi, getting ready for the big game."

Gasp! Heidi must be keeping her close, still suspicious that Deanna sneaked a peek at the handbook.

"Deanna," I say, lowering my voice, "I understand completely. Say 'yes' if you think Heidi is onto us."

"No, I don't think so," Deanna assures me, "we're just going to grab some dinner at Heidi's house before the game."

"Good. I'll see you at the game."

"Love you, too, bye."

I lie back in the empty bathtub, staring absently at the crystal chandelier hanging above me, its base centered perfectly in the complicated retro wallpaper pattern that covers the ceiling.

I don't mean to fall asleep, but when someone rattles the handle to the door of my private sanctuary, I wake with a start and then freeze, trying not to make a sound. The person outside the door has frozen too, and I can hear whoever it is listening to me.

"Hello?" It's a girl's voice, and she knocks on the door. "This is a staff bathroom," she says loudly, knocking again. "No students allowed!"

She stands there listening for a while longer, and then I hear her walk away down the hall, mumbling about having to get the janitor. I check my cell phone.

"Crap!" I yank on the costume, shoving the heavy head down over mine, stuff my clothing into my book bag, and after listening at the door for a second, open it and hurry down the hall toward the gym.

I need a minute alone with Deanna, but I doubt Heidi and Aloha will let her out of their sight. As I get closer, I can hear the gym is full to capacity, the crowd cheering loudly and stomping their feet. What is it they're saying?

When I get to the double doors, the two first-years on ticket duty yank them open in front of me. "They've been waiting for you!" one of them squeals, practically pushing me inside.

"Bring out the horse!" the crowd is yelling, and when they see me, they go wild. I knew that my routine was good; I even knew that people liked it, but this booming cheer is more than I could have hoped for. If they knew it was me, they'd probably attack.

Even though the horse head is the same, I took it upon myself to change up the rest of the god-awful mascot costume. Gone is the matted full-body shag carpet and unwieldy "hooves." Instead, I ordered some stretchy black sequined material and fashioned myself a seriously cute micromini (with swishy tail), tank top, and sneak-peek-proof ruffled granny panties with sequins spelling out the word NEIGH! I also bought a sheet of black foam and cut out four hooflike shapes, which I attach to my wrists and ankles. It took me a few games to get used to the horse head—I spent a lot of time running from one end of the gym to the other, trying to keep from tipping over—but since

I got the hang of it, I've been able to do some pretty amazing things. I have a whole little routine. It involves leaping and waving my arms, encouraging the crowd to stand up and cheer. I also do this thing where I rear up and charge at the other team's cheerleaders like I'm about to hoof them in the face. And I've managed to do not quite a cartwheel, but this signature move where I put my (horse) head on the floor, brace myself on its giant snout, and raise my legs into the air. And I don't think they cheer just because my sequined underwear shows.

And tonight the cheers are deafening before I can even get my legs up in the air. Through the horse head eyeholes I can see Deanna and most of the other Cheerleaders clapping and shouting, and Heidi scowling at me, clapping halfheartedly from the bottom bleacher, where she sits with Aloha and Daphne.

I brace my hands and carefully lift my legs into the air. I have this plan to do a sort of scissors kick while my legs are up, to really get the crowd going. I've just gotten my balance when everything goes all topsy-turvy—something heavy crashes into my side, but instead of tipping all the way over, my body falls, my head staying firmly planted on the ground inside the horse head. My knees crack on the gymnasium floor, and my wrists are bent back painfully as they try to catch my fall. I can't see anything, and the horse head is suddenly too small, and there's not enough air and I'm so dizzy and I can't even take a breath to scream.

And then I feel a dozen hands on me, firmly but gently moving my body and the horse head so that they are again in line instead of perpendicular, and then someone is carefully pulling the horse head off, and I can see through blurry eyes the wooden floor and the shoes of Cheerleaders and basketball players and my own hooves. I am gasping for air now, and somebody is gently patting my back. At first I think the sound of my breathing is so loud that it drowns out all other noise, but then I realize that the gym has gone quiet.

"You could have really hurt her, Heidi!" I hear Deanna's voice and carefully stand up straight, my hands holding on to whoever it is on either side of me. The court has emptied, and both teams are gathered around me, backing up a little now, giving me space. The Cheerleaders are here too, holding me up and glaring at Heidi, who stands close by, her hands on her hips.

"Seriously!" Simone yells at her. "She could have been paralyzed!"

Around her neck Simone wears her locket, the one I said I'd lost. It was in my bathroom drawer all these years. I can't even say that I really thought I'd lost it, or that I forgot about it; I just never wanted to have to deal with the awkwardness of returning it. It was better just to pretend it was lost, until now. Simone touches the locket and smiles at me.

Heidi snorts, rolls her eyes, and spits out, "I just wanted people to see who they're cheering for." She looks up into the crowded bleachers. "It's Gigi Lane!" she yells, pointing to me. "That's who you're cheering for!"

"We know!" comes a voice from the back of the crowd.

"Yeah, we're not idiots," Farley 2.0 calls out.

Heidi looks disgusted. "But it's *Gigi!*"

"Get over yourself, harlot!" This from Farah, who is getting cozy with Fred in the front row. She gives me a happy little wave.

Heidi stays very still, staring into the crowd. She focuses her gaze on a few people—the ones that spoke, I'm guessing—and then says, "You are all going to be very, very sorry."

"Let's get back to the game!" the coach from the opposing team yells, and it's like everything is set back in motion. The ref blows his whistle and the teams get ready to play again. Heidi stands on the sidelines with arms crossed, fuming as Aloha whispers in her ear. Heidi shakes her head, Aloha whispers again, and Heidi growls, "Fine!" She stomps out of the gym, followed by Aloha and Daphne.

I sit on the bench, enjoying the cluster of Cheerleaders who are offering me water and asking if I'm okay. Deanna sits next to me, and I can see it's generally acknowledged that the trauma just experienced by her former best friend is enough to warrant her being excused from cheering for the rest of the game.

When the rest of the Cheerleaders head to the floor to get into a pyramid, I whisper to Deanna, "Were you able to get a look at the book?"

Deanna shakes her head and whispers back, "Heidi wouldn't let me—or her book bag—out of her sight all afternoon."

"Deanna, we have to get a look at that book." I try to keep my voice down.

She nods. "But why? I mean, besides the fact that if Aloha found out, she would tear Heidi's hair out."

"I don't know, I just . . . I feel like something's not right. I think . . ." But I can't finish because the pyramid has crumbled and Heidi has kicked open the gym doors and is walking quickly back over to us.

"They need you on the floor, Deanna," she orders, glaring at me.

I snort. "I'm fine, thanks for asking."

"I didn't," she snaps. "Deanna, on the floor. You're team captain now, you need to start acting like it."

Deanna stands up, and when it becomes obvious that Heidi wants to talk to me alone, Deanna gives me a quick wave and walks away. As Deanna leads the Cheerleaders in a rousing cheer, Heidi steps closer, so that she is leaning over me.

"You're not going to be any trouble, are you, Gigi?" she asks.

"Me? No, I'm out of the trouble game." I scratch my nose with a hoof-covered hand.

Heidi nods, like she thinks she's scared me into some sort of submission. She starts to turn to walk away, but stops when I add, "But just out of curiosity, what kind of trouble were you referring to?"

"What?"

"What kind of trouble were you referring to when you asked if I was going to be any trouble?"

She narrows her eyes at me.

"I'm just wondering," I assure her, "so I can be sure to avoid it."

She nods and seems to think about leaving but isn't so sure.

"Because it seems like the only sort of trouble I could be for you would be if you were hiding something and I found out about it."

She moves her jaw back and forth, not unlike a horse, but doesn't say anything. She stares at me for a long time, in what I'm sure she hopes is an intimidating way, then finally turns on her heel and walks past the other Cheerleaders and out of the gym.

"Bingo," I whisper as Deanna looks over at me. I smile. Game on.

"So you knew they were keeping a secret?" Deanna asks that night when she comes over after the game.

"Not really, not until she freaked out when I brought it up."

"Wow, what are they hiding?" Deanna wonders.

"Deanna, what a pleasant surprise!" My mom comes into the kitchen and doesn't even drop her bags before giving Deanna a hug. "We've missed you around here! Are you staying over?"

"Ummm . . ." Deanna looks at me, unsure.

"Can you?" I ask. "I mean, do you have Saturday practice tomorrow morning?"

"Not till ten. Plus, I'm the captain." She smiles. "I can be a little late."

"Great!" My mom smiles. "Did you girls eat after the game? Who won, by the way?"

"We got clobbered, per usual," Deanna answers. "And now that you mention it, I'm kind of starving."

"Me too," I agree.

"Me three," my mom says. "I've been in the city all day. It took me forever to get home."

"What were you doing in the city?" I ask my mom as she opens the fridge and starts rifling through it to see what we have to eat.

"How about breakfast for dinner?" my mom asks, her head inside the fridge. "We can make pancakes and turkey bacon. Deanna, that okay with you?"

"Works for me, Dr. Lane," Deanna chirps. "No weigh-ins in my immediate future."

My mom pulls some stuff out of the fridge, still not answering my question. Finally she says, "I had a meeting with my agent today about a new project."

"Really? A new Girlie Bird book?" Deanna asks. "I thought you were retired!"

My mom winks at me. "Not exactly. But I'd been having trouble coming up with a new topic. And now that I've thought of the topic, I just have to write it."

"What's the topic?"

"Oh, you'll see," my mom says with a smile.

We're almost done with our pancakes when my dad comes home, and my mom gets his plate of food from where it's been warming in the oven. Even though we're done eating, and even though I'm anxious for us to talk alone, Deanna and I stay in the kitchen with my parents for a long time, talking and laughing, just like old times.

• • •

"We have to get a peek at the handbook," I say later on, when we've changed into our pajamas and are sitting up in bed. "Whatever the secret is, you can bet it's in there."

"How will we get it, though? They never let it out of their sight, especially now."

"True," I agree. "There has to be some sort of schedule as to who has it when. It might be now that Aloha just holds on to it all the time; she might not trust Heidi or Daphne anymore. We just have to find out for sure."

"I'll take care of that," Deanna says with a mischievous smile.

# CHAPTER TWENTY

## This School Sucks.
## Oooh, did I hurt your feelings?

**(Good!)**

The sophomore Hottie Hopeful looks up at Deanna with wide eyes. "Wait, you want to talk to *me?*" she asks. "Really?"

"Really!" Deanna breaks into her most camera-ready smile and sits down on the bench, patting the empty seat beside her. Saturday cheerleading practice is over, and we're back in the locker room, where this unfortunate Hopeful has the duty of installing a hefty-looking combination lock on Heidi's locker.

"I'm . . . I'm not sure I'm supposed to talk to you," the Hopeful falters, looking first to Deanna and then to me, before finally sitting down. "I had to wait until everyone left today to even come in here."

I lean against a locker and watch as Deanna nods in understanding. "Of course you did—you're here on official you-know-who business, aren't you?"

The poor little sophomore looks like she swallowed a prickly pineapple. She slips the new lock from one hand to the other. "Sort of?" she finally croaks out. She looks fearfully at the door. "You guys really should go. It won't be good for any of us if they catch you in here."

"I understand," Deanna says, standing up. "I'm sorry we bothered you. Come on, Gigi."

I'm about to be very vocal about my objections to abandoning the plan to interrogate this obviously very fragile and talkative sophomore, when Deanna winks at me.

"Hey, Dear Heart, before you go, can I ask you a favor?"

What the second-year doesn't see is that before she can even pull the carefully folded magazine cover with Deanna's picture from her book bag, Deanna already has her favorite autograph pen uncapped and ready behind her back.

"Aw, of course! I'd be happy to!" Deanna chirps, whipping out the pen and pausing. "Who should I make it out to?"

"Um . . . me. My name's Izzy." The girl, Izzy, leans over and watches anxiously as Deanna scribbles a messages on the magazine and signs her name.

"Short for Isabel?" Deanna hands Izzy back her magazine. "I *love* that name. So, you're a gymnastics fan?"

The girl shrugs. "Um, not really. But my mom wanted me to get your autograph in case it's worth something someday. You know, as an antique."

For a second I don't think Deanna knows whether to laugh or cry. She looks at me, and even though she's just a couple feet away, it's like I'm looking at her from a great distance. I'm about to make some sophomore mincemeat when Deanna finally forces out an amused, "Ooof!" She clutches her chest and chuckles, "Right in the heart."

"Sorry," Izzy says with a shrug, though she doesn't seem that sorry at all. She holds up the lock. "Look, I don't want to get in trouble, so you guys had better—"

"Not until you tell us what we need to know," I interrupt her, pushing myself off the locker and stepping right into her line of vision.

She smirks. "And what do you *need* to know?"

"Listen, you little tart," I growl, "last time I checked, you were still a sophomore and—"

"And you're a total loser." Izzy chortles. "You two are like the Has-Been Hall of Fame. I wish you'd still be going to school here by the time I'm Head Hottie. I'd make you both tattoo monkey butts on your face."

Deanna is doubled over laughing at this point, slapping her good knee and rasping, "Monkey butts!"

"And just how are you so sure you're going to be Head Hottie?" I snarl through gritted teeth.

She looks at me like I'm the dumbest thing that's ever lived.

"Duh! Because I already have seventy points, and you only need one hundred to be Head Hottie. You get five a day just for wearing the tunic and bringing Aloha her favorite snacks."

"Oh my GOD!" I howl with laughter. "They have you on a *point system?*"

Some of Izzy's premature confidence evaporates. "Um, yeah? Why? Didn't you guys do the point system?"

I pat her on the head. "Sure we did, Tizzy, you just keep on believing that."

Deanna's mostly composed herself, wiping tears from her eyes, still hiccupping with laughter. "Just humor your has-been elders and tell us, who has the handbook?"

"We'll leave if you tell us," I point out. "But if you don't, we're going to stay here until Heidi comes back to check your work."

"Fine," Izzy snaps. "They used to take turns holding on to it, but now Aloha won't let anyone else touch it. Happy?"

"Elated!" Deanna purrs, reaching into Izzy's book bag and pulling out the magazine she just signed. "And I'll just hold on to this."

The whole next week we spend on reconnaissance. At first Deanna doesn't want to go along with my plan to act like we're still not exactly friends, but in the end she agrees that we don't want to raise our profile—yet. So I keep to my schedule of solitary lunches, and Deanna keeps to the Cheerleaders.

By that Friday after school we've figured it out.

"It looks like she has weekly appointments at that place, Trudy's Zen Den."

"Of course she does," I say bitterly. "The Founder's Ball is just weeks away—she's already started her primping. Does she have an appointment tomorrow?"

"She—and by 'she' I mean 'I'—called to confirm just this afternoon. She's going in at nine a.m. Their first appointment. They're booked for the whole day."

"Or so they think," I growl, feeling deliciously sneaky.

Trudy's Zen Den is in a very un-Zen-like location. It's the middle storefront in a five-store strip mall. At least the little mall is new, made of clean red brick, and they've obviously spent a ton of money on the large potted plants that dot the cement walkway. Deanna and I are sitting on two of those stone plant holders in front of the Zen Den's black-tinted glass door at 8:30 a.m. on Saturday, sipping large Dunkin' Donuts coffees, when a roundish woman with angry-looking red hair pulls into the empty parking lot, stares at us from her car for a few moments, then gets out and walks toward us carrying her own jumbo-size take-out cup of coffee.

"I'm sorry, girls, but we're not open yet," she says. "You're going to have to come back in a half hour."

"Are you Trudy?" Deanna asks.

"Yes." The woman eyes us suspiciously.

"I called yesterday, hoping for appointments this morning. I thought maybe if we got here early—"

"It's eight thirty," the woman interrupts, "and our computers aren't even on yet, so you're going to have to come back."

"It's just that . . . ," Deanna falters, "we're trying to get in before the press comes."

"The press?" The woman looks closely at Deanna. "Why would the press get here?"

"Um . . ." Deanna looks at me, laughing and almost crying at the same time.

"You don't recognize Killer Pixie?" I ask the woman, my voice a little harder than I intended.

The woman looks again at Deanna. "Oh," she says, nodding, "I heard you lived around here. You're the gymnast, right?"

Deanna nods. "I was."

"And you're what . . . afraid the paparazzi are going to follow you here?" I can tell by her question she doesn't really think there's a risk of a press mob. I want to spit in her face.

"No," Deanna assures her, "not the paparazzi. *Sports Illustrated.* They're trying to break the story that I'm going back into competition, and if they see me here, they're going to know I'm getting deep-tissue massage and detoxifying mud baths, and they'll go blabbing it to everyone."

Trudy considers this.

"And if I do go back into competition," Deanna pushes, "I'll be sure to mention the fact that I came to the Zen Den to detoxify and get my muscles worked."

Trudy narrows her eyes at Deanna, considering. "All right," she finally agrees. "Come in."

We follow her inside and wait while she turns on the overhead lights.

"Well, my computer isn't on yet," Trudy says, going behind the front desk and setting down her coffee. "What is it you girls are interested in having?"

"We'd like to see the full menu," Deanna says.

Trudy takes a glossy brochure from the neat stack on the counter and hands it to Deanna. "You'll have to wait till I'm ready."

"Thanks!" Deanna chirps, and we sit down next to each other on the overstuffed brown leather chairs. With a wet *thunk*, the wall fountain next to us comes to life, and once Trudy lights a bunch of vanilla-scented candles, the waiting room is transformed into a rather peaceful oasis. Deanna smiles at me, and I'm actually excited for more than the handbook.

We read over the menu together, choosing carefully and slowly, because Trudy looks like she'll kill us if we interrupt her coffee again. We watch her turn on the computer and stereo, filling the waiting room with the sort of calming music that involves pan flutes and wind chimes.

"I'll be back in a moment." Trudy's shrewd voice is gone, replaced by a low purr that I think is supposed to be soothing. As soon as she's through the door, Deanna is across the room and behind the counter, clicking things on the computer. It takes her just a few moments, and then she's back on the couch, next to me, looking up blandly when Trudy comes back down the hall. She has a glass pitcher full of water, sliced lemons floating prettily on top. She places it on the end table next to the couch and says with an affected softness to her voice, "Please help yourself."

"Oh, thank you." Deanna smiles sweetly.

When Trudy goes back behind the counter, Deanna leans close and whispers, "Aloha's getting a mud bath and then a facial. We can take the handbook during her mud bath, make the copies, and get it back into her bag by the time she's done."

"Have you decided on what you'll be having today?" We look up to find Trudy smiling down at us. She's taken her hair out of the ponytail, changed out of her sweat suit, and put on an off-white tunic and pant set and leather sandals. The whole look seems to say, *Calm yourself*. It also seems obvious that it was the inspiration for the uniform Aloha makes the Hottie Hopefuls wear.

"Yes, we'll start with the full-body mud bath. That includes a face mask too, right?"

"It is full body," Trudy assures her.

"Right, so you just drop us in the mud and leave us in the room for an hour?"

Trudy nods.

"Great!" Deanna claps. "That's perfect. So we'll do that. And then we'll each have the yogurt bath—"

"Are you sure? That's another of our resting treatments."

"We're seniors," Deanna says seriously, "we could use the rest."

"And would you like to end with a mani-pedi?" I can see the

dollar signs flash in Trudy's eyes. "Perhaps a salt scrub or massage?"

"Let's just see where the day takes us."

Two twenty-something-looking goth girls dressed in head-to-toe black come in. They look startled to see us.

"Your nine thirties are here early," Trudy informs them, and the girls nod and hurry down the hall. A few minutes later, the girls come back. Gone are all goth effects, and they wear the same tunic getup as Trudy. They have a quick, quiet word with Trudy behind the counter and then motion to us to follow them.

"Enjoy, ladies," Trudy calls after us.

The first stop is the changing room, with a stone floor (heated, we find when we take off our shoes and socks), slatted wooden benches, and showers with curtains that look softer than most blankets.

"Do you think she'll put it in a locker?" Deanna asks.

"No, I think she'll keep it with her. But if she does leave it in a locker, we'll have an idea which one it is." I open a locker by turning its key, which is strung on a velvet ribbon. "You have to take the key to lock it."

A few minutes later we're in our robes and rubber flip-flops, standing behind two claw-foot bathtubs that are filled with some sort of sludge. There is a third bathtub in the room.

"I'm sorry," Deanna says, shaking her head and looking at the baths, "but the mud baths are communal?"

"Of course not!" replies one of the goths—Svetlana, her

name tag says—sounding offended. "You are each in your own bath, there is no sharing."

"Yes, but . . ." Deanna gulps, looking to me for help.

"Is this the only mud bath room here?" I ask.

"Yes," Svetlana snaps. "You don't want the mud bath?"

"It's just that . . . ," Deanna begins.

"We're a little shy," I offer. "You know, don't want other people seeing our bits."

"Ah!" the other goth, Kristina, says, moving between the tubs. "Here." She reaches up toward the ceiling and pulls down on the heavy white cloth that hangs there. It's like a giant window shade, unrolling to create a barrier between the tubs. "Privacy. You see? No one will see your . . . bits."

"Wonderful!" Deanna says, giving me a reassuring wink and stepping behind the curtain. I hear her step into the tub with a happy groan. "Now can you lift it back up so that we can see each other? We like to chat while we detox."

"You'll lower the other shade, though, right?" I ask, my head already groggy from the warm goop surrounding me. "The one between us and the other tub?"

Svetlana, or maybe Kristina, grunts in affirmation. They wait until we've sunk in to our shoulders before sitting on the rolling stools and scooching them up to where our heads lie against the tubs.

"Wooooow . . . ," Deanna moans, and I know we have just entered the same sort of bliss. First a cool gel is slathered onto our faces, warming almost on contact. But it's not too warm, though, because chilled slices of what I guess are cucumber are placed over our eyes. And then comes the head massage. When I was little, my mom would get me to go to sleep by running her fingers through my hair and gently rubbing my scalp. It would pretty much render me useless in two minutes flat. I think this time it takes thirty seconds.

"Oh, holy crap, that feels good." I wake with a start when I hear the voice. I open my eyes to an opaque whiteness, the cucumbers. I listen, waiting for the voice again. The mud bath is still warm, but now that I'm awake, it's too warm, trying to pull me back to that wonderful, weightless, cozy . . . no. I sit up a little, letting the cool air of the room hit my shoulders where the mud slips off.

The voice groans again, and I know for sure I recognize it now. It's Aloha. I sink back down in the tub, realizing I don't know if they've lowered the shade. I slowly lift my arm from the mud and fight the urge to dunk it right down again. The air in the room seems so cold, so not conducive to napping, but I lift my arm all the way out, letting the mud fall off, and then lift the cucumbers from my eyes. I blink; even though the room is dimly lit by warm candlelight, it's much too bright after such a warm, dark sleep. I carefully turn my head, pressing against the bottom of the tub to push myself up so that I can peek over the side. I do, quickly, and see Deanna totally comatose in the next tub over and, next to her, the closed shade. It's harder than I thought to brace myself against the slick bottom of the tub, and my feet lose their grip and I slip back down, dunking myself up to my eyeballs. I try not to freak out, but I have to sit up or die a muddy, naked death. There is a slight wet, sucking sound as my body leaves its mud bed, and I hear the sound of the rolling stool and Kristina ask, "Okay over there?"

I attempt to raise my voice a few octaves from its normal pitch. "Mmm-hmmm."

I hear Aloha sigh impatiently, and I stifle an evil laugh. I'm totally destroying her Zen Den experience. The rolling stool moves again, and I hear Kristina stand up.

"Leave it," Aloha growls.

"But your bag may get—"

"I said leave it or you won't get a tip."

Kristina doesn't answer, and a moment later I hear the door close behind her. I hope they pee in Aloha's bathtub next time she comes in here. My heart is racing. The book is here! It's so close!

I look at Deanna. She is out cold, her head lolled to the right, the side of her face dipped in mud. I reach out but am too far away to touch her arm where it rests on the lip of the tub. I sit up straighter, this time pressing both feet against the side of the tub and pushing myself almost halfway out so that I can reach across to Deanna's tub.

I tap her on the arm. She doesn't move. I look to the privacy screen, listening closely as Aloha begins to snore. There's a reason we made her sleep out in the hallway at slumber parties. I reach out again, poking Deanna harder. This time she makes an annoyed face and shifts her whole body to lean against the other side of the tub, her right arm slipping into the mud, making Deanna smile blissfully in her sleep.

Crap.

I press my feet harder against the side of the tub, my body so far out that my stomach lies across the lip of the tub. I can't reach anything but Deanna's face, so I reach out, take hold of what I hope is one eyebrow hair with my mud-coated fingers, and yank.

"Ow!" Deanna's shout echoes as she's jarred from sleep. She sits straight up, then loses her balance, dunking all the way under and coming up coated in brown mud. "Thpppp . . ." She spits mud and clumsily wipes away the cucumbers, still stuck to her eyes. She waves her arms wildly as her butt slips again, and her left hand knocks into the shade, leaving a mud brown splotch, before the shade, with a horrifying zipping sound, flies back up to the ceiling.

In the next moment Deanna looks at me, horrified realization on her muddy face. I'm still halfway out of the tub, my palms on the floor. Our eyes connect, and I push myself back into the tub, glancing at Deanna as we both drop back down, covering our faces in the thick brown paste before coming up for air.

"What the hell!" Aloha says, the first words groggy sounding and the last full of her usual energetic spite. "What just happened?" I don't move. I don't say a word. And neither does Deanna.

I guess that Aloha takes off the cucumbers, because she

says, "Goddamn shade went up. That's what happened. Cheap piece-of-crap spa. I should sue." Two seconds later she is snoring again. I sit up, carefully, and see Deanna doing the same. She points at me, covering her muddy mouth with her other muddy hand, her shoulders shaking with silent laughter. So of course I start laughing too, except I don't cover my mouth and end up spitting a big mud ball right across the aisle into Deanna's face. I think I might die. I think I might suck in a mouthful of mud and choke to death laughing at the look on Deanna's face. The hissing sound of our stifled laughter is echoing, and I'm seriously considering making a naked run for the door, before I look beyond Deanna to Aloha's tub and see her backpack leaning against it. I catch my breath, wiping muddy tears from my face, and point. Deanna looks at me and nods. Of course, being a gymnast with superhuman flexibility and strength, Deanna has braced herself against the tub and has managed to lean all the way out in one graceful move. She wipes her hands on the towel on the bench next to her tub, reaches out with both hands, and unzips Aloha's bag. I hold my breath. A moment later my heart leaps, the black book firmly in Deanna's hands. She slips it into the folds of the towel on the bench and lowers herself back into her tub, smiling at me in triumph.

So we smile at each other in triumph. And then we smile some more, and then as our smiles falter, Deanna mouths what I was just thinking, *Now what?*

Before I have time to shrug, Aloha sits straight up with a grunt. Panicked, Deanna sinks back into the tub. From my

muddy cocoon, where I wait for Aloha to sit back down, I wonder what the hell we're going to do. I can't hold my breath any
longer, so I quietly sit up a little, and hear Aloha settle back in
her tub. Deanna comes up a second later, mouthing, *Crap, crap,
crap.* I wave my arms to get her attention. *Just go!* She nods and in
a flash is up and out of the tub, grabbing the book. She opens the
door and peeks out for a second before dashing out. One minute
later she's back, and not a moment too soon.

The door opens again and Kristina and Svetlana come back
in. I hear them whisper something to each other, and then they
tap us on the shoulder and whisper, "Okay, time to get out."

I fake a yawn and a stretch, glance at Aloha's tub, and mime
pulling down the shade. Svetlana nods in understanding and
walks over to lower the shade, making curious noises about the
mud splotch.

"Am I done?" Aloha asks, still leaning back, her eyes covered
by cucumbers.

"No, dear, half an hour more," Svetlana whispers.

"Okay," Aloha grumbles, "that stupid shade went up and
woke me."

"I'm very sorry about that." Kristina is helping Deanna out
of the tub, as if she needs help, and as they both turn to face
me, I see the silhouette of Svetlana through the shade, adjusting
Aloha's pillow and spitting into her bath. Ha! Take that, you
salty wench.

We're led back to the locker room, muddy footprints in our
wake.

"Here now, shower." Kristina points to the showers. "Then come for second bath."

"We're starving," Deanna groans, clutching her stomach. "I actually think we're going to go out for a snack before the next bath."

"Snack?" Kristina and Svetlana exchange a glance. "We have apples and crackers."

"Oh, come on, you know that's not enough," Deanna teases. "I'll bring you back an Egg McMuffin, if you want."

"Mmm, okay!" Kristina smiles eagerly. "And one for my sister, too? And hash browns?"

"Of course!"

"Don't let Trudy see, she will think the grease will come out your pores and curdle the yogurt. You can sneak out the back, where we bring the trash."

Five minutes later we've taken quick showers that don't even begin to get off the caked-on mud, and are sneaking out the back door of the Zen Den. Just like Svetlana said, this is where they take out the trash. We see it's just a narrow extension of the parking lot bordered on each side by trees, and we easily sneak around the corner of the building and jump into the Jones Family Minivan.

Kwik Kopies is a tiny print shop in one of those A-frame huts that used to house a photo-developing business in the supermarket parking lot. The roof is made of bright red tiles and, from the sharp tip of its peak, reaches almost all the way down to the asphalt. There is a counter sticking out and a wide window that slides open when people walk up to get copies made. A surly-looking teenage boy with a neck tattoo and eyeliner sits behind the glass.

He waits until we're standing right in front of him before he opens up the window. "Welcome to Kwik Kopies, where copies are quick. How can I help you?"

Deanna's got the bag with the Hottie Handbook clutched to her chest.

"We'd like to make a copy of something," I inform him.

The boy closes his eyes, clamps his mouth shut, grips his hands into fists, and breathes really fast out of his nose five times, his nostrils flaring.

I look at Deanna. She shrugs, backing away a little.

The boy opens his eyes and stares at us. Then he grins. We both jump back. He's showing us all his teeth, but his eyes aren't smiling at all. His voice is a careful calm, and he speaks through his grinning mouth, his teeth gritted. "I know you would like to make a copy. *What* would you like me to make a copy of?"

"Oh . . ." Deanna hesitates. "We don't want you to make it, we want to copy it ourselves."

The boy closes his eyes again, sucking his lips from that awful grin until they are sucked between his teeth. He lifts a hand and, eyes still closed, points to a piece of paper taped to the window. Written in black marker is DROP-OFF SERVICE ONLY.

"Look," I reason, leaning close to the window, pulling my most winning smile out of retirement. "It's really important we make these copies ourselves. Can't you just let us in? Who's gonna know?"

The boy, who is still pointing at the DROP-OFF SERVICE ONLY sign, and who I'm guessing has practiced opening his eyes in a way that makes you feel like the cold black light of death has focused on you, points with his other hand toward the ceiling of the booth. I duck a little to look in, and see a security camera.

Still pointing with both hands, he asks, "Do you want me to make a copy or not?"

"Well, is there another copy shop close by?" Deanna asks.

"In Acton," he answers with a smile, starting to close the window.

"Wait!" I cry, reaching out to stop him and narrowly avoiding getting my fingers chopped off. Acton is twenty minutes in the opposite direction from the Zen Den, which means it would take us almost an hour to get there and all the way back. "Deanna"—I reach out for the bag—"we have to do it here."

She nods, releasing her grip. She stands next to me when I unzip the bag, and we take the book out and hand it through the window. The boy takes it with just his thumb and pointer finger and holds it up in front of him like he's holding a dead rat by its tail.

"The whole thing, please." I offer my best smile. "Every page."

The boy closes his eyes again, but before he can do the rapid-breathing, nostrils-flaring thing, I press on, "We have an appointment to get to. So either you make us the copies fast, or we find out who it is that watches you on the camera, and we tell them what kind of job you're doing. And don't go peeking, either."

He gives one nostril flare for effect, then slides the window closed, turns his back to us, and brings the book over to the copy machine.

"I can't believe we did it!" Deanna squeals breathlessly, and we both lean against the counter, trying to watch the copy action. We watch him open the book to the first page and slap it facedown on the copy machine without looking at it. She squirms a little. "I think I've got mud in my butt crack."

"Me too," I say, squirming, as the kid studies the copy he just made, shakes his head, pulls the book out of the copier, and brings it back over to us.

He opens the window and hands me the book. "Very funny."

"What's the problem?" I ask, opening the book, wondering if maybe it's written with some sort of spy ink that can't be copied. My heart stops. "Oh my God." I hold the open book out to Deanna.

"Oh, no, no, no, no, no," she says as we flip desperately through the pages. Every single one is blank.

Copy Boy closes the window, sits back in his stool, and crosses his arms over his chest, staring at us, the sides of his mouth twitching.

"What does this mean?" Deanna asks. "Why is it blank?"

"Oh my God, Deanna, it's blank."

"I know it's blank, Gigi, but why?"

I close my eyes, trying to make sense of it. "I don't . . . I don't know." I check the time on my cell phone. "We should get back."

We drive back in silence, remembering to make the promised stop at McDonald's on the way. "Gigi, I think we've been set up." Deanna shakes her head, handing me a hash brown. "I bet Aloha knew what we were up to the whole time she was snoring in that mud bog."

I groan, filling with dread. "And now she's waiting for us in the locker room, with her stupid face."

Deanna laughs. "Her face *is* really stupid. So, what do you want to do? We can just not even go back. Let her come find us if she wants her precious blank book."

"No," I sigh, "we should just go back to the Zen Den and get it over with. Besides, we promised the girls we'd bring them breakfast."

"You're right," Deanna says as we pull into the parking lot. "Let's face the music."

We drop off the food to Kristina and Svetlana in their break room, making sure to dodge Trudy, and walk into the locker room.

It's totally empty except for a couple of well-coiffed-looking women putting on robes. They eye us suspiciously on their way out of the locker room, and I remember we still have mud coating our hair.

"So she's not in here." Deanna does a little dance, a huge smile on her face.

"No, she most certainly is not. Deanna"—I squeeze her arm—"I think we may have gotten away with the greatest heist in history!"

"Almost." Deanna pulls out the blank book and heads for the door. "Let me just slip this back in her bag, and then we can get out of here!"

It's the longest thirty seconds of my life. Deanna hurries back into the locker room. "She's still out like a light! Let's go!"

# CHAPTER TWENTY-ONE

(Headline redacted due to obscenity.)

We tip Svetlana and Kristina extra big in our rush to get out of the spa, apologizing for canceling our yogurt baths. An hour later we're in Deanna's living room, its wood-paneled walls hung heavy with plaques, and a huge glass bookcase filled with trophies.

"The big comfy couch!" I squeal, doing my customary flip over the back to land on one of the overstuffed cushions. "Can we have snacks?"

I'm in a good mood. I can't help it. It's been forever since I've been over to Deanna's house, and I realize how much I've missed everything about it.

"Sure," Deanna answers, "you know where the good stuff is."

I make a beeline to the cabinet over the refrigerator and pull out a bag of Cheez Doodles. "Do you want soda?" I call.

"Juice for me," she calls back.

I pour some for both of us and head back into the living room.

"I just don't get it," I wonder aloud. "Why would Aloha be carrying around a blank book? Do you think it's a dummy, and the real one's at home or something?"

"Who knows," Deanna says with a shrug, plopping down next to me on the couch. "This year's Hot Spot boggles the mind. I bet they're not even reading the Hopefuls the cautionary tales from the handbook."

I laugh. "I actually *loved* hearing the cautionary tales! They were, like, the scariest stories ever! That's why I was hoping to see the handbook, to see if 'The Legend of Gigi Lane' had been added yet."

Deanna sighs. "I guess we'll never know. At least we got to hear about Lydia Jarmush."

"Oooh, she was my favorite!" I laugh. "'The Forbidden Dancer'! In her too-tight jeans and red cowboy boots!"

"Right!" Deanna laughs. "And she was dating a kid who lived with his aunt and uncle and slept on a foldout couch."

"Yes! He was from the wrong side of the tracks, a total rebel, which she *loved* because her daddy was the town preacher and had outlawed dancing and . . . what?"

Deanna is giving me a really strange look. Her head tipped to the side, an odd grimace on her face.

She jumps up, and a moment later she is pulling a cardboard box of DVDs out from behind the TV. "Do you remember my third-grade floor exercise?" she asks, flipping through them.

"Kind of?"

Most of her gymnastics routines kind of blend together.

"The whole routine was my mom's idea, based on one of her favorite movies."

"Which movie?"

"Aha!" Deanna pulls out a DVD but won't show me which one it is. She sticks it in the player and sits down next to me on the couch.

"Oh, I remember this movie!" I stuff a handful of Cheez Doodles into my mouth. "Your mom used to let us watch this during sleepovers."

"Mmm-hmmm." Deanna reaches out and takes the bag of Cheez Doodles from me, setting them just out of reach. "Keep watching."

Ten minutes into the movie I jump up off the couch and point at the TV. "Oh my God!" I look at Deanna, my mouth hanging open.

She nods.

"That whole Lydia Jarmush story? That's just the story from—"

"*Footloose*," Deanna finishes. And she's right. It was one of our favorite movies when we were younger, and watching it now, I don't see how we missed it.

"I don't believe this," I murmur, watching Kevin Bacon

dance his way through dusty shafts of light in an abandoned barn. "They made Lydia Jarmush up."

"Those dirty, rotten liar faces." Deanna grimaces.

I shake my head. "And now Aloha, Heidi, and Daphne are using the same made-up story to scare underclassmen into submission. They should be ashamed of themselves."

Deanna looks at the clock. "It's noon on a Saturday. I bet Aloha's done at the spa and back at school by now."

"On a Saturday?"

"Don't you know? She has everyone working weekends now. I say we go give her and the rest of the Hot Spot a piece of our mind!"

"Deanna Jones, you are *on!*"

Just like Deanna suspected, school is buzzing with Hottie Hopeful activity when we get there. "I just can't believe Ms. Carlisle allows this," Deanna says as we walk down the senior hall and see that all of the area rugs have been pulled up and shoved to the side, exposing the scuffed wood floor below.

"She's too busy getting spray-tanned to care," I laugh ruefully. "Did you see how much color she had after winter break? They must have been giving a two-for-one special at Tans R Us. Where do you think everyone is?" I ask, stepping over a crumpled rug.

We enter Founder's Path and see the portraits all hanging crookedly on their pegs as we pass. "This," I growl, trying to stay calm, "this is *not* okay."

We can see Aloha and the rest of the Hot Spot standing under the chandelier in the foyer, their backs to us, a whole crowd of tunic-wearing Hopefuls gathered around them.

I place my finger to my lips, urging Deanna to stay quiet. We step to the side behind a column and listen in.

"You will find it," Aloha is saying, "or none of you will be in the Hot Spot."

"But . . . but we've looked," a teary-sounding voice says with a sniff.

"I don't care!" Aloha screeches. "Find it!"

*Dude!* Deanna mouths to me. We peek out and see Aloha hovering over some poor Hopeful. Aloha's hair is shockingly bad, sticking out every which way. Her clothes are rumpled, and I see Daphne and Heidi exchange a look behind her back.

"I want you OUT OF HERE!" Aloha roars, and a moment later someone runs by us, sobbing into her tunic. We duck back behind the column and watch her turn the corner to the senior hall. "Anyone else?" Aloha sneers to the crowd. There is only silence in response. "Good. Now get back to work." There is the hushed shuffling of feet, and Deanna and I make sure the coast is clear before hurrying back to the senior hall.

"I think ˙I know who that was," I realize aloud when we're safely outside and in the car.

We find her at the Two Scoops Ice Cream Shoppe in the center of town.

"Aloha said I wasn't cut out to be a Hottie," Do-Good Margot says with a hiccup, her eyes red rimmed and glassy. The tunic lies crumped in her lap, and she looks oddly naked in just a T-shirt and jeans. "She said I wasn't cute enough, smart enough. She totally humiliated me."

She sniffs and shakes her head.

"But, Margot . . ." I tread carefully, glancing at Deanna, who gives me a *Speak gently* look. "You're a senior. There was no way you could get into the Hot Spot."

Margot glares at me. "They said I would be a special case. That as long as I helped complete the Hopeful task, I could be in the Hot Spot for the rest of the year."

"But there's barely more than a month left," I push. "How could *this*"—I motion to her tearstained face—"be worth it?"

Margot snorts. "Because the Network is forever, you know that. And five weeks of access to the DOS would be worth more than this." She mimics me, motioning harshly to her tearstained face.

"What was the task?" Deanna asks.

"The same thing you guys had to do," Margot sighs. "Find the Den of Secrecy. Except . . ."

"Except what?" I encourage, leaning forward and pushing the banana split closer to Margot. She stabs at it with her spoon before taking a big bite.

"Except that I think we're finding it for Aloha."

"How do you mean?"

"I mean I don't think she knows where it is."

I snort. "Of course she knows where it is, she's Head Hottie."

"Well, if she does, the Hot Spot never meet there." Margot

takes another big bite. "They hang out in Ms. Cady's old bathroom sometimes, or in the encyclopedia section at the library."

I lean back in my chair. "Interesting."

Margot groans into the melting remains of her ice cream. "Can I go now? I haven't showered in a week, and I have to prep my Sunday-school plans for tomorrow."

"Of course you can go!" Deanna chirps. "Take care of yourself, and we'll see you in school on Monday."

We watch Margot leave, dumping her tunic in the garbage on the way out. Deanna leans back and looks at me. "The handbook is blank."

I nod. "And correct me if I'm wrong, but does it seem to you that there *is* no Den of Secrecy?"

Deanna nods. "And if they lied about Lydia Jarmush, what else did they lie about?"

"Everything," I answer. "They lied about everything."

"What are we saying, Gigi?" Deanna asks.

"Think about it, Deanna. No handbook. No DOS. We don't even know if there's a *Network*. If there is, where are they? Have we ever actually seen anything the *Network* has done? No. All we have are stories about things that happened before we came to school. Anyone with a computer, a credit card, and an inflated sense of their own worth could have sent me to Alaska."

"There is no Hot Spot, is there, Gigi?" Deanna asks.

"No," I say, shaking my head, "what there is is a bunch of bullies who have co-opted a really beautiful Swan's Lake tradition for their own evil deeds." I tell her about the Benevolent Sisterhood.

She closes her eyes. "What are we going to do?"

"We're going to expose Aloha and Heidi and Daphne," I answer, getting an idea. "At the Founder's Ball. We're going to expose them for the liars they are. But first," I say, breaking into a smile, "we're going to have a little fun with them."

She raises an eyebrow.

"Deanna, I think Aloha just might have some competition for queen of the Founder's Ball."

# CHAPTER TWENTY-TWO

**Suck It, Swans!**
**There, is that enough of a headline for you?**

**(Who knew the Vox Foxes were such whiners?)**

Spring break.

Last year at this time I was standing in front of my bathroom mirror in my bikini, picturing myself on the beach in Cabo San Lucas with Aloha and Deanna on the annual Hot Spot spring break trip. Supposedly, a Hot Spotter from maybe twenty years ago owns a fancy hotel there and gives the Hot Spot a suite for spring break, complete with free food and booze and a butler.

Now I realize they probably just trolled the Internet for discount plane tickets and cheap hotel rooms like everyone else.

The fact that they're probably right at this second getting barfed on by skeevy, drunk frat guys makes me feel a little bit better about the fact that my spring break is being spent in Swan's Lake. Deanna's at a cheerleading convention, and my mom and dad are away for the week. To be honest with you, I'm glad for the privacy. The sort of heavy overhaul I'm about to go through won't be pretty. At least until I'm done.

If I'm going to expose the Hot Spot for the liars they are and get myself voted queen of the Founder's Ball, I'm going to need some serious help. I have to undo months of Cheez Doodles, sweatpants, and scrunchies, and I can't do it alone.

"Everything?" Trudy asks when I call the Zen Den. "You want everything on the menu?"

"Yes," I answer, my Alaska money burning a hole in my pocket. "And most things I'll want twice."

Over the next several days Svetlana and Kristina buff, polish, slough, moisturize, and deep-condition my body until I glow like a newborn baby. I bring them coffee in the morning, and most days I go with them on their lunch break while they flirt with the moody kid at Kwik Kopies, before stopping for cheeseburgers (I get a salad) on the way back to the Zen Den.

Thanks to my running schedule, my body has skinnied itself almost back to normal, though I am staying friends with doughnuts so that I can keep my newfound butt. I skip the mall to avoid seeing anyone from school and instead point and click myself a new wardrobe.

"Sign here, please," the postman says when he drops off the

last set of boxes toward the end of the week. He glances up at me. "You look different. No more overalls."

"No." I smile, taking the box from him. "No more overalls."

"Oh, dear GOD!" Jean-Claude yells when I walk into his salon the Saturday before school. "What did those monsters at the mall do to you?"

He pushes me down into a chair, running his hands through my hair and grimacing. "Your snotty friend . . . what's her name? Bonjour? Auf Wiedersehen? You know who I mean. She told us you had taken some sort of vow of ugliness, but I had no idea it was this bad." He turns the chair so I'm facing him. "You should have called me! I would have made a house call!"

He turns me back around and flinches at my reflection. "Leech, heat up the wax. This one's turned into a little hairy monkey." He winks at me. "But don't think I can't see that cute little figure under your sweatpants. You can't fool me. You're no ugly duckling, Gigi Lane, you're a swan."

"Ready, lady?" Deanna asks as we pull into the parking lot on Monday morning. I nod. She drives past the empty parking spaces along the side to three empty slots at the top of the hill, the ones reserved for the Hot Spot. A Hopeful is there with a broom, the sleeves of her pressed tunic rolled up, a red silk handkerchief holding her hair back as she sweeps the parking places.

She looks up as Deanna pulls closer, raising a hand above

her eyes to shade them from the sun, trying to see through the windshield into the car. We see her hesitate, leaning forward a little, and then walk to the driver's side window.

When she sees it's Deanna driving, she smiles and knocks on the window. Deanna rolls it down.

"Hey there," Deanna calls.

"Hi, Deanna." The girl looks so young, it's hard to believe she's a sophomore, let alone in high school. She has a hard time looking Deanna in the face, and I realize she's probably one of those girls that have a poster of Deanna carefully folded away in a scrapbook. "I'm really sorry, but you can't park here."

I lean over Deanna. "Hey. What year are you?"

"Eighth."

"You're in eighth grade and you're rushing the Hot Spot?"

The girl shrugs. "They said we can start this year and build up points for when we're in high school."

I lean farther over Deanna's lap, looking closely at the girl. "Wait, aren't you a Linney? Do your sisters know you're doing this?"

The girl flushes a deep red. "Just because my sisters are in the Voice of the People doesn't mean I have to be."

"Oh, really?" I scoff. "You think you can just throw away five years of Linney family nepotism?"

The girl shrugs uncertainly.

"Your sisters worked really hard to get into the Voice of the People and to secure you a chance at a place in a really decent clique."

"I don't want decent." She sticks out her lower lip. "I want the Hot Spot."

"Aw, bad news, short stuff." Deanna snaps her fingers. "Those hussies you're sweeping up for are a bunch of wooden nickels."

"What do you mean?" the little Linney asks.

"Wait and see." I wink.

"Hey, didn't you used to be Gigi Lane?" she asks, tilting her head to see into the car better. "I thought you dropped out."

"I'm dropping back in." I sit back in my seat with a wry smile. "Deanna, let's park this boat."

We get out of the car, and behind us the long downward slope of student parking places is starting to fill up, though there's no sign of the Hot Spot yet. It's going to be one of those warm early-spring days, and the air already has the scent of the earth warming up and drying out. A few other juniors and seniors are out of their cars now, and they all automatically glance up to the Hot Spot's parking places, as if they are checking a clock to see if they are late. I see them blink, at first not recognizing the strange car in Aloha's place. They stop whatever they're doing—closing their car door, slinging a bag over their shoulder, tucking their hair behind their ears—and look confusedly from the minivan to Deanna and me as we walk toward the back door.

I look at Deanna. "Killer Pixie?"

She nods. "I'm ready. You?"

"Let's do this," I growl, leading the way up the stairs.

The hallway before us is, as we hoped, empty when we get

there, save for Beatrice Linney, who is leaning against Aloha's locker, one foot propped daintily behind her, texting away.

Deanna looks at me inquisitively, and I whisper, "I tipped her last night."

Beatrice doesn't look up until we're standing right in front of her. Even then she types in a few more words before glancing in our direction. She looks at me for a long moment turning her gaze to Deanna.

"Interesting," Beatrice finally murmurs, typing as she talks, "the Return of Gigi Lane." She looks up from her phone. "And the question is, Lane, do we end that statement with a period? Or the accursed question mark?"

I raise one plucked eyebrow. "What do you think?"

Beatrice smiles like a wolf that's stumbled upon a broken-legged deer, and then pointedly presses the period symbol at the end of the sentence. "I have to go." She pushes off and hurries away, calling over her shoulder, "Thanks for the heads-up, Lane. I always knew you had some fight in you yet."

She is around the corner before I can think of something cool to say, like, "You have no idea," so I settle for just smiling in her wake.

"Do you think she'll do a special midday edition?" Deanna asks.

I shake my head. "I think she'll do a breakfast edition."

Out of the corner of my eye I see someone pass by the entrance to the senior hall. She walks quickly, on her way some-where. From the way she's dressed, I'm guessing to the theater.

Someone else follows, a Greenie, her peasant skirt poofing out behind her.

"Any minute now," I say, turning to the back entrance, the one the upperclassmen will start coming through any second.

Our fellow Swans enter from both ends of the hall. They're flushed with vacation, with the knowledge that we'll be leaving Dear Olde Swanny in a matter of weeks. They walk with arms linked, laughing, squealing, giggling. Like two waves coming faster and faster toward us, growing in size and speed and strength to meet in the middle, where we stand. They come closer and closer, and I exchange a nervous look with Deanna. Will it work? Will they even notice we are here? They are closer now and all I can taste is fear. Had I gone too far? Had I really disappeared? Can I ever come back?

"Whoa." And with one word from the first girl who sees me, who really sees me, everyone's attention turns to me. Sunflowers toward the sunlight. The crash of waves stops, leaving Deanna and me standing, suspended, in the empty space between them.

Veronica, the Glossy, is the first to speak. "Gigi, ohmygod, you look amazing!"

"Oh, do I? Thanks. It was really good to rest over spring break."

"Oh. Wow."

"I believe you know my associate, Deanna."

There is a chorus of "Dear Heart!"

A ripple is moving through the crowd from the far end of

the hall, like a giant sea serpent mounding the water as it swims closer and closer. A few of the girls glance nervously at us as they shift their positions, and a moment later:

"What the hell is this?"

Aloha breaks through the crowd, her shirt extra white against her tanned skin, a new gold bangle hanging from her wrist. A pair of sunglasses is nested on her head. "Why are you all standing around . . ."

Heidi and Daphne, with their own tans and new accessories, shove through the crowd and stand beside Aloha, who is now staring at me. I wish I could say she is staring at me in silent horror, but it's more like silent summing up.

"Who the hell said you could pluck your eyebrows?" she finally asks me. Heidi and Daphne laugh on cue. The rest of the crowd titters, but I'd like to think it's more from nervousness than actual amusement.

I don't say anything. I just stand there, a smile playing on my lips, my head cocked ever so slightly to the side. This just may be the happiest moment of my life. Try as they might, the Hot Spot can't hide the fact that they are just the teensiest bit scared shitless. Out of the corner of my eye I can see Deanna with her legs planted a little farther apart than a lady would allow, her hands on her hips.

Aloha sighs, a signal to the crowd that she is over whatever this little charade is already, but she's going to play along, for good humor's sake. "So . . . what?" she asks. "You went to fat camp or something? I mean really . . ."

I don't answer, I don't even move, I just let my smile get a little wider.

Heidi glances at Aloha, whose face has gotten just a shade pink. "Full-body lipo?" Heidi offers weakly.

I slowly level my gaze at Heidi, saying nothing, staring until she gulps and snaps, "Shut up."

Daphne is last to speak, and she tries for Aloha's bored tone. "I don't care if you got your teeth bleached and shaved your legs, Gigi, you're still an asshole."

Shocked laughter ripples through the crowd, and for a second I find myself with nothing to say. "That was really mean, Daphne."

She laughs. "I'm sorry, what did you just say?"

"She said that was really mean, Daphne, and she's right," Deanna scolds. "Where's your sisterhood?"

"Oh, gee, I'm sorry. I didn't realize I had to be nice to the girl that once filled my locker with dog food. *Wet* dog food."

I take a deep breath. "I'm sorry I did that, Daphne. It wasn't very sisterly of me." And the truth is, I *am* sorry. Being mean to Daphne felt so necessary at the time, but now I don't know why. I mean, just looking at her now in the clothing I'd left for her, I don't feel the same sick rage I used to feel when I looked at her. Now I feel something more like pity.

"Oh," Daphne says, glancing at Aloha. "Well . . . thanks."

"What are you playing at?" Aloha growls, stepping close to me.

"Nothing." I make sure to lean back a little, as if intimidated.

"Whatever, Gigi." Aloha tries to dismiss me with a roll of her eyes. "So you don't look like a hairy troll anymore, so what's it mean?"

"It doesn't mean anything." I try for a good-natured laugh. "Who knew that me taking a shower would start such a ruckus!"

"Nobody cares if you take a shower or not, Gigi," Heidi sneers. "You're nobody now, remember? You're not in the Hot Spot, you're—"

"And you are?" I ask with a smile. Heidi and Daphne flinch, but Aloha calms them with a slight shake of her head.

"I'm more than just 'in the Hot Spot,' Gigi," she says, "I'm Head Hottie."

"Ooooh." I feign a frightened shudder.

Aloha turns and works her way back through the crowd, followed by Heidi and Daphne. Before they are out of sight, I say loudly and sweetly, "Oh, and I'm running for Queen of the Founder's Ball."

I can see Aloha's shiny head stop in the crowd for a moment, but she doesn't turn around. She and the rest of the Hot Spot keep walking until they're through the crowd and heading down the back stairs to their Den of Secrecy, where they'll no doubt sit on paint cans and lament the fact that I came back to school at all.

The exit of the Hot Spot breaks the spell, and the waves of girls crash together, hurrying to their lockers on their way to homeroom.

# CHAPTER TWENTY-THREE

## Everyone Here Is So Much Stupider Than They Think They Are.

### (Yes, that means you.)

The plan is simple. Get the whole school to turn against the Hot Spot and vote for me as queen of the Founder's Ball, and then expose the Hot Spot for the sham they are. But first I have to do some damage control.

First up, the Gizmos.

I find Farley 2.0 and the rest of the Gizmos meeting in the main conference room, seated around the long oval table. The heavy door creaks when I open it, and I lose all hope of quietly slipping in and waiting until their meeting is finished.

"Well," Farley says with a grimace, leaning back in her chair at the head of the table. "If it isn't Gigi two point oh. We heard your operating system rebooted itself. Looks like it's true."

"I . . . don't really know what that means."

There is a tittering chorus of snickers from the rest of the Gizmos until Farley, in an impressive and barely perceptible move, twitches her pointer finger and silences them.

"Look," I say, taking a deep breath, "I just came by to—"

"You're not allowed to touch anything, you know that, right?"

I nod, trying to keep patient. "I know. I don't want to touch anything, I just came to—"

"What?"

This is not going how I planned. I finally manage to stammer out, "Do . . . you know who Belinda Fowler is?"

There is a long silence. Finally someone croaks, "How do you know who Belinda Fowler is?"

"She's, um, she's a fan of my mom's. They met at a conference or something."

"So?" Farley tries to keep her voice steady, but I can tell she's interested.

"So, I guess she used to work at Apple—"

"That's never been confirmed. Do you have confirmation on that? Because Apple says she's never worked there."

I shrug. "I don't know, she said she did."

"You *met* her?"

I nod. "And I told her about you guys, and the sort of work you're doing, and she said that she used to be a Gizmo, except at her school they called them the Nerds or the Dweebs or something like that—"

"Get to the point, Lane."

"Right. Anyway, she started talking about something she said you guys might be interested in, something about an L56LUT—"

Almost in unison everyone at the table yells, "What?!"

Farley 2.0 says, "The L-LUT"—she pronounces it as one word—"is a myth. Apple says it was never even a project there. . . ."

Someone else says, "Yeah, but they also say that Fowler never worked there. . . ."

"What'd she tell you about it? Did she say how it worked? *If* it worked?"

I slip my hand into my back pocket and pull out the sleek, silver piece of electronics. "I don't know, why don't you see for yourself?"

"You have one?" Farley asks, her voice shaking.

For a second nobody moves. They stare so hard at the thing in my hand that I suddenly worry if the L-LUT isn't some sort of explosive. One by one everyone looks at Farley. She stands up slowly and walks the length of the table toward me, then she stops and holds out a shaking hand.

"May I?" she asks, her eyes wide, like she's afraid I'm going to snatch it back the moment she has it.

"Sure." I guess I hold it out sort of fast, because everyone jumps and Farley gasps and scoops it out of my hands.

"What is it?" I ask.

"Only the most sophisticated piece of interface ever. They said it was a myth. . . ."

"But you never believed them," someone says, standing up and laying her hand on Farley's shoulder. "You always believed in this."

"Thank you, Gigi Lane, thank you."

"No problem. Oh, and just a little FYI—I'm hoping to get crowned queen of the Founder's Ball. You know, show Aloha a thing or two about what it means to be a Swan."

The woman walks ahead of me even though I'm supposed to be leading her. I was expecting someone more . . . earthy. Maybe with loose braids and a scent of campfire. This woman is . . . intense. She is strutting down the hallway in high leather boots with six-inch heels, her strides remarkably long for a woman in a pencil skirt. Her jacket, in matching gray flannel, cinches in at her waist before flouncing out ever so slightly just above the curve of her hips. Her hair, jet black and scented jasmine, is pulled tight into a bun. Her lips are red, red, red. As I hurry to keep up with her, I worry suddenly if I've called the wrong person. If perhaps I've accidentally summoned a dominatrix to Swan's Lake. I'm going to get in so much trouble if she stuffs a sock in someone's mouth and spanks her. I look closely at the back of her skirt, trying to discern if there's a panty line made by a leather corset. I'm looking so closely I don't notice that she's stopped, and I run right into her, butting her shoulder blades with my forehead like a bull.

I gasp, taking a step back. "I'm so sorry!"

She glares at me for a moment, twisting her red, red mouth at me in stony silence.

"Is this the classroom?" she asks finally, trying to subtly adjust her bra.

"It's the next one," I say, giving her a wide berth as I hurry past her. I stand on my tiptoes, peeking through the small window placed high in the door of the science lab. The class is paired off, in goggles and plastic aprons and rubber gloves, pouring a blue liquid into a white liquid. Smoke comes out. Mr. LeBron is at the front of the classroom, and through the door I can hear his squeaky voice punctuating the words he thinks are important. "Acid!" and "Base!"

I yank open the door, but everyone's concentrating so hard they don't all turn their heads like I thought they would.

I clear my throat, and a couple people look up. I know Mr. LeBron notices, but he ignores me. I take a breath, trying to figure out what I should say, when a voice, annoyed, behind me says:

"Farah Soon?"

Madam Steelner, highest-ranking officer of the Outdoor Girls, slips between me and the door, giving me a none too subtle jab in the gut with her elbow as she passes.

She gets everyone's attention. They freeze at the sight of this pencil-skirted hottie.

"Farah Soon?" she asks again, her voice losing patience.

In the back of the room there is the sound of a high stool scraping on the concrete floor, and then a voice, "I'm here."

It comes from behind a contraption of tests tubes and beakers.

"Show yourself."

Farah steps out, her pale face whitened to something like cottage cheese, her spray of freckles looking painted on.

"Step forward."

Farah stands before us, her head bowed.

"Farah, I have been informed that your expulsion for un-Outdoor-like conduct in second grade may have been improper. I have been informed that it was not you who added nonregulation materials to your campfire. Is this correct?"

Farah looks up, and I open my mouth because I think she's going to silently plead with me for permission to give me up. Apparently, though, she doesn't need my help.

"Gigi Lane did it," she says quickly, looking right at me, "and told me if I didn't tell on her, she'd be my friend."

"I see."

I left out that part when I called and pleaded with the madam to come visit.

"In light of these new developments"—the madam pulls a small piece of cloth from her purse—"I hereby reinstate you as an Outdoor Girl, level one—Newt, with the opportunity and encouragement to pursue other badges to bring you fully to your rightful Outdoor Girls level."

The cloth unravels, revealing itself to be the purple sash that Farah has longed for. Farah bends her head, and the madam places it over her. The class claps, and Farah cries.

"I'm really sorry for what I did, Farah," I say. She nods and gives me a hug, and there is a new chorus of "Awww's" from the class, with one very noticeable snort of derision coming from the front lab station. Heidi sits, still facing forward, carefully dividing liquids into test tubes.

"And just so you all know," I say, addressing the class, "I hope that you might consider me for queen of the Founder's Ball."

"NO!" Coach says as soon as I walk into her office. She stands up, her chair rolling hard into the wall behind her. "I was told you'd be coming." She walks around the desk, stands in front of me, and glares. "And while Swan's Lake always respects a girl's mission to better herself, I have a team to look out for, Gigi, and I can't have you coming back on the field and futzing everything up."

I was expecting this. "I know," I say calmly, taking a slight step back. "I don't want back on the team."

"Good, because you can't *get* back on the team."

"I understand."

"So, what do you want, Lane?"

"I want to make it better. I want to say sorry, and I want to make it better."

Coach narrows her eyes at me. "How are you supposed to do that?"

"Well, it's lacrosse season now, right?"

"Very good, Lane."

"I thought maybe I'd get you a new power center . . . not me," I say, before she can yell.

"Who? I know all the Lacrockies, and none of them could take the center position."

"She's not a Lacrockie."

"Cheerleader?"

"No."

"What, some sort of Gizmo?"

"No."

"Who is she, then?"

"She's a Whomper."

"Oh, come on now! You mean those pale kids that hit each other with foam . . ." She pauses, and looks like she's sucking on a Sour Patch Kid instead. "Interesting. Who've you got?"

"Well, she's a junior."

"Good. Time to train her."

"Right! And she's right here."

"You brought her here?" Coach looks around her, like she's hoping she may have stashed a spare tracksuit around here somewhere. "Well, all right. Let her in."

It wasn't hard to convince Farah to volunteer for lacrosse, because she needs a Sports Patch for Outdoor Girls. And for the first time ever in my life, I asked someone to do something without the threat of violence or social expulsion. It was my first experience of "You scratch my back, I'll help you get your Sports Patch."

● ● ●

It went like that with all of the cliques—an act of kindness, and a gentle reminder of my campaign for Queen.

For the Glossies, I spearheaded a *Have you met Veronica?* Day, where I basically parade Veronica and the rest of her invisible crew up and down the halls between classes, introducing them to everyone. Veronica managed to smile through the same sort of conversation a million times: *No, I'm not a transfer student* and *Actually, you've been my lab partner since we were first-years.*

In careful negotiations where it was agreed that the Greenies would not blow the Deeks' cover, the two cliques quietly broke ground on an organic garden in the Deeks' courtyard.

It took me a while to track them all down but thanks to my intervention, the Cursed Unaffiliated have skittered out of the darkened corners of Swan's Lake to take over Ms. Cady's bathroom. And, right outside of the bathroom, I helped the Do-Good's set up shop on the four-poster bed in Ms. Cady's bedroom, where they hold daily *Learn to Love Yourself!* workshops for the Cursed Unaffiliated. They even use my mom's full line of self-help books!

And speaking of books, the Bookish Girls were thrilled to take over the library, especially since Ms. Carlisle seemed to have abandoned her post as fill-in librarian. There was some whining at the start about the lack of key texts, but soon the Bookish Girls happily worked out a rotation of curling up in the sunny nooks of the library to read or write in their journals, hosting lively book clubs, and making uninvited book recommendations to Swans in need of guidance.

I offer the Mr. T.'s what they most want: me. Rather, I offer them my *motivation*. I spend several afternoons sitting onstage in a wooden chair, taking questions from the audience of curious thespians. I let them pepper me with queries about my inner monologue, improvising insults, and how to glare into a group of people and make every single person feel as though my derision is aimed directly at them.

# CHAPTER TWENTY-FOUR

**There Once Was a Girl from Swan's Lake,
Who'd Taken All She Could Take,
She Said Good-bye, but She Didn't Cry,
Because She Was No Longer a Fake.**

"Do you think they're scared?" Deanna asks, stifling a Razzmatazz burp as we comb through racks of dresses, trying to find the perfect Founder's Ball frocks for exposing a sham organization. "I mean, do you think they know something's going on?"

"Well, they're definitely not happy that I'm not hiding out in Ms. Cady's bathroom at lunch anymore."

"I know, they gave you the stink eye big-time the other day!" Deanna laughs.

I smile happily at the memory. I was sitting with Deanna and the few Cheerleaders who aren't rushing the Hot Spot in the almost empty dining hall for lunch. We were surrounded by the people whom I may have formerly referred to as "people in cliques that don't matter," but since I realized that none of the Gizmos, Greenies, Whompers, etc., are rushing the Hot Spot, I've grown fond of them. They aren't exactly warm to me, but most *will* smile at me before looking quickly away. "Deanna," I whispered, "I think my queen of the Founder's Ball plan just might work!" The dining hall echoed with that happy cacophony that happens when finals (which I've aced) are almost over and summer vacation is so close you can practically feel the hot sand between your toes.

The swinging double doors to the dining hall banged open, and Aloha, Daphne, and Heidi burst in, walking quickly down the aisle between the tables, trailed by the Hopefuls, until they came to the beginning of the hot-food line. We all watched in silence as the Hopefuls, their tunics dingy, their hair matted and unwashed, looked longingly at the potatoes au gratin, mashed potatoes, and french fries that made up that day's "Potato Feast!" Aloha and the others turned to the Hopefuls, staring them down until they all looked at the floor. "Are you hungry?" Aloha asked. "Because I would love to let you all eat, but . . ."

"That's it," I whispered, standing up, my knees bumping the table, ready to forget my Founder's Ball plan, just wanting to end the misery for this poor crew of ill-used Swans. Aloha's eyes grew wide, as did her sneer, as she watched me stand. "DISmissed!" she said quickly, and the dining hall exploded into sound as the Hopefuls rushed the hot-food line. I sat back down.

That was two days ago, and Aloha has been avoiding me ever since.

"They should be scared." I hold up a dress, deem it too garish, and put it back on the rack. "Once everyone realizes there is no Hot Spot, Aloha and the rest of them will have to run for the hills, and all those poor Hopefuls will be free to shower."

"I'm going to try these on." Deanna's voice is muffled by her armful of dresses.

"I'll meet you in there. I want to grab a few more."

My phone buzzes with a text message: "South Tower. 9 a.m. Come alone."

*Hm,* I think. *Now, that is interesting.* I've yet to decide on my act of kindness for the Vox Foxes. Maybe this meeting will give me an idea.

The Voice of the People took over the South Tower twenty years ago as their headquarters. They had been in a cramped room off the dining hall, but they were rewarded with new quarters after breaking a story that exposed the school's food vendor as a front for the mob.

The only problem is there was supposed to be an elevator installed, but it never happened.

So to get up there I have to climb a tower of about a billion steps, my hand gripping the curved banister as I climb. When

I'm almost to the top, a voice from above warns, "Better skip the red steps." I look down and see that now every third or fourth step has a red X painted on it. I keep walking up, skipping the marked steps.

"You've never come to visit us before," Beatrice calls down.

"I've never been asked before," I gasp, still climbing, craning my neck up to try and see to the top of the stairs. "Even when I was rushing you guys."

"Yes, I'm sorry that didn't work out better for you. I'm glad you decided to come now," Beatrice calls.

"Of course I came." I take a break to catch my breath.

"You've created quite the dustup with your new look and newfound amiability. People are talking."

"Good." Jeesh, how many steps are there in this place? Looking up, I feel like there's still a million to go. I walk faster, pulling on the banister to hoist myself up step after step.

"I think I may be of some help to you."

"How so?" I'm practically running now, my muscles cramping in protest. "What do you—" I scream as the step, marked with a red X I didn't look for, crumbles beneath my weight, engulfing my leg up to the ankle in a jagged-toothed mouth.

"Have you noticed," Beatrice says, not even asking if I'm okay, "that the school is falling apart around us?"

"I've noticed," I huff, pulling my foot out, careful to avoid splinters. I take the rest of the steps slowly, not wanting to lose a limb in the quest for knowledge. When I finally get to the top, I find an open door to a round room, its walls crowded with desks and two shabby couches. Beatrice Linney sits on the one closest to the door.

"Wow," I say, catching my breath and falling onto the other couch. Tacked all around us on the walls are old issues of the *Trumpet of the Swan*. They are pinned—some neatly, some in a haphazard patchwork—to every inch of wall space. "Do you have all the issues up here?"

"No, most of them are in our archives. These are just favorites from over the years." She flops down opposite from me on a chair that seems to be missing three of its four legs.

"How'd you guys get this furniture—"

"The you-know-whos aren't the only ones with devoted rushees. Lots of Swans want to be Vox Foxes. Lucky for us, they have strong backs."

I lean back, accepting the offer of a can of Coke, which Beatrice produces from a minifridge by the couch. I open it, take a chilly sip, and sigh. "So, Beatrice. What's up? Why'd you call me here? What kind of 'help' can you be?"

Beatrice looks at me. "I want to know what you're up to."

I take another sip. "Up to? I'm not up to anything. Just felt like cleaning myself up a bit, you know?"

"I can make it worth your while to tell me."

"Really? How?"

"I have some information."

I lean forward. "What information?"

She swallows, and it seems like what she's about to say is

hard for her. "I've struggled all year with whether or not to tell you this, Gigi. It's sort of an ethical dilemma."

"What is it?"

"Do you remember that day, toward the end of last year? The day I ran into you in the hallway?"

"I remember."

"I was on a story, but I killed it out of deference to Ms. Carlisle and the first-years involved. Nothing terrible, just a mild rodent problem in the dining hall. But while I was investigating that story, I kind of stumbled on something else."

My eyes narrow. "Okay . . ."

"You were set up, Gigi."

The Coke can almost slips from my hand. I set it on the floor. "What?"

"A few minutes after I ran into you, I decided just to screw it and go back to class. I went to the bathroom first, the one by the door to the student parking lot. There were girls in the last stall, talking."

"Who?" My heart trills in my chest.

"Aloha and Heidi."

Interesting. "Oh, really?"

"And that's not all. Daphne was there."

"What?!" I yell, jumping up and kicking over the can of Coke. "What are you saying?"

I take the paper towels Beatrice produces from under the couch and start mopping up the mess.

Beatrice continues. "That I heard them . . . plotting. I didn't even realize what it was until weeks later, at the Founder's Ball. Daphne was in on it the whole time, Gigi. You were set up. When they were in the bathroom, Aloha told them that if their plan worked, Fiona would be so mad, you and Deanna would get kicked out of the Hot Spot. And she told Daphne and Heidi that if they helped take you down, they would get to take your and Deanna's places in the Hot Spot."

I choke on my own tongue.

"There's more," she says. "The reason you haven't been accepted into any cliques is because Aloha told everyone if they accepted you, she would destroy them."

"People actually wanted to accept me?"

"Well, not at first, of course." Beatrice laughs at my ridiculousness. "You *were* still a bit of a . . . chump."

I sigh, nodding.

"But people noticed you growing more humble as the weeks went on. They noticed you were really trying, that you had a sort of sincerity in your efforts they'd never seen from you before. But everyone was afraid to bear the wrath of the you-know-whos by accepting you."

I decide against mentioning the fact that I was only clearing the cliques to get my severance from the Hot Spot, and my heart warms at the thought that my fellow Swans actually like me, at least a little bit. "Beatrice, how could you not tell me all of this sooner?"

"Because they caught me listening in that day last year in

the bathroom. And Aloha told me it had to be off the record or she'd shut down the Vox Foxes for good next year when she was Head Hottie."

"And you believed her?"

Beatrice looks confused. "Of course I believed her. Gigi, you *know* what the Hot Spot can do to a person."

I look at Beatrice a long time before I speak. "There is no Hot Spot," I say. "They made it all up."

She laughs, and waits for me to laugh along with her.

"Wait, you're serious?" she says, her laughter now a nervous titter.

I nod.

She's quiet for a moment, an intense look of concentration on her face. "That actually makes a lot of sense."

"It does?" I ask, surprised.

She shakes her head. "I shouldn't be telling you this."

"Telling me what?" I lean anxiously toward her.

She talks softly, as if to herself. "When you rushed with us you were so clueless about the way things work, I thought it was an act. I thought you were just keeping their secrets, even though they did you wrong." She looks at me. "Where do you think we get our headlines?"

"Um . . ." I don't want to tell her that this year's *Trumpet* has been a huge disappointment. "Your clever imaginations?"

"No." She leans toward me and says, "We get them from the Hot Spot."

"But . . . but there is no Hot Spot," I stammer weakly.

"I believe you, Gigi. I think the girls that call themselves the Hot Spot have been messing with the Foxes for years, forcing us to print headlines none of us would write. Especially this year. The headlines Aloha emails to us from an 'anonymous' email address every morning are . . . they're just travesties of journalism. We've been treated like fools." She sighs sadly. "Tell me you have proof, Gigi, tell me you can expose them, ruin them, *destroy* them."

"Do I have proof there is no Den of Secrecy, no Hottie Handbook, and no Network?" Beatrice scribbles notes as fast as I can talk. "Of course I do. But I'm asking you to sit on this, Beatrice, and then I'll give you an exclusive with all the proof you need."

"Oh, Gigi, this is too good!" She is flushed with excitement. "How long do I have to wait?"

I think a moment. "Until the day before the Founder's Ball. But I don't want you to distribute it at school. Just e-mail it out to every alumna you can."

Beatrice's eyes grow wide. "Seriously? *All* the alumnae? Because I can get the e-mail addresses for every living alumna there is, and if they don't have e-mail, I can overnight it to them. Do you really want to push the button on this?"

"Beatrice, all of those alumnae lived in fear of the Hot Spot, at least the ones from the last thirty or so years. Did you know, before that the Hot Spot was called the Benevolent Sisterhood of Swan's Lake?" I ask, suddenly knowing what Deanna and I are going to wear to the Founder's Ball. "They were a secret school-spirit group, and they actually helped their fellow Swans, instead of subjecting them to fear and torture."

"This is good," Beatrice says, still taking notes. "So good." She caps her pen. "Fine, you've got a deal. But I want the exclusive once this all explodes, Gigi."

"You've got it."

I think smoke actually comes out of Deanna's ears when I tell her that we were setup, and she immediately agrees to my plan for our Founder's Ball outfits.

For the rest of the week I look at my fellow Swans, those lovely girls that desperately wanted to accept me into their cliques but couldn't for fear of the wrath of the Hot Spot, and I feel something close to fondness for them. I don't push for friendship, knowing they are still too terrified of Aloha to accept, but I do make a point of smiling warmly at my fellow Swans whenever I can.

The day before the Founder's Ball the brass ballot box goes up outside of Ms. Carlisle's office, and the voting cards are handed out in homeroom. All day long I watch Swans slip their cards into the box, and I try to read their faces. Did they vote with their heart, for me? Or with their fear, for Aloha? I wait until the end of the day before dropping my own card in, peeking into Ms. Carlisle's office as I do. I'm surprised to see her there, since I swear she's barely been at school for the past few weeks. She is asleep, with her legs on her desk, her head tipped back and snoring. Lovely.

Beatrice e-mails me a copy of the *Trumpet: Special Alumnae Edition* that she sent out. The headline is perfect: FAKE STUDENT GROUP EXPOSED AFTER YEARS OF SUBJECTING FELLOW SWANS TO FEAR AND ABUSE.

I wake up with a stomach full of butterflies the morning of the Founder's Ball, a year to the day since the start of my social crucifixion. I was filled with so much hope at this very moment last year, holding that cream-colored envelope in my hands. . . .

I wonder if Hottie Hopefuls all across town are waking up to their own cream-colored envelopes on their pillows, picturing the same sort of beautiful initiation ceremony I hoped for.

"Good morning!" my mom says, poking her head into my room and taking a picture, before coming to sit on the edge of my bed, laying the camera beside her. She takes my hand in hers and rubs her other hand over my arm, the way she did when I was little. "I just can't believe my little Girlie Bird is all grown up."

I sit up in bed, keeping my hand in hers. "Mom, can I ask you something?"

"Of course."

"Have you really kept the same affirmation for twenty years?"

My mom is quiet for a moment. "Well, the base of it has stayed the same. Over the years I've added to it, or have found that some of what I was saying was implied, so I've taken words away. But the heart of it, yes, the heart of it has been the same for twenty years."

I sigh.

"Are you still having trouble with your affirmation? Often it's our first instinct at an affirmation that's the right fit. But often it's so audacious, and so true, that we are afraid to take it as our own."

I look at her with wet eyes and sniff.

"Oh, Gigi," she laughs, pulling me into a hug, "people know who they are. Deep down inside we each know our own true worth. It can be scary . . . terrifying, even . . . to admit to ourselves that we are worthy and deserving of every single good thing that comes our way. Love, friendship, happiness. We *all* deserve those things. But the only people who get the wonderful things they truly deserve are the ones who admit they deserve them. Do you understand?" she asks, leaning away for a moment to look into my eyes.

"I think so," I answer, my voice still a little shaky.

"Good. Now," she says, wiping my cheeks and pulling me out of bed. "I don't want you to worry anymore about your affirmation. You've found it already, you just have to listen close enough to hear your heart call your name."

The heels of our dress shoes sink a little into the grass, tipping us off balance and sending us shrieking and laughing into each other's arms. I think of the Cheerleaders who splayed themselves out on this very lawn, spelling out my doom, and I let my heels sink farther into the memory of their bodies.

The cameras *click-click* again and again, and as Deanna and

I steady ourselves, I look up at the small crowd gathered on our front porch. My mom and my dad are dressed for dinner in the city, a celebration of my mom's turning in the first draft of her new book, *Teeny Bird: A Girlie Bird's Guide for Teens on Finding Your True Heart's Song*. It's a double date. Deanna's mom and her bucktoothed boyfriend from the pool are here too, and when Deanna's mom gets teary, he squeezes her shoulder and offers to take the camera so that she can just watch.

The photographer from *Sports Illustrated* has already come and gone, having shot Deanna doing a one-handed cartwheel while gripping a can of Razzmatazz, her last official contractual obligation. "I'm a civilian again!" she chirped once the picture was taken, hopping from foot to foot as she poured out the 'Tazz on the lawn.

"You girls look *beautiful!*" my mom calls, from behind her camera.

Deanna and I grin at each other, knowing that even though we *do* look amazing in our jewel-tone, bias-cut silk dresses, they aren't what we'll be wearing when we walk into the Founder's Ball tonight. "It's our aesthetic sacrifice," I said when I told Deanna my plan. "We have to martyr ourselves for the greater good."

We pose for picture after picture, and for the first time in so long I have this feeling like my skin is vibrating; humming and glowing. *I am a girl that could light up a room*, I realize, my heart swelling, my whole body feeling like it has expanded, like this is the first breath I've ever really taken, and I can feel its cool relief from the top of my head to the tips of my toes. *I am worthy.* I almost whisper it aloud, and I look at my mom and I think she can see I'm having a moment, and she smiles at me and nods, and for the first time my heart sings out its true song: *I'm Gigi Lane and I am worthy of every bit of jealousy that comes my way!*

I cry out, squeezing Deanna's hand just as my mom takes another picture. Deanna looks at me and laughs, asking, "What?" but I can only shake my head and say, "Let's go, Deanna, let's go do this!"

"YES!" she squeals, throwing both fists into the air. "Super gymnastic powers . . . go!"

Our parents wave from the front porch as we drive away, shouting our good-byes out the windows of the Jones Family Minivan.

"Aw, that was cute!" Deanna giggles breathlessly once we've driven away. "Their widdle babies are all growed up!"

We're both too nervous to say much more as we drive, exchanging looks as we pass limos and catch glimpses of our fellow Swans standing on their own front lawns, posing for pictures in their gowns.

We have one stop to make before we go to the ball.

"Pretty, isn't it?" Deanna observes once she's pulled off the road at the top of the hill overlooking Swan's Lake. I nod, staring out the windshield across the valley. I look lovingly at our school's turrets and steepled roof, and the wide front lawn.

"I wish it were really like that," I finally admit.

"Like what?" Deanna asks, crawling into the backseat to pull out the bags we stashed there earlier.

"I wish it really were pretty," I say, a sudden, nauseous chill crawling over me.

Deanna sits back in the driver's seat, the bag on her lap. "What are you talking about?" She glances over at me and stops. "Gigi, what's wrong?"

"I . . . I don't know." I press my hand to my chest, my heart thumping against my fingers. I look at her desperately, trying to explain the awful feeling that's seized me. "We're about to do this crazy thing, and I just don't know . . . if . . . if it's worth it."

Deanna's jaw drops.

"It's just that . . ." I take a shuddering breath. "Swan's Lake is falling apart, Deanna. It smells like old cheese and it's drafty and have you ever noticed how none of the architecture matches? It has architectural schizophrenia!"

Deanna doesn't answer.

"And there is no Hot Spot," I rush on, "and if the Hot Spot is a lie, then it's like Swan's Lake is a lie and we've been fooled into loving a *lie*, Deanna. Swan's Lake isn't a grand old lady. She's a . . . a pig. A pig in lipstick!"

In a flash of her former gymnastic speed and strength, Deanna's hand shoots out toward my face.

Having your nose twisted hurts more when your best friend does it.

I press my hand to my nose, tears running between my fingers and into my mouth, my throat shut tight to the air trapped in my chest.

She points at me, her finger an inch from my throbbing nose. "Nobody talks that way about our old lady."

I can only squeak in response.

Deanna opens the glove compartment and pulls out a Shake It Cold ice pack. She gives it a shake and hands it to me. I press it against my face, my breath finally rushing out and back in again. "You nose-twisted me!"

"And you deserved it."

We sit in silence.

"Gigi," Deanna finally sighs, "Ms. Cady didn't found Swan's Lake so there could be another pretty school turning out more pretty girls with pretty manners."

"I know," I mumble, huge waves of guilt crashing over me.

"She started it to give young women a place to learn."

"I know!" I sniff, trying not to cry.

"And she stuck with Swan's Lake, even when it was burned to the ground. . . ."

"Twice." I sniff again.

"Right, even when it was burned to the ground *twice* by people who didn't like the thought of girls being taught math and science and sword fighting. What happened the day after the fire? Both times, what happened?"

"Ms. Cady taught class in the ashes."

"Right." Deanna nods. "And if desks made of ashes were good enough for our sisters . . ."

"A stinky, drafty, moldy school is good enough for us," I murmur.

"Ms. Cady would be proud of what we're about to do, Gigi." She pats my knee. "For the good of our school is for the good of our sisters."

We change in the van, glancing out the windows at Swan's Lake in the distance, getting darker and darker in the dusk.

Back in the front seat, Deanna turns on the van and punches me lightly in the arm. "Are you *psyched*?!" she asks.

"Honestly, Deanna, the emotional roller coaster of this evening has left me feeling a little —"

"I'm freaking PSYCHED!" she yells, interrupting. "Let's do this! Let's take them DOWN!"

"Deanna, I appreciate what you're trying to do, but I just don't know if I'm in a rah-rah kind of mood."

"Maybe some music would help!"

"I guess." I shrug, reaching down to pull one of the *Set It Off!* CDs from under the seat.

"Wait." Deanna is suddenly serious. "Not that. *This*." She reaches over me to open the glove compartment and gives me a CD with a handwritten label. DEANNA JONES, OLYMPIAN.

"But wait . . ." I stare at the CD. "Is this from . . ."

She nods gravely, answering my question before I can ask it. "Gigi, I haven't listened to that CD since the morning of my last competition. It is the best motivational music mix ever recorded."

I stare at the CD again. "Are you sure?"

"Put it in," Deanna says. "It's time for us to do Ms. Cady proud."

By the time we drive through the center of town, we are *on fire*. I have no idea what we're listening to. Deanna says it's something called triumphant metal, but I am filled with such molten confidence that I swear I could burn through steel. The Ugly Ducklings standing on the picnic tables in their little-girl dresses glance at us as we zoom past, and over the music we hear them burst into a cheer as they look back toward the school and see one of our fellow Swans make her way up the front steps.

"Do you wish they were cheering for us?" Deanna asks, turning down the music.

"In a way they are," I answer. "They're cheering for Swan's Lake, for the place they dream it will be when they start high school. And tonight we're making sure their dreams come true."

"That's my Gigi," Deanna says, turning the music back up as we pass the line of limousines waiting to pull up the school driveway.

As we predicted, the student parking lot is much fuller than it was the night Deanna and I were sworn into the Hot Spot. I recognize some of the juniors' and seniors' cars, and there are bicycles in a pile by the back door, evidence of the first- and second-years under the Hot Spot's spell. Even though it's full of cars, the parking lot is empty of people, which means Aloha's sham "initiation" ceremony must already be under way.

We open the door to the back staircase. I half expect to hear the sound of screams coming from the basement. There is only silence, though from the landing we can see that the basement lights are on. Part of me wants to run downstairs and kick open the basement door, exposing Aloha and Heidi and Daphne for the liars they are and freeing the Hopefuls under their spell.

But we have a much bigger audience in mind.

We make our way down the senior hallway. "Jeesh," Deanna whispers as our shoes scuff the bare floors, "they're still getting the rugs cleaned?"

We peek out at the end of the corridor, looking down Founder's Path to where Chinese lanterns mark a course from the front entrance to the ballroom. There's no one on the path. I glance at my watch. "I think everybody must be here," I whisper.

Deanna nods, and we slip down the corridor, past the lanterns and into the darkened dining hall. We stop for a moment, letting our eyes adjust to the darkness. "Let's go," I whisper as soon as I can make out the aisle between the tables. We hurry to the far end and push open the doors to the kitchen. We trace our fingers lightly on the steel counters as we move through the kitchen, careful not to knock into anything. At the other end are the double doors to the ballroom, each inset with a round window looking directly onto the dance floor. We press ourselves against the wall for a moment and then risk taking a peek. Deanna goes first.

"Wow," Deanna says, the twinkling lights from the ballroom

making designs on her face. She reaches out and pulls me next to her. "Look," she whispers. "Everyone is beautiful."

And she's right. They *are* beautiful. The Whompers in their ill-fitting costume-rental medieval dresses, foam swords strapped to their backs. The Glossies in their slightly irregular designer gowns, half dancing and half watching to see if the Vox Foxes have noticed them. They haven't. The Vox Foxes are too busy swaying and shimmying in their pencil skirts, stilettos carving half circles in the dance floor. The Art Stars and Mr. T.'s dance and goof off together, comparing frocks made of Bubble Wrap and BeDazzled unitards. The Deeks are in the shadows, leaning and lurking and wearing the same clothes they wore to school on Friday. The Cheerleaders are in their uniforms, cheering instead of dancing, throwing one another into the air, trying to avoid the chandeliers. Even the Cursed Unaffiliated are here, sitting alone at tables, beautiful in a way involving too much rouge and imitation leather shoes.

"Oh!" I cry out happily as Margot and the other Do-Goods pull the Cursed Unaffiliateds onto the dance floor to dance in an awkward group near the sound table, where Farley and the other Gizmos sit, taking turns playing DJ.

"Wait . . ." I scan the room, growing anxious. "Where are they?"

"Where are who?" Deanna says.

"The alumnae." I look at her desperately. "I thought . . . I thought maybe they'd come when they got the *Trumpet*. But they didn't. Nobody came, Deanna."

The lights have been dimmed almost to darkness, and we can see in the faces of our fellow Swans what we ourselves know. The Hot Spot is coming. There is an audible chorus of groans, and I can see people rolling their eyes and sighing, and even through the door we can hear comments like "It was fun while it lasted" and "Let's just get this over with."

"Deanna!" I whisper, my heart quickening with excitement despite the absence of the alumnae army I was expecting. "Do you hear that? The huddled masses are not content! There's a chance we may win this thing after all. There's no way they voted Aloha for queen, there's just no way!"

"I hope you're —"

But Deanna's response is cut off by a booming, pulsing drumbeat thundering through the speakers. We press our faces to the windows and watch as a wobbly spotlight cuts through the darkness and lands on the double doors of the main entrance as they burst open and the Hot Spot walks through.

"Holy crap," Deanna whispers, bursting out laughing.

The crowd parts as Aloha leads the way, wearing some sort of leather bustier and micromini skirt, her hair piled high on her head, her eyes painted thick with black eyeliner, thigh-high boots with sky-high heels giving her a towering strut.

"Ha!" But I'm not really laughing, even as Deanna is covering her face in complete hysterics. I'm too stunned to laugh. The sight of Heidi and Daphne in their own ridiculous getups, leading a group of no less than twelve leather-bustier-clad Incumbents to the center of the dance floor, is hilarious, but this is not a time for laughter.

"Some of those girls don't even have boobs yet!" Deanna laughs so hard she hiccups.

If the rest of Swan's Lake thinks the Hot Spot's new look is funny, they don't show it. I get a sinking feeling in my stomach as I watch my fellow Swans watch the Hot Spot. There is no laughter, no finger-pointing and name-calling. There is no cry of "You look ridiculous!" There is only the booming drum music and the respectful distance of the crowd on the dance floor as the Hot Spot moves to the center.

It's devastating to see the power of popularity used for bad fashion. People look to us to show them what "cool" is, and they take us at our word and follow, even as they know they will never look as good as we do. There is a trickle-down quality to style, and seeing this train wreck of leather and chains in the center of the dance floor guarantees at least a year of stricken Swans stuffing themselves into truly terrible clothing, the efforts worse and worse going down the cliques, until finally you see the Cursed Unaffiliated wearing black polyester mesh tank tops with latex hot pants.

"This is a tragedy," I whisper as the spotlight moves from Aloha and her crew to the other side of the room. We shift positions to see the small raised stage at the front of the room, set with light-strewn potted trees, balloons, flowers, and a single microphone in the center.

There is scattered applause as Ms. Carlisle steps behind the microphone. If the Hot Spot's outfits are a train wreck, Ms. Carlisle's clothing is a plague. She wears a bulky neon green sack of a dress, its frayed hem hanging below her knees. Her hair has been sprayed into a mannish bouffant, and the spotlight catches the smudges on her glasses as she pushes them back into place.

"Hello," she says into the microphone as the music quiets. "Hello, my little Swans."

Everyone has turned to look at Ms. Carlisle and the cream-colored envelope in her hand. She holds the envelope up, smiling her awful, toothy smile. "This is what you're waiting for, isn't it?" she asks, her reedy voice making my skin crawl.

"Get on with it!" I whisper.

"Well, then, my little *Swans!*" Ms. Carlisle hisses that last part, and Deanna and I exchange a glance.

"She's so weird!" Deanna whispers as Ms. Carlisle rips open the envelope, pulling out a cream-colored card.

Deanna grabs my hand, and I scan the crowd, hoping to read in their faces who they've voted for.

"And your Founder's Ball queen is . . ."

I squeeze Deanna's hand, the sound of my heart thundering in my ears. My blood racing through my body, my hands twitching, aching for the moment when I can push through these doors and claim my crown.

The thundering in my ears is loud. But not loud enough to cover the sound of Ms. Carlisle saying Aloha's name.

Time stumbles and slips off its track. My head reels back in slow motion, as if I've been shot, my hands struggling to move through the thickened air to steady myself against the door, Deanna's face a frozen mask of horror. My voice is low, unrecognizable, and the word drags out of me as I collapse to the linoleum floor, "*Noooooooo!*" From the ballroom I hear the cacophonous applause, the sound of Swans cheering on a lie. "No," I groan again from the floor.

Deanna touches my shoulder. "Gigi?" she asks.

"No, no," I say again and again, pressing my palms against my face, tipping so far forward my head touches the floor, all my dreams of what tonight could have been burning up inside of me. "No, no, no, no."

Deanna crouches next to me. "Gigi, it's okay. You can still go out there, you can still—"

"I failed everyone, Deanna," I say through my tears. "I failed Ms. Cady and I failed my fellow Swans!"

"It's okay —"

"It's not okay, Deanna! Don't you see, no one cares about Ms. Cady anymore! They didn't come, Deanna, not one of them came!"

She grabs my shoulders and I flinch, thinking she's going for my nose again. But she doesn't. She just gives me a squeeze. "We're here, Gigi. We're here."

I shake my head and pull away. "We're not enough." I get up and wipe my face on my sleeve, taking a deep, shuddering breath. "This was a stupid idea. It's just high school, right? In a week we'll graduate and never have to deal with this place again."

"No, we won't. But they will," Deanna says, nodding toward the window. I try not to, but I can't help but glance through. The music has started again, the same awful thumping drums, and Aloha, Daphne, and Heidi are standing on the stage with Ms. Carlisle, watching as the Hottie Incumbents perform a choreographed dance so filthy that Margot and the other Do-Goods actually cover their eyes. Aloha and Heidi are nodding their approval, and Daphne looks like her bustier is giving her a rash.

I shrug, trying to ignore the guilt tugging at my belly. "So what? She's making them dance."

"So what?" Deanna points out the window. "She's making them dance like they're her little monkeys!" Deanna does a weird-looking jig, her face getter redder and redder, her voice getting louder and louder. "Dance, little monkeys, dance! Stick the landing, get back up on that balance beam, I don't care if you're bleeding, who said you could eat enough to grow boobs?!"

Deanna stops her dance, gasping for breath.

"Whoa!" I gasp.

Deanna shrugs, breathing hard through her nose. "I just think we should stand up for them, Gigi. I just think"—she moves back toward the window and looks out, before looking back to me, the light from the ballroom twinkling on her face—"that we should tell those little monkeys exactly who they're dancing for."

And just like that, the fire inside of me is back, filling me with air so hot I think I might explode. "Let's do it."

I kick open the door as the song is ending. The Hottie Incumbents are finishing their dance with freeze-frame poses most commonly seen on the sorts of websites your mother warns you about. We march onto the dance floor, surprised Swans all around us. "I have something to say!" I shout.

Not everyone can see what's going on, and as we keep moving toward the stage, I see the bobbing heads of girls with their hair in fancy updos jumping up to get a look. The whispers of "It's Gigi Lane and Dear Heart!" rush like wind from one end of the ballroom to the other, blowing me forward toward the stage.

The crowd parts in front of me, giving me a clear path to the stage, and to Aloha. Our eyes lock and she steps coolly forward, daring me to keep coming. I do. Beside her, Heidi stands in Cheerleader fight stance: arms akimbo, black leather pom-poms resting ready on her hips. She sneers at me, her lips moving through a silent cheer. Farther back on the stage is Daphne, staring blankly at me as I approach; she looks distant, her face drawn. I think I see her stifle a yawn. Ms. Carlisle stands next to her, twitching from foot to foot, looking equal parts curious and giddy at the same time.

We get to the front of the stage, and the Incumbents make a semicircle around us. They look expectantly up at Aloha with their raccoon eyes. I look at their faces, the way they are trying to look so tough, so confident, so loyal to Aloha and Heidi and Daphne, so anxious to prove that it was the right thing to vote them into the Hot Spot, to prove that it wasn't a mistake, that they truly belong in the Hot Spot, despite their chubby thighs, questionable pedigrees, and weak chins.

It makes me sad, and not just that itchy sort of sadness you get when you see someone trying so hard to be accepted into a clique so obviously above her station. These girls are terrified that their popularity, their dream come true, will be ripped out of their grasp. I know that fear. I know it well. But there is a difference. There are those of us who were made to be popular. And those of us who weren't.

Aloha looks at me for a long time, seemingly oblivious to the hundreds of Swans watching our interaction. Finally she sighs and snaps, "What?"

"Yeah, what do you want, Gigi Lane?" Heidi shouts, leaning forward off the stage to shake her pom-poms in my face. The semicircle of Incumbents twitch and growl.

"Calm yourselves or I'll have you expelled," Aloha snarls, barely glancing at them. "Gigi, what do you want?"

The flatness of her voice threatens to send me clawing at her eyeballs. I take a deep breath and say, loud enough for everyone to hear, "I have something to say!" Beside me I can see Deanna nodding.

"So?" Aloha shrugs. "Say it. Who's stopping you?"

Oh. I was expecting more of a fight. I look at Deanna; she nods encouragingly. I grab her hand and pull her up on stage with me. "Excuse me," I say to Aloha, stepping between her and the microphone.

"Be my guest." She motions me to go forward. I clear

my throat and open my mouth to speak. "Nice outfit," Aloha whispers.

I swallow, smoothing down the vintage Swan's Lake uniform Deanna and I found in the basement. "Thank you," I say loudly into the microphone. "I wanted you all to know something."

Behind me I can hear Aloha and Heidi snickering with Ms. Carlisle. I turn to glance at them and see Daphne standing a little ways apart.

They don't even look at me. I turn back to the crowd. "What I have to tell you is this." I take a deep breath and close my eyes. "There . . . is . . . no . . . Hot . . . Spot."

"Gigi, no!"

I turn to see Aloha, who seems suddenly very interested in what I'm saying. She rushes forward, grabbing the microphone from me. "What the hell are you doing?" she hisses, her face going milky and pale.

"I'm telling them the truth!" I say, wrenching the microphone back. I face the crowd. "And the truth is you have nothing to be . . ." In the crowd, to my right, I catch Margot's eye, and she smiles. I clear my throat and start again. "The truth is, we have nothing to be afraid of."

Everyone still looks pretty confused. Farah, my Whomper friend, finally yells, "Ummm . . . can you expand on that?"

I nod. "Yes. Yes I can. The truth is, my sister Swans, we've been lied to. Our whole lives we've been told that the Hot Spot is an organization that could destroy us if we crossed it."

"It is," Aloha growls.

"No, Aloha, it's not. All the *Hot Spot*, is is a mean group of girls with enough money to make our lives miserable, to make us fear them as much as we want them to accept us. But the Hot Spot have a secret they don't want you to know. They can't *do* anything to you! Those stories we grew up on were just lies. Dirty, evil lies."

Aloha grabs the mic again. "Gigi, stop it!" I let her take the mic, and I stand at the front of the stage and yell, "There is no Hottie Handbook! There is no Den of Secrecy! They made it all up to control you! There is no Network! There is no Hot Spot!" Yelling these words, I am filled with such joy, such absolute elation, that I swear I am floating like an angel, until a voice brings me back down to earth.

"Oh, *really?*"

The voice doesn't come from the stage.

"Oh, shit."

But that voice did. I turn to see Aloha closing her eyes and shaking her head.

Everyone else turns to the main entrance, to where a well-coiffed woman is marching across the ballroom toward the stage, followed in a neat double line by dozens of other well-coiffed women. The leader pushes through to the front of the stage, the women behind her spreading out to form four even lines that push everyone else to the sides of the ballroom.

"What the hell is going on here?" she barks.

I look happily at Deanna. The alumnae have arrived!

"Um . . ." Deanna clear her throat. "We were just exposing

what everyone thought was a top secret organization, capable of destroying each and every one of us, as a group of really, really mean girls."

I nod in agreement. "They called themselves the Hot Spot and—"

"Gigi Lane!" the woman yells, her face reddening. "Were you unclear on the terms of your permanent exile?"

All around her, the other women scowl at me and shake their heads.

"Um . . . what?" I look helplessly at Deanna.

"You full well know you are permanently barred from saying the name of the you-know-whos!" she hisses.

"Wait . . ." I shake my head, trying to clear it. "You're saying there *is* a Hot Spot?"

"Stop saying our name!" the woman screeches, looking like she wants to claw out my hair. "Of course there's a Hot Spot! There's always been a Hot Spot at Swan's Lake, and there always *will be* a Hot Spot at Swan's Lake!" She glares at me. "Except for this year. This year, because of you and your actions, we were forced to suspend the Hot Spot until next year."

A cool wave of realization washes over me.

"Oh." A smile spreads across my face. "I see. But . . ." I feign confusion. "If there's no you-know-whos this year, then who are they?"

I turn and look to where Aloha and Ms. Carlisle are trying to climb down the side of the stage, and to where Daphne and Heidi are staring at each other in confused terror.

"FREEZE!" the woman yells at Aloha and Ms. Carlisle. The woman points to the center of the stage, and as if controlled by her well-manicured finger, they move to exactly where she's pointing. Then she climbs up on stage and faces them. "Hello, Ms. Carlisle," the woman sneers.

Ms. Carlisle sighs. "Hello, Famke."

The woman, Famke, looks at Aloha. "I know you. Aren't you that *transfer* student we kicked out of the Hot Spot last year?"

Aloha shrugs.

"And I'm to gather that you have led an unauthorized 'Hot Spot' this year?"

Aloha smirks.

"I see." Famke draws out the words. "And just who would have helped you do that, I wonder?" She stands so close to Ms. Carlisle their noses could touch. "Anything to say, Lydia?"

I squeeze Deanna's hand and she looks at me in shock. "Lydia Jarmush!" we whisper together.

"I have *nothing* to say to you, Famke," Ms. Lydia Jarmush Carlisle sneers.

"Oh, really? Well, if I'm not mistaken, you are still completing your severance task as watcher, charged with assisting the Hot Spot in running Swan's Lake."

A breath of air gushes out of me. Severance task? Watcher? What in the world is Famke talking about?

"And since," Famke continues, "there was no Hot Spot for you to assist this year, you were supposed to run Swan's Lake yourself."

"And if *I'm* not mistaken," Ms. Carlisle says, hopping giddily from foot to foot, "my severance sentence ends . . ." She looks up at the clock hanging above the entrance, her eyes wide, her face flushed with excitement. The whole crowd turns to watch with her as the big hand lands on the twelve, declaring it nine p.m. "Now!" Ms. Carlisle yells with a whoop. She digs a hand into her hair and tears it off her head, and blond cascades of glossy tendrils fall to her shoulders.

The entire student body of Swan's Lake is struck speechless as Ms. Carlisle yanks at the neck of her ugly green dress, ripping it from her frame, revealing a black silk sheath that hugs her lithe body. We all watch as with a wet splat Ms. Carlisle spits out an ugly retainer, the white of her teeth shining in the disco ball's reflected light. Her glasses and shoes fly across the stage, and she reaches into the closest potted plant and produces a pair of black stilettos. Slipping on her shoes, she says, "I am *done*, Famke! I have completed your task! And now"—Ms. Carlisle smooths down her dress and fluffs her hair—"I'm ready for my severance." Her eyes are wide with expectation. "Well, Famke?" she asks impatiently. "What is it? Money? Travel? A house? An island? What?"

"THIEF!" The voice does not come from the stage. Everyone in the room turns to the main entrance, where none other than Fiona Shay has just kicked open the doors and is barreling across the floor, followed closely by Poppy and Cassandra.

I hear Ms. Carlisle groan. "Oh, crap."

"She's a THIEF!" Fiona screeches, clambering up on the

stage to stand next to Famke. Clutched in her hand is a sheaf of papers, and she shakes them in front of Ms. Carlisle. "Did you think we wouldn't notice? She's been stealing from Swan's Lake!" she shouts, shoving the papers into Famke's hands. "For *years!*"

Fiona gets right in Ms. Carlisle's face, even though she's still talking to Famke. "She told us the Network didn't care about us anymore, and that as watcher, she was the one in charge. She told us the school was going broke and that it was our responsibility to fix it. The Benevolent Sisterhood, isn't that what you said?" Fiona growls at Ms. Carlisle.

"Fiona Shay"—Famke narrows her eyes, looking at the papers—"what exactly are you talking about? The Benevolent Sisterhood of Swan's Lake, a.k.a. the Hot Spot, has always been responsible for Swan's Lake, you know that."

"Of course I know that!" Fiona snaps. "But Ms. Carlisle took advantage. She's been stealing your donations and then telling us the school was going broke! We tried everything to help! Let's be farmers and grow our own vegetables! Let's build the world's biggest piggy bank—quarters only, please! Hey, Do-Goods, grow out your hair to donate to bald kids! Except we'll really sell it on the black market!"

"Hey!" Do-Good Margot yells from the crowd, touching the nape of her neck.

"Our school is falling apart around us!" Farah yells.

"Yeah!"

"Shame on you, Ms. Carlisle!"

"Where's your sisterhood!"

"And where are the Oriental rugs?" I grab the microphone to ask the question, so it gets everyone's attention. Ms. Carlisle narrows her eyes at me.

"And the chandeliers from Founder's Path!" Deanna pipes in.

"And books two twenty through four forty of the Dewey decimal system!" the Bookish Girls yell in unison.

In just moments the ballroom is thundering with Swans shouting out all the things that have gone missing over the past year. Field hockey sticks, forks, oil paints.

"She's a thief!" Deanna whispers in shocked awe.

"Well, Lydia?" Famke asks, raising her hand to silence the crowd.

"I sold it," Ms. Carlisle says with a sneer. "All of it."

"She's a thief *and* a capitalist!" Deanna gasps.

"At least I would have," Ms. Carlisle snaps, "if Aloha and her crew ever left school long enough for me to move it. But *no*, she had them here around the clock, tearing this place apart, searching for the Den of Secrecy."

At this everyone turns to look at Aloha, who crosses her arms and sneers at Ms. Carlisle, "I wouldn't have had to search if you had held up your end of the deal!"

Ms. Carlisle snickers. "You made a deal with the devil, princess, of course you got burned!"

"What deal?" Beatrice Linney calls from the audience.

Aloha glowers at Ms. Carlisle. "She said if I started a fake Hot Spot, she'd show us the DOS. But once we did, she refused to even talk to us. She just hides in her office, letting this whole place go to shit."

"This place would have fallen apart if it wasn't for Gigi Lane!" Once again, everyone looks to the main entrance. This time the first-years on door duty have opened the door just a crack to shout through.

"Yeah!" the other first-year yells through the crack. "She took over supervising duties *and* gave us life lessons on hair care and accessories!"

I can't help but smile at this, my chest swelling with pride.

Famke takes one step toward the edge of the stage and points. "First-years, you will close that door or I will have your heads shaved."

The door slams shut but opens a second later to a duet of "We love you, Gigi!" It slams shut again and then opens so that they can add, "And you, too, Dear Heart!"

"Is this true?" Famke asks, looking at me.

"Well, they do seem quite fond of me."

Famke grimaces. "Not *that*. Is it true that you took over supervising duties?"

I nod.

She nods.

We nod at each other for what seems like a long time before she points at Aloha, not even looking at her, and orders, "Take that crown off your head."

"No." Aloha grits her teeth. "I was voted queen."

"I didn't vote for you!" someone yells.

"Me either!"

"I voted for Gigi!"

As the shouts continue, my heart swells. "They *do* like me!" I whisper to Deanna.

"Gigi Lane," Famke ordains, plucking the crown off of a scowling Aloha and placing it on my head, "I hereby overturn your conviction of gross misconduct and remove you from permanent exile. Further, you are hereby accepted into the Hot Spot as Head Hottie for the last seven days of the school year and for the summer, and into the Network for life."

"Thank you!" I squeal. "Please, do Deanna, too!"

"Of course!" Famke smiles, laying her hand on Deanna's shoulder. "Deanna 'Dear Heart' Jones, you are hereby reinstated as a member of the Hot Spot. Now, Gigi," Famke continues, "even if there are only seven days left in the school year, you *do* need a third person in the Hot Spot. Who will it be?"

I look at the people standing with me on the stage. Aloha won't even meet my gaze; she already looks like she's somewhere else. Heidi looks at me with her trademark desperation, her pom-poms vibrating as she shakes. Finally my gaze lands on Daphne. She looks back at me and blinks.

# CHAPTER TWENTY-FIVE

**Special Summer Edition**
**Thanks to all the cliques for dedicating their**
**summer to restoring Swan's Lake**
**to her former glory.**

**(Your efforts have been noted.)**

"Another Italian soda, ladies?"

"That would be lovely, Fiona, thank you." I smile drowsily from beneath my sunglasses and fashionably floppy hat, warm and happy in the summer sun.

I open one eye to see Fiona raise her pointer finger just slightly from the arm of her lounge chair. A young woman in a horribly ugly maid's uniform steps from the shade of one of the many stately potted trees that forest the outdoor garden off the Den of Secrecy.

"Yes, miss? How may I help you, Miss?"

Fiona smirks. "You sound Scottish, Aloha, not British.

You'll need to work on that if we are to accept this term of service as punishment."

Deanna giggles from the lounge chair beside me, and I turn to smile at her in her boy-short bikini bottoms and helpfully supportive bikini top. She lifts her sunglasses a moment to wink at me and sips the last of her Italian soda through a candy-cane-colored straw.

"Yes, miss," Aloha says through gritted teeth, stomping across the cobblestone pavers and back into the attic to the Den of Secrecy kitchen.

My first view of the DOS was a shock, and not just because the secret elevator is hidden in Ms. Carlisle's office, the one place we never thought of. The elevator creaks and groans its way up before the doors shudder open and you find yourself in an airy, loftlike space on top of the grand ballroom. The wall surrounding the entire roof hides everything from view without blocking the sunlight that makes the DOS the calm, sunlit space I dreamed of.

The fact that Ms. Carlisle was the only one who knew where the DOS was made it easy for her to take daily trips up the elevator with the things she was stealing from school—Oriental rugs, books, paintings, crystal. Even though she had already funneled millions of dollars of donations into her personal bank account, she planned on taking her final revenge by selling everything that wasn't nailed down at Swan's Lake. The DOS became her storage space, and she stuffed it to the ceiling with her ill-gotten goods.

Fiona makes a little noise in her throat and then says, "Heidi."

"Yes?" Heidi reddens as she hurries forward, sweating in the black leather cheerleading uniform she wore at the Founder's Ball.

"That didn't sound like a cheer," Fiona scolds. "Deanna, did that sound like a cheer to you?"

"It most certainly did not!" Deanna giggles.

Fiona smiles at me and nods, encouraging me to take my rightful place as Head Hottie. I turn to Heidi. "Were you unclear on the details of your punishment?"

She looks like she wants to tear my throat out. "No," she says, glowering.

I sit up, folding my sunglasses and laying them on the arm of the lounge chair, right next to the real Hottie Handbook. "Excuse me?"

Heidi presses her lips together, glares at the handbook and then cheers through gritted teeth, "I understand, yes I do! I understand, how about you?"

I nod, replacing my sunglasses and relaxing back in my chair. "That's better. If you and Aloha would prefer to serve out your sentence elsewhere, you can join Ms. Carlisle. I hear Alaska is *lovely* this time of year. Though her sentence is a bit longer than yours."

Heidi makes a low, growling sound in her throat that turns into, "I want to stay, yes I do! I want to stay, how about you?"

"Good," Fiona says. "I think we have been exceedingly fair.

One summer of service to your sister Swans to avoid having your college acceptance letters rescinded and being sent to vocational school is not a bad deal. Now, go stand in the shade. I won't have you passing out again."

It turns out that Fiona was right about me not truly understanding what it really means to be Head Hottie. If I hadn't been bamboozled out of my rightful place, I would have found out the Hot Spot is about more than just a reign of terror. Even though the name has changed, we really are still the Benevolent Sisterhood of Swan's Lake, charged with making sure our school keeps running. Which is why last year I was forced to steal toilet paper. Without the Hot Spot, how could Swans wipe their tushes? I had no idea the great good I was doing with that act of petty theft. And it turns out that our beloved newspaper, the *Trumpet*, has quietly operated as the mouthpiece of the benevolent Hot Spot for more than a hundred years, publishing headlines that let Swans know exactly what is needed of them. That's why this year, with Ms. Carlisle secretly acting as the Hot Spot's mouthpiece, the headlines got really cranky.

I breathe in the sweet smell of the flowering rosebushes and am just drifting off to sleep when I hear Deanna get up from her chair. "I need a swim. Care to join me, ladies?"

"It *is* rather hot." I ditch my own sunglasses and hat and step to the side of the pool, which is really the inverted dome that covers the ballroom. "Fiona," I say, adjusting my bathing suit straps as she stands beside us, "I'm so glad you accepted my offer to be our honorary third."

"Of course I accepted," Fiona purrs. "The end of my year as Head Hottie sucked stinky dog butt. I deserve a do-over."

And with that, she leaps off the side of the pool and makes a perfect, nearly splashless dive into the clear blue water. The ripples from her entrance lap at the statue of Ms. Cady that stands guard at the far end of the pool, her marble likeness bursting out of a shell, a trident in one hand, water fountaining into the pool from each of it prongs.

Fiona wasn't my first choice for the third member of the Hot Spot. I originally wanted Daphne, a thought that now gives me nausea and gooseflesh, even as I stand in the hot sun. I got caught up in the moment, in all of the sisterly love, so in front of everyone at the Founder's Ball I reached out my hand to her and said, "Daphne, after all you've been through, you deserve to be in the *real* Hot Spot."

Famke and Fiona looked like they wanted to rip out my tongue for offering the spot to a dirty transfer who had helped orchestrate the fall of the Hot Spot in the first place. The Swans in the crowd glared at Daphne, who, I realized, had been their torturer, despite her reluctance, and Aloha, Heidi, and Ms. Carlisle stared at me with a look bordering on hysterical hunger.

It was Daphne who saved me.

"No thanks, Gigi," she said, picking up Ms. Carlisle's hideous green dress from the floor and pulling it on over her black leather bustier. "I think I've had enough. I've had enough of *all* of it. I don't want to be in any clique. I just want to be"—she looked at me with a grateful smile—"a free agent."

It was my proudest moment, my legacy—the birth of a new clique, one that would make its debut next year, along with a new Hot Spot.

The Hottie Incumbents are here now, downstairs in the library, supervising the reshelving of all the books Ms. Carlisle planned to sell. Fiona, Deanna, and I had been careful in the selection of the new Hot Spot. We wanted a group impressive enough to revive the tradition of fearing the Hot Spot, but not so intimidating that it would further alienate the student body. So we chose three girls whose combined assets were the perfect blend of intelligence, beauty, and a connection to a higher power (even higher than the Network) that seemed to assure our fellow Swans that no harm would come to them under the new reign. Simone, the cheerleader; Margot, the Do-Good; and, after signing a written agreement never to open her eyes more than three-quarters of the way, Veronica, the Glossy.

I think all creatures have an innate knowledge of who they are, and where it is they belong.

We may test the waters elsewhere, imagining ourselves a teen queen, a ruthless ruler, a fashion icon, when really all we are is a transfer student in donated jeans who never really fit in anywhere, not even with the artists, who, let's be honest, will take just about anybody.

Or we may want so desperately to be accepted somewhere, anywhere, that we play at being a delinquent, an artist, an athlete, when really what we are is a girl who has been persecuted for the the unavoidable sins of popularity.

I realize now that I have always known who I am, even when I was wearing overalls, eating Cheetos, and not showering. And I've always known my affirmation, my true, simple, perfect affirmation that needs no accoutrements to be true, just like I needed no accoutrements to be truly popular.

*I'm Gigi Lane.*

The rest is just assumed.